Fear
of an
Obsession

By Penelope Lynn

ISBN: 979-8-218-55469-9

To my family and friends Canadian and American. And to
my husband Craig for giving me the opportunity to finally
complete this book.

Table of Contents

Chapter 1

A sliver of sun slanted through the drawn curtains of the apartment on the eighth floor. It was early in the morning, hours before Heath needed to be at work. He examined his hands almost reflectively; they were not the hands of just an average guy. No, these were the hands of a skilled surgeon. Heath had performed thousands of operations, yet he had never set foot in a hospital or a medical clinic. And as far as the government was concerned, Heath did not exist! Could you even put a job title to what he did? Not legally. However, he was skilled—skilled in combat and in hacking just about anything and everything. He was so perfect that he was inhuman, and Grant had worked hard to make him that way.

And soon that higher power would make their move, and when they did, he would be ready to fight them.

***

Elle sat up in bed; she was shaken by another bad dream. It was one of those strange dreams where nothing seemed to make any sense. She was calling out to someone in the darkness, but it was not her—although it never was her but rather someone else entirely, someone wearing her skin.

Everything was worse at night, the dreams and the blackouts. It felt like there was something in this apartment with her, watching and waiting. And if she was not careful, she would lose herself to it. She tucked a strand of sweaty hair behind her ear. Her blue eyes fluttered into each dark corner of the room, searching, but of course there was nothing there.

It was late, and her paranoia would not let her go back to sleep. She glanced absently at the clown night-light—it was embarrassing to her to know she had it. Why couldn't she just be normal, go to work, get married, and have a few kids? She had none of those things and likely never would. Elle could not keep a job, and what guy would want a woman in her late twenties with mandatory visits to her psychiatrist?

She grabbed the night-light from the outlet and went into the kitchen to throw it away. She was done with it.

The kitchen was the only room she found comforting, where she did not feel like she was being watched. Elle poured milk into a pot to heat up; the thought of going back to bed wasn't appealing. She'd had more nights like these than she cared to admit through the years.

Could she pinpoint the day when she lost it? Not really. It had happened slowly at first and then started picking up speed, until finally, she was a mess, which even her mother could not ignore. It had started innocently enough, a few strange drawings in school and a little lost time. But then something happened; the lost time started to take on disturbing qualities. She woke up one night standing before her bedroom wall; there were words written in bright-red paint. Some of it washed off; the stuff that did not, she covered up with anything and everything, posters or drawings, normal ones. She tried to shut out the reality of it; she would go to sleep, only to wake up standing before her walls with the words *They know* or *We are watching* written there. The darkness would threaten to take her away. It usually won, and what was left was anything but her.

Elle's hand reached forward as if trying to reset something in the past. Instead, she burned her hand on the hot pan of milk, which was threatening to boil over the side. She jerked back and forgot to let go of the handle. The hot pan hit the floor; it melted the black-and-white-checkered linoleum before she picked it up. "Shit." The smell of melted plastic and burnt milk filled the kitchen; she had always hated those smells. She could not even heat up a glass of milk without screwing it up. A tear spilled down her cheek; she covered her eyes with her hand until the need to cry passed. She reached for some paper towels and wiped at the spilled milk. She should be using a rag instead of paper towels; it was wasteful. "I guess that's as close to being normal as I can get, being wasteful just like everyone else." Elle's mother, Margaret, would be proud if she could see Elle now. She lifted the lid to the wastebasket to throw away the used paper towel; she saw the clown night-light smiling up at her. If her mother walked in now and saw her looking at the clown night-light—hell, if she even knew that she had one—Margaret would write *normal* on the fridge and underline it. She could almost hear Margaret now, saying, "Elle, you are a grown woman; you're too old to be afraid of the dark!" Elle closed the garbage can; the smiling clown seemed too sinister to plug back in.

Somewhere between puberty and adulthood, it became evident that Elle's blackouts and the lost time were not a phase she was going through. They were not something that she was going to outgrow. That is when the barrage of doctor's started; Margaret had dragged Elle to pretty much every doctor, quack, or psychologist from coast to coast, trying to figure out why Elle was not normal. None of the doctors helped; they just put her mother in debt. One doctor recommended a psychologist that dealt with lost memories, panic attacks, and blackouts. Elle remembered the hopeful look Margaret gave her. But at one point, Elle had had enough; she did not want to be poked and prodded anymore. However, fate had a way of intervening; during a shopping trip just before her eighteenth birthday, Elle freaked out. She trashed the produce section in a grocery store and threatened to hurt a couple people. She had been arrested and had spent a month in a psych ward; a court order had made it mandatory that she see a psychiatrist for help, and that was how Dr. Emma Davis became her shrink. Dr. Davis seemed to think that Elle's problems ran deeper than what Margaret believed. She said it might take years to uncover what was triggering these paranoid delusions and the blackouts.

In the end, she had hoped that this doctor might be able to help her, and that was the one thing that Elle held on to.

***

Dr. Emma Davis leaned back in her chair; she was waiting for Elle to start. Elle always felt safe here, like there was no one watching her. However, today Elle was anxious, she had something important to tell Dr. Davis, and she was afraid of her reaction. Elle was rocking slightly, forward and backward, almost listlessly.

"Elle, how are you doing? You seem a little more agitated than usual today."

"I'm not good. I've been having a recurring nightmare, and it's been keeping me up at night."

"Why?" Dr. Davis questioned.

Elle sighed. "I cannot relax. I'm anxious. It feels like someone is watching me. I'm worried about losing myself when I blackout—I think I become this other person."

"Who do you become?" Dr. Davis questioned.

"I don't know. I think it looks like me, it sounds like me, but it's definitely not me."

"And then?"

"And then I'm back in my body, and I wake up."

"Elle, I want to give you something to help you sleep; if you're not sleeping, you're not recharging, which isn't healthy." Dr. Davis scribbled on her prescription pad; when she looked up at Elle, she seemed to have come to a decision. "Elle, I want you to consider something, something that we have never tried before! I want to try to hypnotize you. I think something traumatic happened in your past. It could be triggering the blackouts and the erratic behavior. If we can get to the root of the problem, you might have a chance at leading a somewhat more normal lifestyle, maybe meet someone."

"I met someone."

"Who?" Dr. Davis asked as she leaned forward eagerly.

"He's in my building, and he's watching me."

Dr. Davis's eyebrows lifted, then settled. "Elle, he's not, talk to him, and you will find out that these are just your paranoid delusions." Dr. Davis handed Elle the prescription. Elle stuffed it in her pocket; she had no intention of taking the drug; she had to be alert and ready to fight off the next blackout.

***

Heath stared at the video camera, he wanted desperately to sleep, but sleep was a luxury he could not afford. Sure, he got a little here and there, but sometimes he was dead on his feet.

"Why don't you go get some sleep; you're bagged."

He looked up into Missy's eyes. She was a couple years younger than him, and right now it really showed. If he had known life was going to turn out this way, working nonstop, he almost would rather the infection had ended his life back then when he was just a kid. Although, Heath supposed, things had a way of working out in a fucked-up kind of way.

As far back as he could remember, his life had been a disaster. Nadine, Heath's coked-up mother, would pass him off to her friends. Some of these so-called friends were almost as bad off as she was. It was surprising that Heath had made it at all; it was even more surprising that Nadine hadn't ended up OD'ing in some scummy motel room.

With no parental guidance to speak of, Heath had gotten himself in a bit of trouble when he was eight. The fast-food joint threw out their garbage daily, and this was worth the wait. It was almost time.

"Hey, kid, want a fix?" asked the Dark Man.

The Dark Man was standing in the shadows. Heath remembered this man vividly, even to this day; no matter how far the man stepped out into the sunlight, his upper torso remained in shadow. But being eight, Heath was not afraid of much. Had he known what would happen, he would have turned and ran for his life. The Dark Man stood over him, casting Heath into darkness. The figure wore a long trench coat and a hat. He had no distinctive facial features, and when he spoke, his mouth did not seem to move. Heath was not even certain that he had lips, but certain details seemed irrelevant at the time. The Dark Man gazed down at Heath, and he felt almost hypnotized staring up into the man's face. The Dark Man reached out one long arm and wrapped his fingers around Heath's upper arm. His fingers encircled him with vicelike strength. It was not so Heath could not run away; no, the purpose of the man's touch was to transfer the infection into Heath. After a few moments, the Dark Man released him. Heath could feel something slithering throughout his body. The anger and the aggression that blossomed within Heath, just from the man's touch, were indescribable. And just like that, the Dark Man was gone, and Heath was left alone in the alleyway, ravenous with this violent rage twisting and turning inside him. A whirlwind of activity followed while Heath's temperature climbed to a boiling point. When Grant found him, Heath had killed two homeless people and stabbed a third with a piece of steel. He had smashed a dangerous hole in his own skull. Heath was self-destructing at an alarming rate.

Grant was a trained physician, and he had enough military clearance to get himself into the Pentagon. He had degrees from Oxford and Harvard and was one of the leading scientists on a top-secret project based out of the Nevada desert. The project consisted of reverse engineering a crashed extraterrestrial spacecraft that the military had recovered from Roswell, New Mexico. Two of the scientists from the project died suddenly when radiation leaked from the cracked fuselage. While an ongoing investigation was held, everyone who worked on the project had been given a temporary leave of absence.

Grant had a way of bringing his work home with him, which was exactly what he'd done when he saved Heath's life. He used an experimental metal, one that was not on the periodic table, to piece Heath's head back together. The recovery was next to miraculous. The metal absorbed the parasites that had gotten into Heath's bloodstream when the Dark Man touched him. What followed were painful skin grafts to cover up the metal plate and make Heath look human again. However, a small portion of Heath's brain had been permanently damaged, and he lacked certain human aspects.

Heath was indebted to Grant; if it had not been for him, Heath would have died. Survival was the basis of a very primitive code that had been hardwired into every human, every strand of DNA. The alien parasites overrode Heath's basic instincts.

Grant knew what he was doing when he saved Heath's life years ago. He needed someone to keep an eye on his daughter, to keep her safe from the evil forces that were out there.

Heath snapped back to present day, staring at Elle on the monitor; he had rigged a camera up in every room in her apartment except for the kitchen.

Grant had disappeared years ago, but during the time leading up to his disappearance, Grant had prepped Heath for the inevitable. Grant had always highlighted the importance of keeping Elle safe. But somewhere along the way, Heath knew he could not do this job entirely alone. Heath had enlisted Jamie, a pickpocket/junkie. Jamie hung around more for the hell of it than anything else. The truly remarkable member of the team was Missy. Heath first met Missy when she was a guinea pig in one of Grant's experiments; she was later released after she had been given a clean bill of health. Missy joined the team after she finished medical school. Heath knew that having another member with medical know-how could be invaluable. He was not invincible.

Grant had insisted on Heath being prepared for every type of scenario imaginable. He programmed him for hand-to-hand combat, surgeries, all-American sniper, and so much more.

Constantly watching Elle was the toughest job he had ever had to do. He was not a robot; sometimes he wished he were because he would not need to waste time eating, sleeping, or taking a piss. If he got shot, he would not bleed; he would just keep going. But despite the hardships he had had to endure over the years, he had no real regrets, other than missing a good night's sleep from time to time.

There were more drawbacks than just a lack of sleep however: he had to keep himself an outsider. Watching Elle deal with her mental breakdowns over the years was difficult. If he went in there and told her why her mind was so fucked up, that her father had permanently altered her memory because of the blueprint he implanted into the core of her brain, his cover would be blown. He would be a sitting duck; he had to bide his time and wait for the aliens to make their move.

Heath raked his fingers through his unwashed hair. It felt too long and unkempt. He would have to get a trim soon. But right now, he was thankful for a quiet night.

Elle did not know it, but he was the key to her survival, and without him she would end up in the loony bin or dead. Heath vaguely wondered why her nervous energy had not taken her there already.

Missy was waiting for an answer. "Nah, Missy, go home; feed your cat; live your life."

"I think you destroyed any chance of that years ago."

"Go grab a few hours of sleep then; we can trade off tonight."

"You're the boss, boss."

A quick surveillance of Elle's apartment showed that there were no intruders. He switched the video camera back onto her bedroom. She had gone to sleep, and she seemed to be having a restful night for once.

Chapter 2

Heath watched Elle through the binoculars; it was almost time for her to leave for her appointment with that quack. He wanted her out of the building before he entered her apartment.

He switched his attention back to the video camera. What was taking her so long? He checked his watch a third time; she was going to be late if she did not get moving.

Heath switched the camera onto her bedroom. She was looking for something in her closet. She pulled out a jacket and put it on over the top of the T-shirt. Then she turned and walked out of the bedroom. He followed her through the apartment with a switch of each camera. She stopped by the door and put on her boots. Then she opened the door and closed it behind her. Heath knew she had not left; she usually spent a few minutes jiggling the door to make sure it was locked. Heath waited; finally she emerged from the building, caught a cab, and was out of the way.

The phone rang. Heath glanced at it before he picked it up.

"Are you going?"

"Yep."

"Do you need some help?" Jamie asked.

"Nope." Heath set the phone down. He walked into the kitchen and stood in front of the counter. He reached up into the cupboard and took down the canister of flour. He rooted through it before he came up with two keys. Heath had paid Jamie one hundred dollars if he could, and would, pick Elle's pocket to get her house keys. When she was keyless, the superintendent had let her back in her apartment, and she thought she had lost them. For a doped-up fuckup, Jamie was incredibly smooth. Heath copied the keys and had Jamie stow them in her purse; she just thought she had not looked hard enough for them. Elle was so sure she was crazy that Heath could manipulate her mind anyway he had to to make things work out in his favor. He did not really like playing mind games with her, but it came in handy now and then.

With his own set of keys, there was never any forced entry; he could come and go as he pleased, so long as she was not home. He pocketed the keys and moved out of his apartment and down the hall. He took the stairs two at a time.

Once out on the street, he looked like everyone else with something important to do. He jaywalked across the street and over to the building that Elle lived in. He put the key in the lock. He held his breath and turned the key to the right. He heard a click as the lock drew back. He walked inside and crossed the lobby to the elevators. The doors slid open, and he stepped inside.

Inside her apartment, Heath could smell a burnt odor lingering. There was a melted spot in the kitchen linoleum, which must have caused the smell. He moved away from the kitchen and into the living room. She did not have much furniture: a couch, TV, DVD player, and a coffee table. Her TV was not that big; it was only a forty inch. He knew she lived off the money her father had left her, and it must've been pretty significant since she didn't have a job. Mostly she sat in her apartment and read books and tried to keep out of trouble.

The wind blew through the living room and lifted the hair off his forehead.

Missy had permanently removed his fingerprints years ago. And if anyone saw anything, Heath would take care of them. He did not need a program for that—that came naturally.

Heath looked around the corner of the door into her bedroom. He did not want to go in there; that room gave him the creeps. Elle had painted hundreds of sets of dark, almond-shaped eyes on the walls. To a sane person, this was crazy. But Heath knew differently; this was what was yet to come—a disturbing glimpse into the future.

Heath crossed the room in two strides, stopping at the window and throwing back the curtain. A hand reached through the window, followed by a leg. Jamie had gotten into Elle's apartment from God only knows, a fire escape or from drain pipe. Heath lowered his gun: Jamie was wearing green cargo pants with pockets from heels to hips, greasy brown hair sticking out from underneath the black do-rag tied to his head, and dark wraparound sunglasses to shield the sun.

"Jamie, you just about got your head blown off. You better be careful; I do not pay dead men. And while you work for me, I would appreciate if you did not get stoned all the time."

"Hey, someone gave me good stuff."

"Yeah, well, you better watch it; nothing is free in this world."

"So, are you gonna bump this guy off or what?"

"Yeah, that's the plan." Heath nodded. He bent down through the window and onto the little balcony. He climbed off the balcony and onto the foot-wide ledge and moved to the right. His hands were slippery with sweat as he reached for a handhold. His hands skittered up and down the wall; he hated heights.

"Hey."

A hand clasped the collar of Heath's jacket, pulling him back. Heath swallowed thickly. "Thanks, Jamie."

"Are you ok?"

"Yeah." Heath leaned against the wall and focused on the window casing from the next apartment. The ten feet separating him from safety and one long fall made him feel lightheaded. He could almost imagine himself pitching off the ledge and plummeting to the street below; if he could make it to the balcony next to hers, then he was home free.

"Boy, it's windy up here," Jamie stated.

Heath did not need to see Jamie to know that he was loving this. This was almost better than his costly high, and this one was free. Four feet remaining and then he would have a handhold; three, two, one, and he was at the balcony.

Heath felt an overwhelming sense of relief flood through him as he took a firm hold of the drainpipe. Then he moved around it, reaching for the balcony railing. He felt his gun slipping from his inside coat pocket. It slid down his stomach to stop in the tight band of the coat. His one hand remained on the railing while he reached up under his coat to pull the gun out before it fell. Deeper pockets, that was what this coat needed. With one hand, he tucked the gun into the waist of his jeans. Then he swung one leg over the railing, and when both feet were firmly on the balcony, he reached for the window, lifted high with one push, and crawled through it. He reached out a hand for Jamie, but he was not on the ledge anymore. Heath knew that Jamie had not fallen; he must have gone back into Elle's apartment. He had not come this far for the scenery; he had a job to do, and if he did not hurry up, he would be late for work. Heath seized his gun— the silencer would keep everything low-key—clasping it tightly to his side he moved away from the window. Heath had never been in the guy's apartment right next to Elle's, but he had a pretty good idea on what the layout was like. He had been in Elle's apartment more than a few times, and most of these apartments were exactly alike. His foot sank into the plush carpet as he edged along the wall toward where he assumed the kitchen was. Why had Heath not asked Jamie where the old fart was? The doorway up ahead should lead Heath into the kitchen. He crossed the distance in three long strides. When he stepped through the doorway, he came into a living room; it must have been laid out opposite of Elle's apartment.

Heath looked up as the old guy entered the living room from the kitchen. The old guy stopped when he noticed Heath. Heath did not hesitate; he pointed the gun at the old man and pulled the trigger. The bullet hit the guy high in the right shoulder; the guy spun around and fell face-first into the carpet. The plush carpet stifled some of the thud. Heath put two more bullets in the old guy's back to confirm the kill. The dead guy had on a long-sleeved shirt. Heath pulled the shirt up out of the dead guy's pants, and along the spine were three small black triangles. They looked like tattoos, but they were not; he had seen the triangles before. They were burned into the skin, like how ranchers branded cattle to keep track of their assets. Heath had been trained to kill; however, he had never been trained to feel remorse.

Before Heath turned, he noticed something moving just under the dead man's skin, almost like something was alive and was burrowing around. Elle's neighbor was infected with a parasite, and that was bad news. Heath dug through his inside coat pocket and pulled out a sealed container of cleaning fluid. He poured the cleaning fluid onto the old guy's back; it ate through the skin and spilled over the bug; the apartment filled with a rancid smell as the acid gobbled up everything in its path. It was a concoction that Grant had come up with years ago; it destroyed the transmitter in the bug so that it could not relocate and infect a new host.

Heath went to the front door to let Jamie in. Jamie was bouncing from foot to foot; he looked like a little kid that had to go to the bathroom. "Hey, remember, only grab anything of value; we have to make this look like breaking and entering," Heath reminded Jamie with a quick shake.

"Yep," Jamie answered as he rushed over to the TV. It was big, at least a sixty inch, and he pulled it off the stand. Heath moved over to the counter and pocketed the guy's cell phone and wallet. Heath threw a few chairs around and scattered some stuff. They went out the door into the hallway and then through the opened door of Elle's apartment. They stowed the TV in the closet of Elle's spare bedroom for now, covering it with a few extra blankets.

"This is a big son of a bitch; you know where this TV would look really nice?" Jamie asked, smiling.

"Not now," Heath demanded. When the dead guy's apartment came up for rent, they would get the apartment and move the TV from Elle's apartment. But for now, it was a safe place to stow the TV. Elle barely used her spare bedroom; the TV should go unnoticed for months.

Hurrying from Elle's apartment, Heath headed back into the dead guy's apartment. Heath surveyed the apartment for anything else of value. The old guy did not really have that much. Jamie was already toting the small stereo out the door. Heath turned and went to the dead guy, looking for some sign of life, but there was not much left—the cleaning fluid had chewed through a portion of the corpse already. Heath picked the keys up off the table near the door and then locked the door. He stood out in the hall and looked up and down the hallway. With the coast clear, Heath threw himself against the door until the lock shuddered under the weight. The deadbolt let go so quickly that it caught Heath off balance; it sent him sprawling on the floor. Heath rolled onto his back; he stood up and threw the keys back onto the table by the door; he needed to get out of there before someone came.

Heath stopped outside Elle's apartment as Jamie was locking her door. Heath held out his hand for the keys, and Jamie deposited them in his palm.

They headed in opposite directions; Jamie would take the opposite stairwell to avoid any chance of being seen together. As for the cameras, Missy had already disabled them; there was no way Heath could be connected to this guy's death.

At the bottom of the stairwell, Heath hesitated; he did not want to risk running into anyone. He pushed the door open a crack and looked out. He could not really see the front door from where he stood. If he moved a step out of the door, it might give him a better view. Footsteps echoed across the hard tile floor. Heath stayed where he was and watched for the person to come into view. Jamie appeared, strolling casually across the lobby. When Jamie was in line with Heath, Jamie turned and looked directly at him. He lifted his hand and gave Heath a one-hand salute before he left the building. Heath waited a couple minutes before he left the stairwell and stepped into the well-lit lobby. He crossed the lobby in ten strides and came face-to-face with Elle just as she was coming in through the front door of the building. He noticed the nervousness wash over her just from the sight of him, and she had no idea who he was, yet.

He brushed past her out into the street; he was already late for work; he disappeared among the people. Even though he blended in, Elle would remember his face, and that was not something he wanted right now.

***

A dark figure stood in an alley watching Elle walk into her building. No one noticed, and no one seemed to care that this stranger was there. Everyone was too concerned with their own lives to stop and observe anything unusual about the individual, to ask themselves if there was something in that alleyway that should not be, to really look. But hey, if they did, that would just mean trouble, a lot more than anyone was looking for.

Hell, they did not even see him, not really; however, that time would come soon enough. And then everybody would see.

Chapter 3

Heath had to run to catch his bus; he was already late for work. He made decent money at the construction site, but his boss, Chace, was an asshole. It seemed to be a perquisite for a boss nowadays.

Chace was standing at the base of the building; it was mostly just a skeleton structure of beams and girders. But one day soon, it would be a skyscraper.

"You're late!" Chace snapped.

"Yeah, sorry," Heath answered as he gathered up his gear, slinging the harness over his head.

"Aren't you going to give me some lame excuse?" Chace demanded.

Heath slammed his lunch box down in the little office trailer. "Nope, don't have one," Heath yelled at him. He could tell that Chace was glaring at him; it was doubtful Heath could avoid a confrontation with his boss much longer. Guys like Chace had a short fuse and could only be pushed so far before Heath would either get canned or would get one hell of a talking-to.

However, not many guys had as much on their plates as Heath did. Chace let him go…for now.

***

Elle's session with Dr. Davis had done her a world of good; she pushed the nervousness aside after bumping into the stranger leaving her building. Today's session only took about twenty minutes, but they had covered a lot.

The elevator came; she stepped in and pushed the button for the eighth floor. The elevator went upward; her fingers tightened instinctively around the rails that were on each wall. Of course, if the cables suddenly snapped and the elevator plummeted to the ground, holding onto the rail would do no good.

The golden numbers flickered from one to the next and so on. The elevator stopped, the doors slid open, and Elle exited. She walked down the hall toward her apartment, hesitating as she dug for her keys. Absently, Elle looked up the hallway to Mr. Wilson's apartment door. Elle noticed that the door had been knocked inwards, and splinters of wood littered the hallway carpet.

"Mr. Wilson?" Elle called softly.

Elle moved slowly toward his door, feeling her way along the hallway like someone blind. She peeked around the door frame into his apartment, terrified by what she might find. Elle listened for any sounds of an intruder, she thought of barricading herself in her apartment, but what if Mr. Wilson was hurt and needed help right now? She stepped slowly in, eyes darting in each direction for some sign that she was not alone. Elle cringed inwardly when her boots squeaked on the linoleum; she was afraid that at any moment somebody would jump out from behind a corner. If they did, she would not be able to keep her bladder in check. Elle turned the corner into the living room. Mr. Wilson was lying face down on the floor; blood had pooled around his body and had soaked into the carpet. The carpet would be permanently stained. The blank spot where his TV had sat caught her eye immediately. They had killed an old man over a stupid TV! Desperately trying to remain calm, she looked down at Mr. Wilson. His back was a sizzling, withering mass of fleshy decay. She had seen enough; it was time to get help. The thought was so simple, and yet it took her a few minutes to get her body to respond. She was staring at her neighbor as if hypnotized by his body's decomposition.

The phone in Mr. Wilson's apartment was right there; she dialed quickly, waiting for an operator; the phone rang three times before an operator came on the line; the voice sounded competent and ready for her call.

"Hello, this is 911. What's your emergency?"

Elle's mouth was so dry; she just hoped she did not have one of her blackouts.

"Hello, is anyone there? Could you please speak up?"

Elle was not handling this calmly. "My...neighbor...has been...murdered."

"Say again, Miss?"

"My neighbor is dead."

"The address."

Elle gave all the other information the emergency operator needed. She put the phone down and went and took a seat away from Mr. Wilson, not thinking about destroying evidence, just thinking it would be nice to sit down. She waited, sitting with her back straight; staring at a spot on the wall, she did not take her eyes off that spot, because the alternative was to look at his oozing, withering back.

When the cops arrived, Elle stood up and went to the door, not that they needed to be greeted. She even held out a hand to one of the officers, he took it after a moment's hesitation, looking at her oddly, but she did not feel it was odd. Good manners were expected since Mr. Wilson had always exhibited them, demanded them. More officers came in; she did not bother to shake any of their hands. They moved about, asking her questions, and did their police work. One officer took an immediate interest in Elle; his name was Officer Carter. He studied her to the point where it made her uncomfortable, so she wrapped her arms protectively around her body as if to shield herself from his harsh eyes. His tone was nasty as he took her statement, going over each sentence, each word, making her go over what she had just said to see if it changed. When it did not, he asked her where she lived.

"But you can't visit me there."

"Why not?" he demanded.

"Because I don't think I like you." Elle knew she was babbling, but she did not care. Everything she had said up until now was sane; however she could feel herself cracking under the pressure. "Can I go home now? I feel worn out."

He eyed her suspiciously. "That's enough for now. But I wouldn't leave town if I were you."

Elle moved out of the apartment like a rabbit walking through a wolf's den. Each one of them looked at her as she went past; they gave her a little bit of a head start before they pounced.

It was not until Elle was in her own apartment with the door securely locked that she had the strangest feeling, like someone had been in there. She did not know what it was that made her think that, just a feeling. At least she did not think anyone had been in. She glanced around, but nothing seemed out of place or missing, and her door was locked. Was this just more paranoia, or had somebody really been in here after she had left for her doctor's appointment?

She took her coat off and threw it on the couch before she moved to her bedroom. One look at the room told her that no one was there. The curtain billowed out from the breeze. She had not had any blackouts in at least a week, and yet she was sure that she had closed that window before she left.

Elle knew it would always feel as if someone had been in her apartment, but this time she suspected that someone really had. But what for, to open a window? It made absolutely no sense.

***

Heath left work with dragging feet; he still had a late night ahead of him. He caught his bus and rode home. He felt like, if he had another day like this one, he would have to quit. There was no way he could work this hard and put in a full night.

***

Jamie had at least fifteen minutes before Heath got home and checked on Elle via the video camera. Elle was always Heath's number-one priority; however, if Jamie entered her apartment, he could easily erase all traces of his visit. The one thing still nagging at Jamie was that there might be a cop still hanging around. He should wait—although waiting had never been his strong suit.

It would be easy enough to do; Jamie had his own set of keys to her apartment; he had them made a while back. Jamie never really thought he would need the keys, but things were different now, and who was to say how long Heath would need him around. He had the shakes and the chills; he needed a fix really bad; he needed it.

Jamie stood outside Elle's building debating; Heath watched and stalked the girl after all, so in a way Heath was crazy, but was Heath crazy enough to come after Jamie and kill him? A resounding yes answered Jamie's question—Heath would. But Jamie did not care anymore; drugs won over common sense. Jamie reached into his pocket and pulled out the keys. He stepped to the locked front door of Elle's building and put the key in it. The lock released and Jamie stepped inside. He pulled the door closed. It closed with a secure *swoosh*. But this security would not help Elle any.

Jamie walked across the lobby to the elevator. The doors opened, he stepped inside, and he pushed the up button. When the doors opened, he stepped out and walked to her apartment. His hands were shaking so badly he could not fit the key in the lock at first. Jamie thought about kicking the door in, but he probably could not do it as easily as Heath did. Heath outweighed him by forty pounds of muscle. Jamie rested his head against the door and took five deep breaths, to try to steady his hands. Then he reached forward and inserted the key into the lock. He turned the key; the soft click told him that he was in. He looked down the hall, smiled, and went in, closing the door softly behind him. Jamie had glimpsed the camera briefly before coming over, Elle had gone to bed extra early. Jamie believed he could slip in and grab the TV before anyone knew he had been there, but if she caught him, he would have to handle Elle and make a run for it.

Chapter 4

Heath emerged from the bus stop; it was only a quarter-mile walk to his apartment building. He was not going to make anything for supper tonight; he just wanted to crash on the couch and put today behind him. How much longer would he have to watch Elle? He already knew the answer to that question: the job would end when either he or Elle was dead.

Heath entered his building and rode the elevator up; he exited on his floor. Once inside his apartment, Heath's eyes drifted to the camera. Jamie had just shut the door to Elle's apartment. Heath flew to the kitchen. He grabbed the flour can out of the cupboard and looked inside. Her apartment key and the building key were still there. But Jamie was in Elle's apartment. Heath grabbed the keys and ran back out. He hit the elevator button. It opened. He got on.

The elevator descended to the lobby, and Heath was out the doors before they had barely opened. He darted through the traffic, and his only thought was getting to Elle before Jamie did. He could feel his killer instinct taking over; it booted up inside him as if he were a computer. And like a computer, he was no longer thinking or feeling; he was acting as the program suggested, as the program was designed to run. When Grant had fixed Heath's mind, placing it back together piece by piece, the metal plate acted as a protective ionized barrier in his skull. It was so high tech that it did a lot more than absorb the parasite; it was like a computer that directed his body and drove him harder and faster than the human body was designed to run. It made him a living, breathing lethal weapon.

A car horn honked as the lights blinded Heath. He was in and out of the traffic; he flung himself at the lobby door, jammed the key in, and twisted it in a jerking motion. Through the door, he skidded across the lobby on rubbery legs; his heart was hammering in his chest, and adrenaline had flooded every nerve—that was still one thing he had in common with humans.

He got on the elevator and pushed her floor number. The elevator rose; it seemed to be taking forever to reach her floor. He should have moved into her building sooner. Why had he pissed around so long? He knew why: he had waited because he wanted to make sure that everything went perfectly.

The elevator doors started to open; he forced them to open quicker and exited with just enough room to fit through. He pulled the keys out of his pocket and thrust them toward her door, but there was no need—her door wasn't locked. Inside her apartment it was deathly silent, a little too silent for a clumsy drug addict; although when Jamie really wanted something, he could be incredibly smooth and focused. Heath knew why Jamie had come to her place; he was after that TV. Jamie appeared before Heath could enter her living room.

An angry violence churned through Heath, and he could not hold back. He reached out to Jamie, clamping his fingers around Jamie's scrawny neck, and squeezed, trying to crush the life out of him. Fear pierced the anger. Where was Elle? He let Jamie go, and he dropped to the ground where he had been released. Heath strode through the entryway to her bedroom. He paused outside her door, hesitating in a moment of fear before he looked inside. There was a lump in her bed, and for the briefest of seconds, he feared that she was dead, that she had awakened and gotten in Jamie's way. He flicked on the light; Elle squeezed her eyes tight against it. He knew she was all right. He turned the light back off and headed to the kitchen before she completely woke up. Jamie was in a sitting position, with the TV right beside him, and he was rubbing his neck. Heath grabbed the TV in one arm and Jamie in the other hand. Dragging Jamie by the collar of his shirt into the hallway, Heath turned back and locked Elle's door before heading to the elevator, Jamie still in tow.

One look at Jamie told Heath that he was on an all-time drug low. Heath should bump him off before something like this happened again. There was too much at stake. Instead, he took Jamie home with him. He really could not say what it was that kept Jamie alive that night; it was not human compassion because Heath did not have any. Jamie was a drug addict, a fuckup, and a pain in his ass. Heath duct-taped Jamie's mouth shut and tied up his hands and feet; he left him lying in a corner of the apartment; Jamie had to sweat this one out. Heath did not usually give second chances, but Heath felt like he needed Jamie to do one last job, and Jamie was the only one who could pull it off. And if he could not, well, Jamie might just become a liability, and Heath always took care of loose ends.

Heath laid down on the couch, and once his head hit the sofa, he was out.

***

Elle turned on each light in her apartment; she was going from room to room to make sure that no one was there. She thought a few minutes ago someone had come into her room and turned on the light, then turned if off and went out. And even as strange as that sounded, she was sure that was what happened. But her door was locked up tight, so no one had forced entry into her apartment. Her windows in her bedroom and in the kitchen were still locked; it did not make any sense. How could someone get in? Maybe it was time for her to change the locks, especially with the murder of her neighbor, Mr. Wilson. It was not safe anymore, not that it ever had been, but it only underlined the reality of the situation.

Elle's eyes hesitated on the closet in the spare bedroom; the closest was slightly open; she always kept it closed. Elle dropped every other thought and moved closer to the closet. She stopped in front of it. Her hand extended inches from the doorknob, then she threw the door all the way open. She almost jumped back, thinking that someone was hiding in there. She flicked on the light inside the closest, throwing the darkness away. Her heartbeat quickened with a jump. But there was no one and nothing in there except a couple of blankets.

***

The onslaught of rain made Jeanie shiver; she had been waiting in the alley for a while. Waiting, waiting, and not for just anyone, she was waiting for the Dark Man; he used his usual calling card; and she would have to be deaf to not have heard it. The Dark Man had powers out of this world, he had skills and ways to handle certain people, and Elle needed to be handled. The Dark Man could change Jeanie's fate; he could make Elle vanish so that not even a trace of her was left. And after all, that is all Jeanie had ever wanted.

Things had been going the way they were, and if something was not done soon, everything could be lost. But with the late hour approaching, she wondered where the Dark Man had gotten to.

25

"Anything to report?" the Dark Man whispered.

Jeanie whirled, suddenly frightened; she was surprised to see him finally. He could stir up so many emotions in her that it was almost too alarming to face him, and yet now that he was here, she could not turn away. Not for anything. She gulped. "Yes, that crazy doctor wants to start digging around in Elle's head. I think we should be worried. Very worried. All could be lost if we're not careful. I don't know how to stop it. Elle has more control than I do."

There was no sign of a reaction on the Dark Man's face. She was certain he was listening, though she dare not question him.

"That doctor can't get inside Elle's head. She's locked up tight, and only the right one can unlock what's inside."

Jeanie wanted to argue, but she was also aware of how the Dark Man was reading her thoughts.

"However, if you're worried, we can take care of the doctor."

"You mean, take care of her…?" Jeanie questioned with a quiver in her voice.

The Dark Man reacted to Jeanie's question almost instantly, he grabbed a hold of her arm, and his screams reverberated through her body. The Dark Man appeared as a man, but he was far from that. It was a facade: when he screamed, he took on the horrific figure of an alien, and his face changed, morphing into a mask of evil. The hot-and-cold fire seemed to completely ignite her thoughts from within. She shuddered uncontrollably; eventually her brain caught on, and Jeanie could only describe the feelings as fire and ice combined into one horrible, slithering touch. The pain then moved on, and it felt like the worst migraine ever.

"No, please, stop it." Jeanie howled as the pain inside her head made her crumple.

"Do you know how you stop the doctor? It's quite simple: you kill her. Her life means nothing to me," the Dark Man stated.

Jeanie was soaked, lying on the pavement, the feeling of death hovering close by. She realized that, in the blink of an eye, the Dark Man could erase her very existence.

"Jeanie, are you listening to me?"

"Ok," Jeanie screamed. "Ok, I will kill the doctor." The Dark Man released her arm finally.

Jeanie's arm was numb, and her head felt about ready to explode from the intense migraine blossoming there. There was only the briefest moment of true despair, when realization sunk in, and she knew she must follow through or it would be her end. Although she knew it could be a lot worse—if the Dark Man had given her the infection, death would be a blessing compared to that. The infection would twist and warp her, inside she would self-destruct, and still she would go on, in pain. Mercy was not in the Dark Man's makeup.

"Get up, my dear, the pain is gone, and it's just you and me."

Jeanie needed all her strength to get up out of the gutter, to get her legs underneath her. When she was on her feet standing opposite the Dark Man, she had one of the strangest feelings ever, as if the Dark Man wanted even more from her.

"Perhaps I've been a little oblivious?"

"Oblivious to what?" Jeanie questioned, out of breath.

"Does Elle have friends?"

"No."

"No? Are you certain?"

"Yes."

"If you're wrong…"

And with that, the Dark Man vanished from the alleyway, leaving Jeanie alone to wonder.

***

A groan from behind the couch jolted Heath from his own slumber; the groan increased in volume, becoming a muffled scream. Heath had not meant to fall asleep, but he had succumbed to exhaustion; Heath listened for a few minutes before his fuse was cut short. He got up and rounded the couch. Jamie had a wild look in his eyes, and he was squirming, trying to get his hands untied. Heath smashed one of his fists into Jamie's head; it quieted Jamie for a few seconds before he started screaming again. Jamie's screams were almost loud enough to alert someone; thankfully this building was a shithole and was only one step away from being condemned. Not too many people cared what went on here, but Heath was not about to take a chance either. Heath reached behind his back, slid the gun out, and put it against Jamie's temple. Jamie's eyes swelled in their sockets.

"Listen, buddy, I don't want to kill you, but keep this shit up, and it will be the last thing that you ever do." Heath whispered, "Boom." It was more than enough to get Heath's point across. Jamie quieted down.

***

Elle hurried down the hall to Dr. Davis's office. She was a little late. She had not slept well at all last night. She was stiff, sore, and felt exhausted. It made the appointment with Dr. Davis more of a pain than it already was.

Sadie, the secretary, ushered Elle into her psychiatrist's office. Dr. Davis was already in her chair with her notebook in hand and an eager look on her face. Her big glasses seemed to magnify her eyeballs and gave the impression that you were a bug being inspected through a magnifying glass.

Dr. Davis had the first signs of gray hair and was an inch or two taller than Elle.

She motioned for Elle to take a seat. Elle moved toward the couch and sat.

"Elle, I'm so happy you made it. We have a lot to cover in this session, so let's get started."

A trickle of fear seemed to swallow Elle. "What did Margaret say?" Last week Dr. Davis had a session with Elle's mother, Margaret, and today Elle hoped to find out exactly what Margaret remembered and thought about Elle's progress, if anything. It was one of the first steps before Elle was to be under hypnosis.

Mostly Elle was ok with not knowing; she had started to care less and less over the last couple weeks. She had only agreed to this crap because it was mandatory and nothing else had been working, and considering her recent and not-so-recent history, she fit into the category of crazy. Maybe she went to the sessions because, secretly, she wanted a little something out of it, and as much as she hated to admit it, she craved some kind of normalcy. But was it possible, somehow? She doubted it was.

"What did Margaret say?" Elle demanded again.

"Elle, your mother has shed some light on your troubled past."

Elle felt her heart stop. Whatever Margaret had told Dr. Davis could not be undone.

"I used to think that your problems had a lot to do with your past, and now I know. A traumatic event when you were a child can have damaging consequences; a child's mind is a fragile thing."

"There isn't a whole lot from my past that I remember."

"Do you remember your father?"

"No, I was very young when my father left."

"Elle, you were nine years old when he disappeared; you would think you would remember something."

"That's not possible."

"Did your mother ever talk about him after he disappeared?"

"Margret has never talked about my father, ever."

"How odd. She said you and him were like two peas in a pod before he disappeared. She said that she thought talking about him would be too painful for you. Elle, you did know your father, whether you remember or not."

"Margaret and dad broke up when I was just a baby. I don't care what Margaret told you. She's lying."

"How can you be so sure, if you don't even remember your childhood?" Dr. Davis questioned.

"I remember a few scattered images, a bad smell, someone screaming. And then I'm older, and the drawings have started, the blackouts and the panic attacks."

"You have no real memories until after you're nine years old. The year you turned nine was the year that your father disappeared. It is as if the time you spent with him never happened."

"Maybe it didn't. If I was nine when he supposedly disappeared, wouldn't you think that I would remember something? How can you explain that? I don't know why, but I don't even have one damn photograph of us together. Margaret is misleading you, maybe for her own purposes."

"Margaret told me she could not stand having the photos around, so she gave all the pictures to your grandmother. You just don't remember because something has blocked, or erased, your memory."

"This is ridiculous; no one has the power to do that."

"Perhaps when your father disappeared, it was such a shock to your system that your subconscious chose to erase it, and you're not ready to face reality. So as far as you're concerned, it never happened."

"Or maybe my mom is creating a story to make herself feel better about me not having a father."

"You are the one with the problems. Not your mother."

"I might have problems, but so does Margaret. I don't suppose you remember everything from when you were young, do you?" Elle countered.

"Not one memory, Elle," Dr. Davis stated. She was trying to remain calm, but she was clearly agitated. She closed her notebook and shoved her glasses up higher on the bridge of her nose.

Elle could feel a migraine start to creep out of the darkness; a crack started to form; and a memory arose, strong and bright. "That's not true," Elle said as she put a hand to her temple to try to ease the pain erupting there.

"Name a memory then, a real one," Dr. Davis demanded.

"It's really bright outside, I know it should be dark out, but I see lights."

"In all our sessions you've never described this memory. I'm trying to help you get better, and you're lying to me."

"No, that memory is real," Elle assured Dr. Davis. "I just couldn't access it until now."

"Perhaps you're remembering the lights from all the TV cameras? When your father disappeared, it made national television."

"I don't remember my father. I just remember all these lights in the middle of night."

"What kind of lights? Streetlights?"

"No, these are different. They're so strong they're blinding me. I can't move."

"Elle, are you sure you're not lying to me to try to create an illusion of normalcy?"

"Ask my mother; ask her what she is so damn afraid of that she has shut out the truth each and every time I've asked her about my father. You ask her; you ask her what she's hiding from me."

"Elle, sit down and relax. Your mother loves you."

"Does she?" Elle had not even realized she had stood up; her hands were clenched into fists. She felt like she was ready to fight. Slowly, she lowered herself back down into the chair. "Ask her about the memory."

"I will. How do you really feel about your mother?" Dr. Davis asked, clearly trying to distract Elle since the memory was exciting her.

"Ok, I guess."

"Are you sure about that?"

"I think in Margaret's own twisted way, she loves and cares about me. But I don't trust her, and I think if I'm not careful, she could have me locked up in a nuthouse."

"What about blackouts? Have you had any since our last appointment?"

Elle did not want to answer yes to that horrible question. Why couldn't she believe that she was getting better? Maybe someday soon she would.

"Elle?"

"I think someone was in my apartment the other night. I woke up because I was almost certain someone turned my bedroom light on and then turned it back off, so I got up to investigate, and then…" It was better to leave it at that. It could take so much out of her when the blackouts hit.

"Why do you think you have this paranoia of people watching you, coming into your apartment?"

Elle said nothing to this response. Dr. Davis obviously did not believe that anyone had been in her apartment. And she probably never would.

"Elle, to try to uncover everything, we really need to get to the root of the problem. Are you ready to move forward with the hypnosis session?"

Dr. Davis liked to ask questions on the course of Elle's treatment and how they approached normalcy. But in reality, if Elle objected to treatment, Dr. Davis could seek a court order, and she had the power to strip Elle of everything she had, simply on her say-so. Freedom could cease to exist in the blink of an eye. Elle sighed, her back was against the wall, and she knew it. "I guess so."

"Good, does next Friday sound good to you?"

"Are you going to hypnotize me yourself?"

"Well, I could, but I think I want to bring in a specialist, someone who has even more experience in this field than I do."

"Do you have someone in mind?"

"I've actually been thinking about this for quite some time, but I didn't realize how delicate the situation was until I talked with your mother."

"What do you mean delicate?"

"We have no idea what we could be unlocking, and if we don't have an expert on hand, your mind could become even more damaged than it already is. Perhaps whatever you've repressed has been repressed for good reason; remembering could send you on a downward spiral with no way back. However, without this regression, we may never know what happened to you, so I think we should proceed, but cautiously. The alternative path, however, is heavy medication and electroshock therapy, and I don't think we want to attempt it unless it's absolutely necessary."

"Who the hell do you think you are, to be playing god with my life?" Elle screamed; she wanted the hell out of here.

"Please calm yourself. I am taking every precaution imaginable. Without this regression, you may never achieve a degree of normalcy. And that is something that everyone has a right to, no matter how damaged they are inside."

Elle knew that this hypnosis session had dangerous consequences, and it was not just what they might find. What if she lost what she already had? Elle could end up in an institution, drooling, with heavy meds running through her system, if things went wrong. Even if by some grace of God, if Elle could convince Dr. Davis not to go ahead with the hypnosis, Margaret had power of attorney over Elle's life, and ultimately it could come down to what Margaret thought.

"Elle…Elle?" Dr. Davis was calling her name.

Elle looked over at her psychiatrist.

"I know it's a big decision. Do you want to sleep on it?"

Elle shook her head. "Let's give it a try."

Dr. Davis nodded. "I'll set things up, and we'll move forward. I have a good feeling about this." She gave Elle's shoulder a reassuring squeeze.

The walk back to her apartment released some of the tension that came with the visit to Dr. Davis's office. That was not how therapy was supposed to work; unfortunately that was how it seemed to work for her, at least lately.

Chapter 5

The apartment finally came up for rent, and Heath jumped on it, snapping it up in minutes. The only thing he owned that was important was the video equipment, and he was going to pack it up and move in as soon as possible. Being next door to Elle, he would not need to rely entirely on the cameras, but it would always be helpful.

Heath started setting up the video equipment in his new apartment, and *new* was definitely the word to describe it. This apartment did not have rats scuttling down the hallways or people sleeping in the lobby.

The hardest part of his move was going to be sneaking Jamie in; he was still tied up behind the couch, this was Jamie's punishment for disobeying, and Heath intended to make him pay. Heath would transport Jamie by duffel bag, making sure to coldcock him prior, just to ensure he did not scream or move. Jamie could draw some unwanted attention to them if he started screaming, and the added attention was not worth the risk.

Heath was looking Jamie in the eyes; he knelt over Jamie and moved, swiftly bringing his elbow down into Jamie's face. Heath worked him over well, until Jamie's body was limp. Heath got the huge duffel bag and folded Jamie up until he fit in it; the zipper groaned as Heath lifted the bag onto his shoulder. When he walked out the apartment and toward the new building, the weight would have been staggering for a regular man, but for Heath, he could make it look normal, as if it were simply athletic gear he was transporting. Nobody noticed or paid any attention. Once inside his new apartment, Heath dropped the duffel bag and unzipped it. He dragged Jamie's limp body from the bag and checked his vitals; he was still alive, just unconscious from the beating.

***

Heath was fine-tuning his system, the cameras on his end in the new apartment. He looked up as Missy strolled through the front door; she was dressed like she had a hot date. Her jeans were tight, and she had a low-cut T-shirt on that barely met her jeans. Her hair was loose and curled slightly;

her eyes were outlined heavily in eyeliner. "You're going to get yourself into a lot of trouble dressed like that," Heath offered, but his focus was on the video equipment.

Missy smiled. "Maybe a little trouble is what I need right now. Why don't you come with me? You're entitled to a night off now and then, like a normal guy."

"You and I both know there is nothing normal about me. This is my life—it's a twenty-four-hour job, no breaks, no extended lunch hours, and no holidays. I do it and that is it."

"How long are you going to live like this, huh?" Missy snapped. Her mood had changed in a matter of seconds when Heath paid her little attention. "Ok, then."

"What's ok?" Heath absently asked as he fiddled with his input and output cables.

"You. You know, Heath, I used to think you watched over Elle because of a promise you made to her father, but now I think you do it not because you have to but because you enjoy it."

"You think this is enjoyable?" he snapped.

"Am I right, or aren't I?"

"You know what could happen to her."

"Only what you've told me. I think that, in some pathetic way, you've been doing this so long that it has warped your sense of reality; the second she finds out about you watching her every minute, it isn't going to make her fall madly in love with you. She is going to look at you in utter disgust. I don't want to burst your bubble, but that's the way it is. Now why don't you come out with me tonight and have one night of fun? Hmm?"

"Don't think I could handle fun at this point in my life," Heath stated.

"No matter how you look at it, Heath, if someone finds out you're watching her, they're not going to give you a medal. They'll lock you up in the Peeping Tom ward with the rest of the pervs."

"Look, once this is finished, I'm finished with anything having to do with her."

"You'll never be finished with her, even when she's dead."

Heath watched Missy stroll out of his apartment. He had tried to keep tabs on her, where she was and who she associated with. But for the better part, he knew he could trust that Missy would not do anything to jeopardize his mission. However, he did detect a slight note of jealousy in her voice; hopefully she would not do anything they would both come to regret.

Heath vaguely wondered if Missy saw Jamie on the floor, duct-taped up. She probably had, and she probably did not care. There was always a kind of tension between the two. He leaned back on the couch, briefly thinking about following Missy, but the idea quickly faded where it had begun.

***

Jeanie met up with Chace. If she was going to take out the good doctor, the time was now, and as midnight approached, so did her determination. She just had to be careful she did not get herself killed in the process. Chace had given her instructions on how to disable the security system from the power pole. That would help get her through the front door and should allow her enough time to do the job.

The quack had a good-sized house, two floors set far back from the street; the place dripped of wealth. Jeanie rolled her eyes—she would enjoy taking out the older woman's jugular and watching as the light in her eyes dimmed.

Jeanie took a towel from her backpack; she broke the glass in the front door as quietly as she could. She used her other hand to reach through the door and unlock it. Once inside, she surveyed the surroundings; fine overstuffed furniture filled each room. She crept to the staircase and headed upward; her heart was hammering so loudly that she could not hear anything else. But she was in a forward motion; the Dark Man told her to do this; disobeying was not even an option.

Once up the stairs, she had a few possibilities, but the first room was only a guest room. Jeanie's eyes had adjusted to the lighting, and she could just make out where the doctor lay in the bed of the second room. Jeanie took a deep breath and crept forward; she felt like something was happening. Her foot jerked forward so violently that she almost lost her balance; she looked down to find a twelve-inch knife gripped in her hand; where it had come from, she could not say. She had initially intended to use a gun with a silencer, but her hand was shaking so badly that she could

35

not take out a gun. It was frightening to not know what you were doing, to have no control over your movements. Jeanie moved to the edge of the bed, stepping up onto it until she was straddling the doctor with her legs. At the last second, the doctor opened her eyes and looked up into Jeanie's; there was a desperate scream before Jeanie plunged the knife down into Dr. Davis's throat; the blood was instantaneous and shot up, splattering everything. Jeanie dragged an arm across her face and wiped some of the blood off.

The quack gargled and gurgled for what seemed like forever but was probably only a minute or so. Finally, the doctor was silent. Jeanie wiped the blood from the knife and got out of there as quickly as she could. She was running by the time she hit the street; panic had spread throughout her body and was fueling a rush of adrenaline.

***

Heath pushed the scalpel deep down. Blood shot up, it was black, and it moved with a life all its own. It covered his hands and slid up his body. Beads of sweat popped out on his skin, and his brain screamed for oxygen while he was washed away in the blood. Heath jolted forward on the couch; he had not realized he had fallen sleep. He had gone so deeply into the past that he remembered one of his very first operations, and the memory had transformed into a full-blown nightmare. It disturbed him deeply, most of his memories were locked up tight. He did not know how long he had been asleep. It felt like only a short while, but when Heath turned the camera back onto Elle's bedroom, Elle was gone. Heath switched the camera onto the bathroom, bedroom, and living room. Elle's apartment was empty.

Oh shit, what have you done?

***

Missy flinched away from Jamie when the door was thrown open against the wall; she tried to pretend like she had not just untied Jamie, that perhaps Jamie had become a master of escape and had worked his hands and legs out of the rope that had secured him indefinitely.

However, Heath didn't seem in the least interested in Jamie's miraculous escape. The room's atmosphere had changed instantly.

"Heath, why aren't you at work?" Missy asked, frightened.

There were big bags under his eyes. His hair was sticking up in places, as if he had been running his hands through it again and again. Heath's hands were curled into fists.

Heath glanced at Jamie for a fraction of a second before he planted his hands flat on the counter. He stared out the kitchen window. Missy's eyes kept drifting from Heath to the bald patch on Jamie's head; the duffel bag's zipper had ripped out a big chunk of Jamie's hair.

"Heath?" Missy was suddenly uneasy as she moved toward him. He was not acting like himself at all. He just kept staring out of the kitchen window. "Is everything ok?"

"I lost her," Heath finally offered, as if it was difficult to admit this.

Missy knew she had heard him wrong. "Excuse me?"

"She's missing, god damn it."

"What do you mean you lost her?"

"I mean I fucking lost her; she disappeared on me faster than a toddler in a toy store."

"How did that even happen?"

"I don't know. I fell asleep. I just felt so wiped out. When I woke up, Elle was gone."

This did not sound like Heath. He never did anything other than what he thought he had to. Anything less was unacceptable. "Umm, well, we'll spread out and look for her," Missy suggested.

"Not him." Heath pointed a finger at Jamie.

"Why not?" Missy asked.

"Because I don't know if we can trust him anymore."

"What happened between you two?" Missy could not help sounding like a concerned mother trying to determine what her boys had been fighting over.

"I came home, and this little maggot was in Elle's apartment."

Missy knew her mouth was hanging open, but she could not help it. Jamie was rather pathetic, pathetic enough that at times you could not help having pity for him. "What were you doing in her apartment?" Missy asked Jamie.

"Why don't you tell her, Jamie?" Heath demanded.

Missy looked speculatively at Jamie. He was still poking at his head tenderly, completely oblivious that anyone was addressing him. She doubted Jamie would listen to anyone, unless they could explain the mysterious disappearance of his hair. Heath impatiently answered for him.

"He was there to get the TV, to pawn it for drugs."

Missy could not help letting a laugh escape her lips; she smothered it with her hand when she saw the look of anger transform Heath's features.

"This isn't funny!" Heath screamed at her.

Missy had to stifle another laugh; she could not help it; the noise had slipped out. "I'm sorry, Heath. It's just that, what did you expect when you recruited a drug addict?"

"Don't start with me, Missy. I fucked up enough in the last twenty-four hours. I don't need the pros and cons of recruiting Jamie for this mission."

"Ok, ok. We'll spread out and help you look for her; she couldn't have gotten too far."

"Missy, we gotta find her," Heath stated.

"I know. But Elle does go AWOL from time to time; of course, you're usually more on the ball than this, but we'll deal with it."

Chapter 6

Elle fell out of the blackout into reality, she was soaked, it had been pouring rain, and she was in a part of the city she did not recognize. It was hard to tell whether it was day or night; there was too little light, if any, from all the rain and clouds. It took her hours to pick her way to the subway and get back home.

Once safely in her apartment with the locks in place, Elle rushed to her phone and played her messages; most were from her mother. The last message was frantic; Margaret was begging for Elle to call her back.

Nothing had changed in her apartment, but it did not need to to know that the past two days were not spent here. The dirty feeling indicated she had not showered in days.

Another image crept up from the dark recesses of her mind, where memories didn't usually return from. The image was of people around her; they were screaming about something. She didn't remember what for, but she knew this was a new memory, a memory from the missing time possibly. What she had done in that time frame was a mystery.

A sharp knock made Elle jump; she felt nervous, as if the boogie man might be the visitor. Sighing inwardly, Elle had to shove these crazy thoughts aside. Going to the door, she looked through the peephole at her mother.

"Where the hell have you been?" Margaret demanded when Elle opened the door.

"Is today Friday?" Elle inquired.

"You blacked out for two whole days. You can't remember what you did or where you were, can you?"

"I've got to get to my appointment. I'm late. I would like it if you weren't here when I got back home."

"Do you know what I went through while you went on your crazy little escapade? Do you?"

"Do you know what I went through when I had this blackout? Well, neither do I, so get used to it." Elle walked to the bathroom. She needed a shower. Her hair felt gritty like she had been sludging through dirt or sand for days. She was slightly tanned and her hair had lightened quite a bit, either from the sun or bleach.

Elle showered and got dressed as quickly as possible.

"I think you should come and live with me. I could put locks on the doors so you cannot go on these crazy escapades."

"You've always wanted to lock me up and throw away the key. I'm not moving back in with you!" Elle screamed at Margaret. "Leave now."

Margaret left, thankfully; Elle could not deal with her anymore.

Elle was hoping that the hypnosis might be able to shed some light on where she had been for the past couple of days.

She made it to the session with no minutes to spare. Dr. Davis was noticeably absent. Sitting across from Elle's usual spot was an older gentleman. Elle estimated him to be at least fifty-five or sixty. His eyebrows were thick and dark, unlike his white mustache and hair. He was well built for his age, no potbelly, and kind blue eyes, eyes that did not seem natural. She stood fixated, taking in all his features at once. Elle had been told not to stare, but she couldn't help it; there was something oddly familiar about him, almost like she knew him. And yet that was impossible.

"Where is Dr. Davis?" Elle asked, trying to break the uncomfortable silence.

The older gentleman introduced himself as Pete, only Pete. And then Sadie, Dr. Davis's secretary, rushed into the room and whispered into Pete's ear.

"I've just been informed that Dr. Davis was discovered dead at her home." Pete stood up, brushing off the knees of his jeans.

"She's dead?" Elle demanded.

"Hon, sit down." Pete was trying to take control of the situation.

Elle felt in awe of Pete; he had complete control of his emotions, something she could only dream of.

She spoke slowly, afraid her words would betray what she was thinking. "How did Dr. Davis die?"

"It seems she was murdered," Dr. Davis's secretary said, looking uncertainly from Pete to Elle.

"If you want someone to talk to, call me." Pete offered his business card, pushing it into the palm of Elle's hand; on it was his cell number and the company he worked for.

***

Missy knew that looking for Elle would be like looking for a needle in a haystack. When Heath texted—"Elle showed up"—Missy knew that Heath would not backtrack Elle, but Missy thought it might be interesting to find out what she could. She had Elle's credit card number and enough info about her that she could not really disappear, at least not in a modern city. And though Elle was the mission, it was worth checking out to know everything there was to know. Missy did not like surprises.

***

When Elle arrived back at her apartment, she felt out of sorts, as if she should be ashamed of herself. Although for what, she couldn't say. She felt little to no remorse for her doctor's gruesome end. If anything, there was this feeling of unfinished business, and the more she thought about it, the more she wanted to call Pete and go ahead with being hypnotized.

Margaret was waiting at Elle's apartment when she arrived. "Thought I made myself clear that I wanted you gone. If you want to commit me, do it already. the constant threats are getting tiring," Elle stated.

"That was a quick session," Margaret said.

"The fucking quack didn't show up." Elle had no intention of telling Margaret the whole truth, surely she would find out when she called Dr. Davis's office, but for the moment, Elle just wanted quiet.

Margaret left with that, stomping down the hallway to the elevator.

Elle sat in the living room flipping Pete's business card end over end. She dialed the number slowly, hesitating before pressing the next number.

"This is Pete." He answered on the first ring.

"Hi, Pete, this is Elle. I was wondering if I could talk to you about things that I can't remember. Dr. Davis thought you could help. Do you think you could still do something for me?"

There was silence on the other end of the phone as Elle waited for Pete to reply. "I don't think I can help you unless you're hypnotized. I can't break behind that wall."

"What wall?"

"I think something happened to you to keep those first nine years of your life locked up tight. I read Dr. Davis's report on you. I don't deny that you need help, just maybe not the kind of help Dr. Davis could've given you."

"Well, that's not even an option anymore."

"I know, dear, but if you want to get to the root of your problems, talking about it is not going to unleash those memories. I have years of experience hypnotizing patients. If you want to uncover your past, you need to be hypnotized. But ultimately, it must be your decision."

***

A knock on the door almost made Elle jump out of her skin; she had to learn to not fear the unknown. If she could not cope with the unknown, then how could she cope with everything else.

She looked through the peephole. Pete's dazzling blue eyes looked back—it was unmistakable who was on the other side of the door. Elle was flooded with relief; she had been afraid that it was Margaret again.

Elle slid back the deadbolt to let Pete in.

"Come in," Elle said, standing back; she held the door wide for Pete. She felt a moment of unease as his blue eyes touched on her; as if he could read her thoughts. "Thanks for coming." She hoped she had not made a mistake.

"Not a problem. I work with people who are in situations like yours all the time."

"Should I be afraid?"

"That's something I won't know until we begin. Dr. Davis wasn't interested in healing you; she was interested in something else."

"What do you mean?" Elle asked, instantly alarmed.

"Some people claim that they have the kind of technology to erase memories, and I believe someone wanted to keep you from remembering."

Elle was skeptical. "What kind of people would claim to have that kind of technology?"

"That's the thing—they don't actually fit into the human category."

Elle could feel a prickly sensation at the nape of her neck. "Pete, I think you've lost me. What are you referring to?"

"Elle, I know you're skeptical, and I can understand that. For years I didn't want to admit what was right in front of me. But an event with your dad made me a believer."

Elle jumped to her feet, knocking her chair to the floor. Elle's heart was hammering in her chest; suddenly she no longer wanted to know what was in her past—she was more worried about her future. She was trying to put as much distance between herself and Pete as she could in her small apartment, because now his blue eyes were not friendly—now they scared the hell out of her. It was not a coincidence that Pete had known her father. But Pete was quick, and before she could put much distance between them, he had her by the neck, and he was strong. He had one of his hands clamped tightly over her mouth before she could scream, and thrashing uncontrollably did no good—he only strengthened his hold on her.

"I don't want to hurt you," Pete said quietly through clenched teeth. "Keep your mouth shut, and I won't."

"You got a funny way of showing it," she tried to say, but her screams were muffled by his hand clamped tightly over her mouth. His blue eyes drilled into hers, looking away was impossible, and slowly the fight in her seemed to drain from her body, until she was limp in his hands.

Pete lowered her body into the easy chair; she knew he was talking, speaking directly to her subconscious; she was sinking deeper and deeper into this hypnotic state. It had happened so slowly that she was not even aware at first that it was happening.

***

Pete took a step away from Elle, he had a good grasp on her mentally, and it really had not taken much, but then he already knew that would be the case. He had used a trigger word to unlock her mind, and in he had swept, just like the old days.

"Elle, I want you to remain calm, to remain conscious. I need you to think before reacting. You're not going to get excited by what I am going to tell you, and we are going to have a nice discussion. Is that ok with you?"

Elle nodded.

"You have a voice; answer me when I ask a question," Pete demanded.

"Ok," Elle answered.

"Good, I want you to think back to your earliest memory, and you *can* remember that far back. You remember everything that was locked in the far recesses of your mind, and you will remember now while we are having this conversation and when I end it; you will remember only what I want you to remember; is that understood?"

"Yes."

"Good. Elle, what do you see?"

"I see the lights in the sky, they're not the streetlights, but they're from a craft hovering above our house."

"Of course. Are you afraid?"

"No."

"Good, Elle, do you remember what happened next?"

"Yes, Mom is paralyzed on the front lawn, and…"

"And what?"

"Dad is standing there; he's moving toward the light."

Pete could see Elle's fingers clench down hard on the chair, fingers digging until her knuckles were snow white. "Elle, remember to remain calm."

Elle's fingers relaxed on the chair's arms.

"Then what happened?"

"Oh god, Dad, noooooooooo…" Elle was screaming.

"What happened, Elle?" Pete asked, alarmed. Elle was getting emotional; she was violating Pete's instructions.

"They took him?"

"Ok, let's try to remain calm. Do you remember your basement?" Pete questioned, trying to change the subject; he already knew that Grant had been taken. It was a test to see just what all, if anything, she could remember.

There was a knock on the door; Pete looked up; annoyance creased his forehead deeply. "God damn it." Pete went and answered the door.

Chace was there. "Did you get what I need?"

"I need more time. It's a mess in there."

"Look, I want what she's got, and we're paying you a lot to get it out," Chace snapped. "Hurry up."

Chace was working for the Dark Man, and he was annoying to deal with. Pete had accepted this job simply because he had made a promise to Grant years ago, to try to keep Elle safe, but this job was really starting to have its downfalls. If Pete was able to extract the info Chace and his goons wanted, they might just spare Elle's life.

"How did you know my father?" Elle questioned.

Pete broke out in a cold sweat. "You've got to go; she is breaking through the hypnosis; I need to regress her again." Pete had Chace by the shoulder and was shoving him toward the door.

"Pete, who are you really working for?" Elle demanded.

Pete looked over his shoulder uncertainly; Elle was on her feet. She wasn't completely out of the hypnosis, and this was not normal—she should be putty in his hands, and she seemed to be resisting him. Her head was hanging like she was drunk and it took an enormous amount of strength to keep it up. "Gooooo…" Pete said, breathing at Chace.

Chace shrugged his shoulders and left with one final smirk over at Elle.

Pete closed the door and locked it up tight; he needed the time to put her back under.

Elle took a step uncertainly toward Pete. God, it was scary to see her move, jerky like someone else was in control, something unholy and unnatural. Pete had to get her under control before something bad happened, before she broke completely out of the hypnosis. It was uncertain what all Elle had gone through years ago and just what Grant had done to her.

"Elle, calm down, we're going deeper into a relaxing state, and you will respond to my commands and not speak or move unless told to. I want—"

Elle responded instantly to something else in her head, and she rushed forward, grabbing Pete by the neck. Her hand encircled Pete's neck; one-handed, she was lifting him off the ground. She was so strong; it surprised and scared the hell out of Pete. Elle had become inhuman…

"That won't work." Elle hissed at him; she threw Pete across the room as if he were a rag doll. He struck the opposite wall, sliding down into a crumpled pile of arms and legs. Pete felt as if he had been in a bar fight and not just up against a single small woman.

"What the hell did Grant do to you?" Pete asked through gritted teeth; he was grimacing in pain, and he was scared for his life.

Elle smiled a devilish grin. "He put in a little insurance, a safety clause, if you will. Now, Pete, what part do you play in all of this?"

If Pete wanted to salvage this, he needed to be honest or she would rip him apart; in the current state she was in, he was no match for her mentally or physically. Her mind was operating on a level he was nowhere near; she would not succumb to suggestion or planted thoughts. Her one-word trigger would not put her under now. He had to be very careful from here on in. "Grant came to me to be hypnotized when he was just a kid. I was a young man just starting out, and he was the first patient that I had, with such an extraordinary situation. He told me about his father and how he did not want to end up like him. Grant wanted to find out if there was anything wrong with him so he could start to correct things before everything got out of hand. Later when he was older, he told me about you and how much he wanted it all to stop. I tried to help him, but they had this plan from the beginning, and we're no match for them." Pete slouched over his trembling legs.

"What did my father want stopped?"

"He wanted to stop the abductions and being afraid of what they were doing."

"He was abducted?"

"Grant and others, and like him, and like most of them, they can't remember what happened when they were abducted. Most people are controlled; they're more robotic than human now."

"That's where you came in."

"But nothing I have ever heard over the years has scared me as much as what your father said under hypnosis, when we had our very first session."

"What did he tell you?"

Pete handed Elle a folded-up letter that Grant had written for her years ago. It was a piece of slightly yellowed paper with neat handwriting.

"Dear Elle, I love you so much. I suppose, if you are reading this, I am no longer with you. I guess you might say this is my last will and testament; unfortunately there is nothing that I will be leaving, except an ugly truth that will turn your world upside down. If, of course, it isn't already. You are the one that can stop what is happening to us, to free us from what has been done. But first you must learn to understand why they want us, why they want you. After you were born, I designed a blueprint; the blueprint had a much greater value than I ever imagined. The Dark Man found out I had it, and I realized in my own head, the blueprint wasn't safe any longer.

"When you were almost nine, I programmed it into you for safekeeping. You are the only one who has access to the blueprint. It is not accessible through a key word or any methods like that. I cannot tell you how to do it either; just because you don't know how to get it out, it doesn't mean that the Dark Man can't find a way of his own in. Since you are reading this, I know they haven't. They might try another course of action to get them out, and they will do just about anything. They'll turn people against you, good people you've known forever. And pretty soon they will get the plans out one way or another. They have no breaking point, no line they won't cross; they will keep coming until they get what they want.

"Unfortunately, destroying the plans is not an option; without them, you will die and quickly. As long as you have them, you still have value. It will buy you some time! You'll have to figure out on your own, like many other things, who to trust and who not to. But there is one silver lining to this gray cloud that has enveloped you. When I installed the plans, I programmed someone to help you. I programmed your own personal protector; they are around your age, and their goal in life is to protect you from the Dark Man and his kind. You are what the protector lives and breathes for. But remember, just because I have programmed them, it does not mean that you have met them already. They have been trained to decide when it's time to make their existence known to you—when you will believe things without question and when you need the protection the most. This person I programmed is someone that can't be taken over by them. He is immune to them and their ways of control. He is the one person that you will bestow all your trust in during this journey.

"And finally, I want you to know that the things Margaret may say or do to you are not of her own accord, much less what some of the other people do.

"Keep up with what is going on with baseball, just because I'm not with you. You always loved it so much when you were little. We used to go catch a game every chance we got; if you get the chance, don't pass up the opportunity.

"I'm proud of you, Elle. Love, Dad.

"P.S. Everyone is the enemy, and remember to watch out for anyone with a tattoo of three black triangles. They are usually burned along the spine, but they may be on another part of the body. You cannot lift everyone's shirt up, or check behind their ears, but if they act a little weird, maybe their behavior is unorthodox, then chances are, they are being controlled by a higher power, and nothing can be done to save them."

Elle had broken completely out of the hypnosis; she was conscious and seemed aware of everything that had happened, or at least most of it. Whether she remembered Chace being in her apartment, Pete could not say. It was strange how she had converted from a destructive, powerful being back to her normal self—if she could be considered normal—and seemingly with no side effects and no interest of resorting to her powerful self again.

"Pete, who is this person that is supposed to protect me. Is it you?"

"Elle, this person is your age. I'm more than a few years older, a lot more."

"What do they look like?"

"I don't know what he looks like. I haven't seen him since he was a kid."

A blunt knock on the door seemed to rattle Elle to the core. "Elle, let me in."

"Is that Margaret?" Pete asked.

"Yes, it's my mother." She folded up the letter from Grant and put it in her jean pocket. She walked to the door. She stood in front of it trying to look normal before she opened the door.

Her mother seemed to still herself when her eyes met Pete's. Elle seemed to feel her mother's hatred for this man.

"Pete, it's been a long time," Margaret offered.

"Yep, Margaret, it has. You left without saying good-bye," Pete stated.

"Some things are better left unsaid. Besides, you can only take so much of the crazy before you start to worry about it rubbing off on you. My husband goes missing, and everyone assumes that aliens got him."

"It was one of the theories," Pete answered.

Elle looked back and forth between her mother and Pete.

"I've tried so hard to make you better, Elle; you just don't know how much I want you to have a normal life," Margaret said.

"Define normal?" Elle questioned.

"Don't get smart with me; all your life, you have wanted to be like everyone else. You know what you want; you have always known. Do not let Pete come into your life and fill your head with this nonsense."

"It's not nonsense, Margaret; why don't you tell her why her father was taken," Pete demanded.

"Stop it; stop it." Margaret hissed.

"Tell her!" Pete screamed back.

"For Christ's sake, what do you want her to know, that her grandfather was crazy and spent a better part of his life in an asylum? And then her father tells her these lies when she's just a child, lies that he really can't handle himself, that he really seems to believe, that scare him so badly that suddenly he disappears. Of course, everyone assumes aliens got him, ignoring the more likely possibility that he just wandered off into the desert."

"That's not what happened, and you know it's not."

"All we really know is that you weren't there, I wasn't, and if Elle was, she sure as hell can't remember. Your grandfather said he was there when they cleaned up the spaceship that crashed in Roswell, New Mexico, in 1947."

"Elle doesn't need to know about that."

"You wanted her to know things. I'm just doing what you wanted. When Grant was just a little boy, his dad started to patrol their house, carrying a gun like he was still in the war. Delmar said that he wasn't going to let them get him, them meaning aliens. Grant was never allowed out at night; your grandfather, Delmar, said that if he ever caught Grant outside after lights out, he would kill him, that Grant could not be trusted, that he might one day turn on his own parents. He said that someone who went against the rules of the household was doing the devil's work. Grant's mother, Jean, told Grant to just stay inside at night, and no problems would ever arise. She believed that Delmar would not really hurt Grant. The summer your father was eight, he had a best friend; the friend convinced Grant to meet him in the valley to set off bottle rockets. Either Delmar didn't sleep at night or your father just wasn't that lucky. Delmar caught Grant sneaking back into the house; he almost killed Grant that night. It took Jean and three cops to tear Delmar's hands from Grant's throat. Grant ended up with a concussion and a broken collar bone.

"Your grandfather told these lies to anyone and everyone about being there and seeing the bodies and knowing why they had come. Grant only followed in his father's footsteps, and now you are following. Every generation has been crazy, and I wanted you to be sane, for once in this bloodline. There is nothing out there. That was just a weather balloon that fell that night," Margaret stated placidly.

"That's not the whole story, Margaret, and you know it. Grant went out to meet his friend that night. The friend never made it out of there alive, and Grant almost died. The other boy was found a couple days later, or what was left of him. Rumor was that he died of unusual circumstances. At least that's what the police and the coroner stated. Delmar was not crazy, your father was not crazy, and, Elle, you are not crazy either. They are out there, and they really did get a hold of your grandfather. Then they got your father. Now they're after you. I cannot fight them. I'm just an old man. I might be able to help you, but it is up to you. When you are ready, find me, hopefully before it's too late."

Chapter 7

Pete left and with him any hope of releasing Elle from her past. Elle sat down on the floor, she could see that she had a lot of people to fight, and she wasn't sure who to trust.

"Elle, get off the floor; this is silly. I want you to consider moving to an institution; it will protect you from these visitors, from yourself. They've had progress with people like you. Elle, are you listening to me?"

"Mom, did we used to live in Roswell, New Mexico?"

"You're intolerable."

"Margret, why don't I have any memories of Dad?"

"Oh, honey, when your father went missing, I think it hurt you more than I realized. I couldn't help you. I couldn't help myself. I was overwhelmed with depression, and I was struggling to keep our heads above water. Your father left us with a sea of debt. You were looking for answers, and I wasn't there when you needed me. Your mind started to unravel, and by the time I got myself under control, it was too late for you. You had put up this wall, and no one could get past it."

"I have a lot to think about. I need to be alone," Elle said, holding the door for Margaret. There was one thing that Elle knew for certain, her father never left them with a sea of debt. He had a left bank account in Elle's name to live off. What else was Margaret lying about?

"Sure, honey."

Margaret smiled, she left, and Elle barricaded herself in her apartment."

***

Heath knew he felt his heart skip a beat or two, something was going on, and he wasn't sure what. Over the past few days, things had happened and not in his favor. First Elle had disappeared, and then her psychiatrist, Dr. Davis, had been murdered. It saved Heath from having to take care of her himself, but who else could have had a grudge with her, an escaped patient that didn't like being sent to a psych ward? Dr. Davis had been messing with Elle's mind, and it was starting to worry him, not just what she would find but who it would draw in.

That, in itself, was frightening, but when Pete showed up at Elle's front door, it was a blast from the past. It had been years since Heath had seen Pete, he did not trust Pete then, and he did not trust him now. Heath did not like watching Pete climb inside Elle's head. He was on his feet and getting ready to intervene; he had his gun drawn and was turning to go through the front door when things started to get very interesting. Grant must have left some kind of special orders or commands in Elle's subconscious, and just as Chace showed up, Heath's boss of all people, Elle broke freakishly out of the hypnosis and threw Pete across the room. Elle clearly had been programmed to keep intruders out; tossing Pete was no easy task, considering Pete was a good-sized man of well over two hundred pounds. The way things were progressing, it was getting time for the Dark Man to make his move; once things changed, there was no going back.

***

Jeanie unlocked the door carefully using two pieces of very thin wire. The lock drew back, and the door creaked open a few inches. She stepped inside the house, shutting the door softly behind her; she was getting more comfortable with the new roll the Dark Man had given her.

She moved through the house with a relaxed and undisturbed confidence, stopping now and then to look at some article of fascination. She stopped in the living room before heading to the mantle above the fireplace. There was a picture that had caught her eye. Jeanie clasped the picture frame tightly in her hands. There was enough moonlight coming in through the bay window to distinguish who the two figures in the photograph were: one was of Grant Mackowski, Elle's father, and the other was of his partner on the project, Vincent Striker.

Jeanie was so engrossed in the picture that she didn't hear movement in the living room.

"Elle?"

Jeanie glanced up for the briefest of seconds before returning her eyes back to the picture.

"Hello, Jeanie. Sorry, you're standing in the dark over there; sometimes it's hard to distinguish between the two of you."

"It's ok, honest mistake, Vincent. When was this picture taken?"

"Right before Grant got discharged from the 'Project' in Nevada," Vincent answered.

"Oh." Jeanie nodded absently.

"What the hell was Chace doing this morning?" Vincent demanded.

"I heard about that."

"And what are you planning to do about it?"

Jeanie studied the picture, ignoring Vincent's question. She might have been working with Vincent in the past, but it did not mean she liked what they would inevitably be doing to Elle. Hell, she would have to be stupid to continue along the path they were taking. She did not trust Vincent; if anyone turned on her, it would be him. "You know, I don't think you're going to be able to help us get the information we want. It seems Grant did not trust you very much, even back then." She looked over at Vincent.

"I know a hell of a lot more than you do; if Elle were in a mental institution, we could work 24/7, not a few hours a week. And with the right drugs, Elle's mind would relax. We could get inside with no problem."

"Doubtful. Pete already tried to manipulate her mind; she broke out of his hypnosis. I'm afraid, if we let you try things your way, you will fuck everything up."

"What do you mean?"

She could hear the shock and confusion in his voice, his voice was empty of fear, but that did not matter. "You don't know how sorry I am, Vincent." She reached into her coat pocket and pulled out the gun. She pointed it at Vincent and allowed just enough time for fear to contort the expression on his face. The bullet blew out his right kneecap, knocking him face down into the carpet. It was so unexpected that he lay there for a few minutes, seeming to not even know what had happened, clearly in shock. The blood was seeping through his pajamas, soaking into the rug. "You think I was going to let you put Elle in a loony bin and let them torture and feed her toxic drugs? Is that what you thought?"

"You need what Elle has more than I do, or you will never be free of the Dark Man."

"Shut up; just shut your lying face."

Vincent rolled onto his back, favoring his leg.

"I think you need a matching set."

"Huh?"

Jeanie circled around in front of him. His good knee bent in the thin blue material of his pajamas. She pulled the trigger. The noise exploded into the house, making the gun barrel smoke slightly.

"*Aaaaahhhhh!*"

He screamed like a girl. Jeanie waited.

"Oww, goddamn you!" Vincent screamed. He was slowly dragging his body toward the phone.

"You know I can't let you leave." Vincent looked over his shoulder at her. His eyes wide with fear, he was not wearing his glasses anymore. His eyes almost looked normal for once. He rolled slightly over as if to ward her off. She jumped, landing on him, knocking him flat on his back. He screamed, clawing at her face. She used the gun to slap him in the face. Jeanie grabbed his hair and smashed his head backward into the floor. She brought the gun to his temple. The bullet barely made a noise as the side of Vincent's head blew off and splattered against the wall, dripping where the picture of him and Grant had once stood.

When Jeanie had bought the gun, she had made sure to pick up a silencer. But it did not matter if the neighbors heard. Jeanie smashed the fancy frame, removing the picture from the glass. She pocketed it before moving back out of the house and into the night.

She had one more thing to do before her work was done for the night, before she could rest. She walked out of the house and to the rental car parked in front. She got in and drove back to Elle's.

Jeanie unlocked Elle's front door; she felt like an intruder, but the feeling quickly diminished. She deposited the keys on the little table, alongside the gun she had used to kill Vincent. She looked down at the landline, a smile spread across her face, and Jeanie picked up the phone and set it against her ear. She looked down at the numbers; an anonymous call would be the best; Elle would be arrested and would spend the night in the loony ward. And without Vincent pumping her full of drugs, the reality of Elle murdering the two doctors would put her into a fragile state of mind, where the plans could be unlocked from her subconscious. Jeanie believed that fear would be Elle's trigger. Once the Dark Man had the blueprint, things would finally move forward.

***

Elle fell out of the darkness. What had brought her back, she had no idea. She lifted her head off the pillow, staring sleepily, listening carefully. Had she heard someone in her apartment again? She did not know what had awakened her this time. Wait a minute. There it was again. It was the phone ringing that had brought her from a deep sleep. She got up, throwing back the blankets and grabbing her housecoat. She stepped into the living room and moved toward the phone. She hesitated for a few seconds, her hand hovering just above the phone. It kept ringing, and she looked at it, unsure of what she was so afraid of. She glanced nervously toward the front door—the top lock of the door was not done up. She had locked it before she went to sleep, which meant someone had been in here. She stared uneasily at the front door, trying to figure out just how they had gotten in, the ringing of the phone almost forgotten. A creepy sensation traveled down her spine. She picked up the phone just to silence the noise; she could not think. "Hello."

Silence was the only answer, and it stretched out. Elle wanted to scream. Was this the person who had been in her apartment earlier, and now they were calling to torment her? Or was it just a robocall?

"Get out of the building," the voice yelled at Elle.

"Who is this?" Elle asked.

"Get out of the building; they're coming for you."

Elle looked down, finally noticing for the first time the gun that was lying beside the phone. "Who is this?" Elle demanded, but it was no more than a whisper. Desperation had planted her feet to the floor.

"Now, damn it."

Elle had been scared plenty of times growing up, especially when the blackness seeped over her, dragging her down into the unknown. Elle dropped the phone and raced for the front door in the middle of the night, wearing only her pajamas and the housecoat. She did not dare to look back.

Where had that gun come from? She did not own a gun.

Elle headed for the stairwell; she felt like she could get cornered if she took the elevator. She threw the door open to the stairwell, a sinking in her heart as she assessed the stairs; there was metal grating on the edge of the stairs to prevent people from slipping. Noises from the hallway, of cops shouting, of feet pounding out of the elevator, helped make up Elle's mind. It was too late to go back for shoes. The grating dug into the bare soles of her feet, tearing them to bits, leaving a trail of blood in her wake.

By the time Elle had reached the third floor, the bottoms of her feet were coated in blood. A few more steps and she slipped in the blood. Everything happened at once: Elle reached out for the guardrail too late, she was falling, then she hit the stairs and rolled down. She slammed onto the landing with a cry of pain. The pain shot up through her shoulders. She lay there for a few moments, trying to catch her breath. Her pajamas were torn and her shoulders hurt, and the bottoms of her feet were in tatters.

She reached out with her right arm to clasp the guardrail and pulled herself into a sitting position. The knees of her pajamas were completely missing, big gaps where her raw knees poked through. Elle pulled herself to her feet and started limping down the stairs slowly. Her body had responded to the fear. She was still trembling from the phone call.

"Halt, ma'am, put your hands on your head and stand still."

Elle looked up to the landing above her. There were two police officers pointing their guns at her. Her hands slowly rose from her sides and did as they demanded, but she knew this had to be a mistake. What could they possibly want with her? She had not done anything!

"Ok, surround her, men."

Four cops came slowly up the stairs; all their guns were pointed at Elle. The first cop spoke to her again, "Kneel down, keeping your hands on your head."

Elle did as they demanded, afraid that they would shoot. The stairwell filled with cops pounding up and down the stairwell. Her hands were jerked off her head and pulled painfully behind her. The cuffs dug into the flesh of her wrists, and she knew that there was no mistake. She was the person that they were after, for whatever reason that had been created to entrap her.

A pair of hands lifted her to her feet. The cop read her Miranda rights.

"Hey, boss, she's bleeding pretty bad." The cop pointed at her feet. The landing of the stairwell was covered in her blood.

"Can you walk down here, ma'am?"

"Yes." Elle walked down with an officer holding on to each of her arms so she would not fall. They exited the stairwell and rode the second-floor elevator down to the lobby. There were reporters waiting outside. They swarmed around Elle and the arresting officers—the cops shouted for the reporters to get back. Elle actually welcomed the back of the cop car.

"Why did you do it?" one reporter asked.

"Did you know what you were doing when you did it?" another asked.

"What do you have to say for yourself?" a third yelled through the window of the cop car.

At the hospital, the staff was waiting with a gurney. Elle was escorted from the cop car and laid down flat on her back. Elle was strapped down tightly; she had to take shallow breaths to breathe. She was so overwhelmed by everything, so much so that she barely felt her feet anymore; she felt numb from head to toe. Tears overflowed, running down her cheeks, distorting everyone and everything. Elle closed her eyes, the cops were talking to her, but they faded into the background until she could not hear them. They had to wait outside the emergency room while the doctor and nurses cleaned and bandaged her feet. She felt worn out; after everything that she had gone through, she just wanted to shut everything out.

A few memories came out of nowhere, memories that Elle had never had access to before, possibly being released due to the high levels of stress she was under. Elle let herself drift backward in time. She felt free, even if for just a little while.

Elle was about six, she was playing in her backyard, and she could feel eyes on her. She dropped the chalk she was using to draw on the sidewalk to look at the fence enclosing their backyard; she could just make out a pair of eyes watching her from the vertical boards of the fence.

Somewhere along the way, Elle fell asleep, and this was where she wanted to go most of all. In sleep, no one and nothing could hurt you. Dreams came and went, and one memory of long ago erupted from where memories usually did not return from.

***

This was a quiet night; Elle was watching a long movie and had been glued to the TV all evening. Heath had abandoned her to make supper. When he turned back to look at the video feed, he was shocked that there was nothing but static on the video camera. What was going on? Nothing should have interrupted the feed. The feed was from a cable that ran directly to the various cameras in Elle's apartment; nothing ran off Wi-Fi.

A soft flicker of light caught Heath's attention; the light was interrupted by someone's shadow standing just outside his apartment door. Heath moved back out of the line of his front door, just in case someone started shooting. The lights in his apartment flickered, and then everything went out, shut off. He heard footsteps retreat after a few seconds, heading far off down the hallway. The lights came back on, Heath looked toward the video camera, but only static remained on the feed. Heath unlocked his door and stepped quietly out into the hall. There was no one in the hallway anymore that he could see. He moved cautiously, looking in the direction he was headed and back over his shoulder. His left hand felt up under his shirt to the silenced gun tucked into the waist of his jeans. Heath pulled the gun out. God, he was craving a cigarette, but that would have to wait. The hallway was dark, a few light bulbs had burned out, and that created a gloomy atmosphere for a killer to lurk. This was a weird change of pace: usually he was the killer, and now he had become the hunted.

The corner was right there, he could have stepped around it, but instead he retraced his steps back to his apartment and went around the other way. The hallway was a complete square; he would try to come up behind them. He pulled his keys out of his pocket while walking around the first corner; he rounded another corner; there was one more to go before he would be in line with the other corner. Heath hesitated, jiggling the keys noisily as if he did not have a care in the world. He rounded the last corner, gun held out in front of him. But no one stood in the hallway.

Had the visitor stepped into the elevator or taken the stairs out of sight? Keys jingling, gun in the other hand, Heath headed back toward his apartment. He kept walking though, moving more slowly. Where had the stranger gone? Heath moved down the hallway, listening for any sound. The silence seemed to fill the apartment complex. Heath stopped at one door, listening, wondering if the stranger was hiding behind this door. He did not care if someone came down the hallway and found him lurking outside someone else's apartment. His eyes scanned up and down the poorly lit hallway for any sign of movement.

He did not see it when it happened—he heard it, just a fraction louder than a whisper. The door he had just passed squeaked ever so softly.

Every muscle was tensed and ready for action, and he heard the softest noise, someone cocking a gun on the other side of the door. Heath dropped the keys and whirled, pulling the trigger; a return bullet whizzed by Heath's ear. The head ducked back into the apartment, completely vanishing behind the door. The second slug almost hit Heath in the head; if he had not jerked his head back, it would have hit him in the side of his face. The guy was firing straight through the closed door at him. A few droplets of his blood peppered the opposite side of the hall from the splinters of wood flying everywhere. Heath kicked the door in; he fired two more shots into the darkened apartment. A soft *oomph* resounded within the apartment. A person fell forward into the hall. Heath tried the light switch just inside the door, but the lights did not work. He felt for his phone, hoping it was there in his back pocket. It was.

The stranger was not identifiable; Heath grabbed a hold of the stranger's head and dragged them back into the apartment. He leaned the door against the frame as best he could. He reached for his phone in the back pocket; his hands fell away as he realized, for the first time, that he was not alone in the apartment. The toe of his boot dipped in the spreading puddle of blood; he moved softly forward, feeling in the darkness for the presence. He closed his eyes, letting his instincts take him to his enemy. His hands reached out, holding the gun tightly—the grip would be permanently etched in his palm after this. Something to the left, he turned slightly. Fired.

Labored breathing filled the small apartment; it made Heath's skull ache. The pressure was inches away. He pulled the trigger, emptying the cartridge until the rapid breathing stopped.

Heath palmed his cell phone and held it inches from the dead body; the bullets had gone through the stranger's neck and had embedded in the drywall behind. Her hand had gone instinctively to her neck; blood poured between her fingers. The other bullets had hit the wall at least two feet from her, except for one that had gone through her right shoulder. Beside her on the floor was a gun; she must have dropped it when he had wounded her firing through the closed door. Her eyes were closed, and her hand slipped away from her neck, falling limply into her lap. Her palm distinctly had three black triangles tattooed there. This only confirmed that they were controlled by another force; thankfully, they could be killed easily.

One good surveillance confirmed that he was the only one in this apartment alive. It also told Heath everything he needed to know; one of the walls was covered with hundreds of pictures of Elle—people she bumped into on the street, her riding in the elevator, getting on the subway, carrying groceries home. They were documenting her life to try to locate him, but he never followed her outside. He just watched her from the safety of his apartment. That is probably why it took them so long to pin him down.

"Fuck, it's tonight," Heath whispered. It had to be. Why else would they come to his apartment? They now knew what he looked like and were going to try to get rid of him. They had screwed with the feed on his video camera to try to distract him, intercepting his camera equipment with their technology, scrambling the signal.

Heath bolted out of the apartment not caring about the gun still in his hand. He flung open the door to his apartment and raced inside. This was no fucking coincidence; when things happened, they happened for a reason. He picked up the phone and hit one on the speed dial of his landline. He reached for the pack of smokes while the phone rang, grabbed the lighter, igniting the end of the cigarette. Pick up the goddamn phone, Elle, Heath screamed in his mind. He willed her to pick it up, unless she had already been taken.

It rang and rang; long spaces of time seemed to separate the ring tones. Deep puffs of smoke escaped Heath's lips. Waiting was driving him nuts; he was about ready to go through the fucking wall that separated their apartments. Elle surprised him when she finally picked up. He choked on the smoke, inhaling everything; he had not done that since his first cigarette when he was a kid. He held his hand over the phone so she would not hear him coughing—hell yeah, he was embarrassed, embarrassed as if he were an amateur rather than a full brother of Marlboro.

"Hello."

He gasped for breath, trying to force the smoke out of his lungs so he could grab fresh air. The smoke cleared making room for air. He sucked it down, removed his hand from the phone, and spoke. "Get out of the building."

"Who is this?" Elle asked.

"Get out of the building; they're coming for you."

There was a hesitation on Elle's end. "Who is this?" She demanded in a whisper.

He wanted to slam down the phone; he knew she was afraid; she knew this was not a prank phone call by the fear etched in her voice. "Now, damn it," he yelled at her. He thought about grabbing her the second she came out the door, but it might not be safe to do that; he had not planned on the Dark Man making his move so soon. Heath needed to plan everything out carefully; maybe that is why they choose tonight, because they knew Heath did not think it would be so soon. Were they watching? His only hope, up till now, was that they did not know what he looked like—his face was not on the wall of pictures.

He heard someone running in the hallway; he hoped it was Elle. He turned to go, not bothering to grab anything but the manila envelope and a box that contained his police scanner. He tucked the gun away before entering the hallway, pulling a ball cap down low to shadow his face. The elevator dinged, the doors opened, and four police officers rushed out, knocking Heath aside as they headed into Elle's apartment. They paid no attention to Heath as he climbed onto the elevator; he didn't fit the description of who they were looking for.

He was too late; the cops were now involved, which meant he had to be very cautious; he did not have the manpower to take out the entire police force. It was not safe to get anything from her apartment either; they were already crawling all over every inch. He had to get out of the building and as far from here as possible so he could not be tied to the killings just down the hall. The forces that be had created a reason to go after her, so no one would suspect anything when Elle was arrested. Most of the population was under their control already; there were only a couple hundred thousand people that were not.

Heath rode the elevator to the lobby, then he headed out the front door. Two cops were guarding the entrance; they let him through after he informed them which apartment he lived in. Outside the building, there was a buzz of activity, more cops, and a bunch of reporters.

He left and walked down the street; the darkening night rumbled from the thunder; the rain started. Heath walked to his bike in the parking structure, he drove to a coffee shop, and there he pulled out his cell phone under the fluorescence.

He needed Missy's and Jamie's help; he hit Missy's number; she picked up on the sixth ring.

"Yeah."

"It's tonight."

"What's tonight?"

"The night we've been waiting for."

"What do you want us to do?" Missy asked.

"You know what I want you to do." The scanner picked up the story he was waiting on: Elle was arrested and being taken to Mass General Hospital for non-life-threatening injuries. She was wanted for murdering her psychiatrist and taking the life of another doctor tonight. He could not rule Elle out of killing her psychiatrist, since Elle had gone missing that night and had been missing for a while before she came back home. But as for taking the life of another doctor, she had been home all evening and couldn't have done it. It was clearly a setup. "Is Jamie with you?"

"Yeah."

"Ok, tell him to meet me outside Mass General Hospital tomorrow before eight o'clock, near the emergency wing where the ambulances wait. Missy, I want you to get on the road; you need to arrive before we do; get everything ready; you will need to be on the opposite side of the roadblock."

"Ok," Missy answered.

"Good luck."

"You too."

"Don't forget to take your gun; you could run into trouble."

"I already got it," Missy stated.

Heath ended the call and headed to the airport; his bike wove quickly through traffic, which at this hour was light. He had a bag stowed in one of the lockers there, with everything he needed. The stuff Missy needed was stored an hour from the city limits, Grant had hammered into Heath the importance of being prepared for almost any type of scenario, and Heath had done just that.

Chapter 8

When Elle woke up to the opaque white of a hospital room, she had been asleep for a while, and she had slept well. The feelings of peace were quickly replaced with dread, she was lying in a hospital bed along the south wall, and her hands were cuffed to the aluminum railing surrounding the bed. There were few furnishings in the room, only a monitor and a chair. Nothing was within reach.

The room was illuminated by the sunbeam coming from the eastern window. So many questions raced through her mind, questions of why she was here, but nothing came to mind. Then it all came back to her: the mysterious caller and the urgency in his voice for her to get out of the apartment building, fleeing down into the stairwell, how the soles of her feet were torn to shreds, and how she was arrested. But who had called her? How did they know what was going to happen only minutes before she was arrested? She was not going to go to jail for something that she did not do—or at least for something that she could not even remember doing.

Elle had to get out of there, a higher power had put her there, and Margaret was likely to blame.

"Hey, are you ready for visitors?"

Margaret peeked in through the door; her heels clicked rhythmically on the floor. It was a rhetorical question of course; Margaret plowed right on in with a bouquet of flowers.

"What am I doing here?" Elle snapped. Margaret's brow furrowed. "Elle, I wish you had not done what you did; however, you can plead temporary insanity. And this way, you can get the kind of help you need. Dr. Davis, bless her heart, did what she could for you. But you need full-time care."

Elle gasped for breath. "What is it that everyone thinks I did?"

"Elle, don't you remember what you did last night?"

"No!" Elle screamed at Margaret. "I don't remember anything other than the cops coming for me."

"You killed Vincent Striker, and they think you killed Dr. Davis too."

"No." Elle was shaking her head.

"Elle, I'm afraid you did kill Vincent, and now they're trying to match your prints to those found in Dr. Davis's home."

"No, I didn't kill anyone."

"I wish that were true, sweetheart," Margaret answered sadly.

Elle felt panic. She knew she had not killed anyone; this was completely out of character, even for her. Even if she had blacked out, she had never done anything like this before—or at least she did not think she had. "This isn't happening," Elle chanted softly under her breath.

"Honey, you didn't know what you were doing. Maybe in some messed-up way, this is a good thing; you can finally get the kind of help you need."

Margaret was reacting very calmly to all this. "You got me put in here, didn't you? Now get me out," Elle stated. She felt so cold; if given the chance, she was not sure what she would have done to her mother.

Margaret shook her head. "There is a guard posted outside that door, and you are cuffed to the bed. I know you don't believe this, but this is the best place for you right now."

Elle started to cry; she wanted so much more than sitting in some padded room, drugged into a drooling, induced stupor.

"Elle, whether you knew you were doing it or not is irrelevant now. You're guilty; your prints were all over the gun used to kill Vincent Striker."

"Someone else did it. You have to get me out of here, before it's too late."

"You're not in your right mind."

A sound distracted Elle from what Margaret was saying.

"Move in there, fat stuff, or you're going to get a bullet through your guts."

The security guard came through the door, walking backward with his hands on his head; he was followed by a kid of no more than twenty. The kid's brown hair was stringy, and it hung down from underneath a do-rag. He wore a baggy T-shirt with Beavis and Butthead on it. The shirt was so worn that it looked see through except for where the characters were still emblazoned on the front. He had on a pair of camouflage pants with pockets all the way from his feet to hips. A pair of sunglasses hung from the neck of the shirt. It looked like he needed them; he kept blinking his bloodshot eyes uncertainly at the Elle, Margaret, and the cop. His arms were skinny except where a small amount of muscle bulged. His appearance had distracted Elle from the silenced gun in his hand.

"Hey, girlie, are you Elle?" He waved the gun in her direction when he referred to her.

Elle felt shock paralyze her, and it took a few minutes before she answered. "Who's asking?"

"You're the girl. I'd know your voice anywhere."

It was a statement, not a question. He started snorting and kind of laughing at the same time. He seemed to forget about the guard and leaned over the railing of the bed to pat at her feet.

"You're pettier than I remember. He never let me look at you when he was watching you." The kid was shaking his head, a big grin ear to ear.

"Jab your emergency button, Elle," Margaret said, edging toward the door.

With Elle's one hand, she could just barely reach the button, but she made no attempt.

"Hey, shut it," the kid squealed.

The kid rushed Margaret. He snapped out with the gun and hit Margaret across the temple; she fell backward onto the floor. Blood poured out where her scalp had been split; the kid stayed focused on Elle. The cop took a step to toward the kid, and his pants rustled as he drew closer. The kid was on high alert and whirled on the cop, focusing the silenced gun on him. The cop bolted for the door.

"Any last words?" The cop fell forward as the bullet tore its way through his back and out his chest. Blood poured out of the bullet hole and across the floor toward the door. It became concentrated into a thin stream of blood, with a mind of its own, as it seeped out of the guard. The blood continued with an abundance of momentum, heading toward the hallway as if to warn people that something in this room was terribly wrong. It flowed away from the guard toward the door, never wavering or going off course. Most blood pooled around the victim's body but not this guy's blood. A sane person would have assumed that the floor was not level, but that wasn't the case. The stream of blood continued getting closer to the hallway. The kid grabbed an extra blanket from the foot of Elle's bed and threw it into the blood's path. The blood soaked into the blanket, slowing it down considerably. The kid spoke quickly.

"We've got to get moving."

Elle could barely drag her eyes from the blood. "Who are you?"

"I'm here to help you."

"You're my protector?" Elle felt astonishment; she had expected someone grander, but she guessed that beggars could not be choosers.

He didn't answer her. He just pointed the gun at the metal cuffs that connected to the railing. Elle whipped her head away and pushed it into the pillow. The bullet from the silenced gun made the metal fly apart. He had not even warned her what he was going to do. Her left arm was no longer connected to the bed, although the cuff still encircled her wrist.

Elle felt the fear of almost being shot and called out before he could pull the trigger again. "Maybe the guard has a key."

She waited for a little while before turning her head out of the pillow. The kid lowered his gun and looked at her for a few seconds. Then he moved over to where the guard lay. The kid checked two of the guard's pockets and came out with the key after checking the third. He put the key in and unlocked the part of the cuffs encircling her wrists. There was a deep groove in her flesh where they had been.

She stretched down to her ankles where two Velcro straps were wrapped, holding them tight against the bedding. She pulled the Velcro straps free and kicked at the railing. It fell down, and Elle slid off the side of the bed, planting her bandaged feet down hesitantly. This was weird. She had been paranoid of everything and everyone, yet she had no problem going with a stranger, a very weird stranger at that. Probably the thought of spending the rest of her life in a mental institution had something to do with it.

The kid rifled around in the guard's pockets and came up with a pack of smokes and his wallet. He took out the money and put the smokes in one of the zippered pockets of his pants. Then he tore the white sheet off the bed and threw it at Elle.

Elle looked at the sheet confused.

"Wrap it about yourself. Get rid of the gown; they could have a tracking device on it."

When he turned, Elle flung the hospital gown to the floor and wrapped the sheet tightly around herself.

The kid seemed satisfied by the general look of things and moved to the door. He pulled it open a crack and looked out into the hall. Seemingly pleased that it was clear, he stepped over the blood-soaked sheet and out the door into the hall. Elle followed. They moved down the hallway together, keeping close to the wall. Elle held the sheet tightly to her body so as not to lose it.

There were not any doctors or nurses moving about, or people in general, inside this wing of the hospital. It seemed eerily quiet. The kid headed to the nearest exit. They pushed through the double door and headed out across the green lawn. The kid ran to a red Jeep Cherokee parked in the guest lot and hopped in. He fiddled with some wires, and it started up.

"This is stolen?" Elle demanded.

"Borrowed."

"I'm not going with you. You're going to get me in trouble."

"What do you think you're in now? You killed two doctors? They're going to fry you for what you did. Now get in."

Elle knew the kid had a point. She climbed in the passenger side. The kid threw the Jeep in drive, and they were out of the parking lot, tires squealing.

"So, what's your name?" Elle asked.

"Why do you want to know that?"

"So I don't have to call you kid."

"Jamie."

"Ok."

The kid pulled onto the highway. He drove fast and wove in and out of the traffic. Jamie kept looking in the rearview mirror at someone. Elle looked back, trying to get a glimpse of what he was looking at; there was shiny black sports car racing behind them. The windows were tinted black. It was impossible to tell who was driving. They could pass the Jeep easily enough if they wanted, yet they stayed the same distance behind, no matter how many cars came in between the Cherokee and the sports car. If Jamie wove in between two cars that you could not imagine the Jeep fitting through, as soon as there was enough space, the black car swerved between them, making a path for itself.

"I think that black car is following us." Her eyes trailed it as it let another car come between it and them.

"Don't worry about it," Jamie informed.

"Don't worry about it? According to the police, I killed my psychiatrist and a doctor I don't even know. My fingerprints are on the murder weapon. I have no memory of killing anyone; if in fact I did, and on top of everything else, I just broke out of the hospital where I was being held. For all I know, you could be the one who committed the very crimes I'm suspected of doing. And the only reason I tried to flee my building in the middle of the night was because I got a disturbing phone call minutes before the cops showed up. You killed the cop that was watching my room, you stole a Jeep, and now we are currently being followed by a black car. And you tell me not to worry about it? Let me ask you this, what the hell should I worry about?"

"Look, he's working with us."

"Who is it?"

"My boss."

Evasive behavior. Elle had a feeling that, no matter how she grilled Jamie, he would not tell her the truth. Right now, she would give him the benefit of the doubt.

While they drove out of the city heading southwest, Jamie pushed the Jeep faster and faster; the black car kept pace with them. They were almost out of the city when the cars ground to a halt. They inched their way ahead with the other cars. Elle looked ahead to see if she could locate a traffic accident; it was not more than two or three miles away that there were flashing lights.

"A check…stop!" Elle said alarmed. She had meant to keep her thoughts to herself. Maybe they were looking for illegal drugs—or wanted criminals who had just broken out of the hospital that morning. The more she thought about it, the more she knew it was the beginning of the end for her.

"No big deal," Jamie said; each word echoed into the space that separated him from Elle.

"We'll never get through. They're looking for me." A phone rang, interrupting Elle's fears. "Who's that?"

Jamie reached into his pocket and pulled out a cell phone. He pushed answer on the phone and put it to his ear and listened.

"Yeah, she's ok."

There was a pause as Jamie listened to the person on the other end, keeping his eyes straight ahead.

"No, she's ok."

Another pause.

"Yeah, I guess."

Another pause followed the first two; Jamie said nothing, seemingly listening to whoever was on the other end. Jamie looked over at her and away from the highway, letting a few inches creep between them and the car in front. She could not help feeling like they were talking about her. She pulled the sheet tighter around her body.

"She won't shut up."

The smile disappeared from his face as a car length separated them from the car in front. A car somewhere behind honked its horn before Jamie pulled ahead again.

"Who the hell are you talking to?" Elle felt anger toward Jamie for referring to her as yappy.

"Shut up. I can't hear what he's saying," Jamie said to her.

Elle dove for the phone—she wondered if the voice on the other end of Jamie's cell phone was the same voice who warned her to get out of her building. This whole situation was making Elle's skin itch. She dove across the center console for the phone, jerking it away from Jamie's ear. He did not react for a few seconds, shocked by her sudden action possibly, and let her have the phone without a fight. But his docile demeanor did not last; he seemed to awaken and lunged for the phone, ripping it away from her head before she could hear anything. Elle fought back; she tried to twist it out Jamie's hands; he made grab for the sheet that surrounded her chest, waist, and legs. In those few seconds, she had to decide what was more important, the guy on the phone or being totally naked in front of Jamie. Elle could hear a guy's voice shouting on the other end of the phone; she could not quite make out what he was yelling, but it sounded to her like "What the fuck is going on?" Then there was a pause, and then the guy yelled, "Jamie?" Elle secured the sheet more tightly around her waist and chest, thankful he had not seen anything.

Jamie put the phone against his head and started to talk to the guy on the other end. Elle looked over at Jamie; he noticed her eyes on him. "*No.*" He reached into another pocket and pulled out his gun. He pointed it at her, and she ignored him and his gun; she did not like the idea of letting go of her sheet anymore. She could hear the guy screaming at Jamie. Jamie's head whipped around and stared out the window, as if someone had bitten him through the glass.

"Yeah, sorry about that, boss, but the bitch grabbed the phone away from me."

There was quiet while Jamie listened to the guy. It was quite a while before Jamie said anything. When he did, he looked over and scowled at Elle. He lowered the gun and put it back in the side pocket of his door.

"Yeah, I understand how important she is," Jamie answered into the phone.

Jamie and Elle both listened.

"No, you don't need to knock me silly. I understand."

Time stretched outwards, Jamie said nothing while he listened intently to the guy on the other end of the phone. Finally, Jamie answered. "Ok, yeah, you count on me." There was another pause. "No, I'm not going to apologize for what I did. She had it coming…" Another pause. "No way. She started it…oh, Christ. Fine, I'll do it." Jamie ended the phone call and put the phone back in his pocket and moved the Jeep a few inches forward. "I'm sorry for grabbing your sheet, but you're just going to have to trust us; either that or you can talk to one of those cops up at the check stop and find out what they are going to do with you. We are your best chance of keeping you alive. I suggest you be patient."

This was a completely different approach to her. "You got chewed out, didn't you?" Elle inquired.

"Yeah, because of you. Look, I don't want any more trouble. You want to stay out of the loony bin, then keep your head down when we get up to that check stop and don't try anything. And we might just get through this, if you behave," Jamie reminded her.

Elle was astounded that Jamie got his ass chewed out. "So you can't tell me who is in that black car—why?"

"I'm just doing what I'm told."

"You're not my protector, are you?"

"What do you think?"

That answered that question. Jamie was not organized; he had bloodshot eyes and was following orders from someone higher up. It scared her not to know who was in that black car. However, Elle really did not have other options; maybe she could plead temporary insanity for killing Dr. Davis, but why should she, if she knew she did not do it? And in the end, why get punished for something that she did not do? She would be cautious, and if she could get away from Jamie and the black car, then she would take the chance. Unless when the time came, and she met whoever was in the black sports car and felt she could trust them, then she might stay with him.

"One question."

Jamie looked at her through the corner of his eye. He nodded his head after a moment.

"Was that my protector you were talking to?"

"He's just my boss. That's all I can say."

"Who's your boss?" Elle questioned.

"I don't know who this protector is that you're referring to; my boss sent me to get you. That's who was on the phone."

For all she knew she could have passed her protector on the sidewalk and she would not even know him from anyone else. She certainly did not have access to many memories, and no one came to mind. Hell, she could not even remember her own father—how was she supposed to know her protector?

She knotted her fingers in the sheet, trying to calm herself down. The Jeep was closer to the check stop; she kept her eyes down so she would not have to see it.

"They will recognize me and stop the Jeep."

"No, they won't."

"Do you have a plan?"

"Nope."

"Boy, you're a complete dipshit—you break me out of a guarded hospital room only to be caught at a check stop, three miles out of the city. Be honest, you sniffed glue as a child, didn't you?"

"Shut up. You fucking talk too much."

There was maybe a mile between them and the check stop. The distance was disappearing.

"Get on the floor," Jamie demanded.

Elle could see out of the driver's window—the black car was wedging itself between the Jeep and the Bronco in front of them. Grasping the sheet tightly in her fists and shoving the seat back as far as she could, Elle could just barely squeeze into the foot space between the seat and the dash. She pressed her body against the dash and the floor, trying to disappear from everyone's view. The minutes ticked by; the Jeep moved ahead, stopped, moved ahead again, and stopped again. She faced the driver's window, waiting for them to discover her.

"You might want to plug your ears?" Jamie quipped.

Elle was looking into his face, and Jamie was lowering himself in his seat as if trying to disappear into thin air. Jamie was not invisible, and neither was Elle, though she desperately wished she were in her heart of hearts. It started to become hard to breathe, possibly from anxiety. It was only a matter of minutes before they would be discovered. An explosion rocked the Jeep hard enough that her head smacked against the dash. Elle pressed her palm to her mouth to stifle a scream; flames seemed to lick at the Jeep. Elle shot up off the floor just in time to see everything in front of the black car get vaporized with flames. The front end of the black car lifted slightly, as if from an aftershock; the cars lined up behind them either turned around and headed back into the city or the occupants fled on foot. Elle was too scared to move. After a few minutes, some of the smoke cleared, the black car's tires started to squeal, and the car shot forward, disappearing into the flames and wreckage. Jamie punched the Jeep's gas pedal and followed suit. He was laughing crazily, drumming his fists on the steering wheel and hollering. Elle grabbed for her seat belt as they rocketed after the black car, flames and smoke completely blocked out all visibility, it cleared, and they were free of it and on the other side. They raced past the oncoming traffic waiting on the other side of the check stop; most people were too scared to move and looked on as they raced by, the black car in the lead and the Jeep following. Twenty miles up the road, they were coming up to a crotch rocket sitting on the side of the road. Jamie slammed on his brakes, coming to a stop in the middle of the highway. The rider was dressed in black leather and seemed to have a woman's body. Long red hair trailed out of the helmet and darkened face guard. The leather-clad woman had what Elle could only describe as a rocket launcher strapped to her back. Elle wanted to pull on Jamie's hair and tell him to get them out of there, but Jamie hopped out and opened the back door of the Jeep. The woman threw the rocket launcher onto the back seat. Jamie was laughing. She saluted him, got back on the bike, twisted the throttle, and disappeared back the way they had come. Elle knew that she was sitting there with her mouth wide open.

"Whhhoooo was that?" Elle asked when she finally found her voice.

Jamie shrugged; he was shaking his head as if he were still in disbelief over what had just happened. He was loving the excitement.

The black car stayed in front for a little while before it slowed down. Its dark-tinted windows did not let eyes penetrate as it pulled even with the Jeep and then fell behind them. Jamie pushed down on the gas pedal as the traffic started to dwindle. He drummed his hands on the steering wheel before he reached down to the radio. The radio station was playing Metallica, "I Disappear." His choice of music was harder than Elle's tastes. However, the song held significance; maybe she had just disappeared from everyone's radar, the cops and her mother included. This was basically a road trip with an unidentified escort. Elle leaned back against the seat. Everything passed by in one long blur of color and scenery. She did not even identify what the colors belonged to anymore. The heavy metal rock station was somewhat comforting, practically a lullaby to all the bad things that happened over the past twenty-four hours. The adrenaline that had surged through her veins earlier was long gone. She felt physically, emotionally, and mentally exhausted. Somewhere along the highway, Elle fell asleep, putting her life in Jamie's hands— maybe not the most intelligent decision she had ever made.

She did not know how much time had passed. She could feel herself surfacing from the heavy blanket of sleep. Someone was talking; they sounded far away, far enough away that she would never be able to identify their voice, even if she had heard it a hundred times a day. But the words that were spoken were clear.

"How far away are we?"

"A long way—we're practically in the middle of nowhere."

The stab in her arm brought Elle to the surface. A circle of light brightened, she could identify Jamie, but before the light could widen enough to include anyone else, the light was cut off, and she was submerged into the darkness again, but not before she heard the other voice.

"She didn't see me, did she?"

"I don't think so, but even if she did start to wake up, the drugs will hit her pretty quickly. Your identity will remain hidden for another day, boss," Jamie answered sarcastically.

There was darkness and panic. Why had she trusted complete strangers? Elle felt a prickling sensation at the back of her neck, the feeling she got when she felt like someone had lied to her. Jamie told her he was working for his boss, she just assumed that he was working for her protector, she had accepted his answers easily enough, and now she was fighting to open her eyes, but the drugged sleep was too strong. Someone picked her up and moved her to another seat; this she was still aware of. This seat was almost flat, so she could lie down. There was not as much sun where she lay now. It was not burning her closed eyelids. A car door slammed, and she rolled her head in the direction, but she could not force her eyelids open, no matter how she struggled, and before she knew it, she was fast asleep.

Chapter 9

Heath had taken care of most everyone at the psych ward, leaving only the security guard for Jamie, and even that he had almost messed up. Heath had walked in like he owned the place; he had picked up a white coat from a doctor after he'd knocked him senseless. The orderly buzzed him in, barely glancing at Heath, everyone had become complacent, and Heath capitalized on their overconfidence. Within seconds of entering the secure site, Heath threw down a canister of tear gas—Missy had gotten one from a cop friend. While everybody was gasping for air, Heath slipped on a gas mask; he moved quickly, slapping each hand before they could sound the alarm. He knocked two orderlies out with a single punch. He pulled out a gun on the fourth and fifth security guards and shot them point-blank. He did not care; human life meant very little to him when he had a mission to complete. Jamie and Elle had basically walked out the front door of the hospital, receiving a few odd glances from several housekeeping staff. But nobody dared to get in their way; there was a time and a place to report breakouts from the psych wards, and now was not that time—unless they wanted to find themselves six feet under.

But with the check stop quickly approaching, Heath felt the need to update Jamie with instructions. Hopefully Missy had gotten out of town long before the check stop had been set up, and she was ready. He hit Jamie's number on the cell phone.

"Jamie, how is she?"

"Yeah, she's ok."

"Does she trust you, or do I need to worry? Once we get up ahead, Missy is going to take out the check stop."

"No, she's ok."

"What the hell does that mean? She's ok or she's scared shitless?"

"Yeah, I guess," Jamie answered.

"Well, she's high strung, and she needs to feel at ease with you so she don't freak out and make a break for it."

"She won't shut up."

A car horn blared. He could hear Elle in the background. "Who the hell are you talking to?" she yelled at Jamie. Geez, Heath wished he could be in the vehicle with them; she would be more at ease with him, after all Pete had told her about him. Pete hadn't told her about screw-up/drug-addict Jamie.

"Shut up. I can't hear what he's saying," Jamie said to her.

Then all hell broke loose, and there were muffled screams and grunts. Heath knew she had made a grab for the phone. Damn it, he wished he was in that car with them, that he could get control of the situation before she got away and started to run down the highway; that type of incident would be hard to recover from. Heath needed Elle to know that she was safer with them than with the cops so she wouldn't try anything. Heath's temper exploded. "What the fuck is going on?" Heath started yelling, "Jamie?" Heath waited for a few seconds. "Are you seriously letting Elle get the better of you?"

"No," Jamie answered; he sounded like a defensive schoolboy.

"Good, now get the situation under control." Heath yelled.

"Yeah, sorry about that, boss, but the bitch grabbed the phone away from me."

"I made a promise to Grant to protect her and what she's carrying, and if you harm one hair on her head, you're a dead man." Heath saw that Jamie had lowered the gun and put it away.

"Yeah, I understand how important she is," Jamie answered into the phone.

The hamburger churned dangerously in Heath's stomach. He wanted to slam that fancy little black car into the Jeep. But that would only grab unwanted attention. His fingers dug into the smartphone, cracking the screen. "Do I need to knock you silly?"

"No, you don't need to knock me silly. I understand."

Jamie looked out the window toward Heath. Jamie probably could not see the look on Heath's face, which was a good thing. His skin was the color of a ripe tomato, it felt prickly hot, and he knew that the skin had fallen back, letting his veins stick out.

Heath could feel his patience hanging by a thread; it took a few deep breaths to get his heart beating somewhat normally; if he was not careful, he would do something that he and Jamie would both regret. Jamie would die here and now in Heath's bare hands. "Do you? Because you were pointing a loaded gun at her, and if I have to knock the ever-fucking life out of you, I will." Jamie had let Elle get the best of him; she had taken the phone; that much he had seen from behind and in a lower view from the black sports car. But what Jamie had done to get Elle to drop the phone, Heath knew he would not like, and he would find out about it soon enough.

There was a pause; all Heath could hear was Jamie's breathing, low and choppy.

Heath reached for a cigarette; he was so angry he could barely think; a cigarette would calm his nerves. His lips twitched; he grabbed a pen off the dash and stuck it between his lips so as not to grind his teeth while he looked for a smoke. The package was in the back seat. He twisted around, straining his back, almost making it groan in the process. His teeth ground into the plastic pen like an addict. He grabbed the package off the back seat, opened it up, spit out the pen, and put in a real cigarette. The lighter flared, and Heath took a steadying breath before speaking. "Listen up, Jamie." His voice was calmer. "I don't want you to ever use guns while she is in the vicinity; she is too goddamn important."

"Ok, yeah, you can count on me," Jamie answered.

"Don't ever threaten her; now apologize to her for what you did," Heath demanded.

"No, I'm not going to apologize for what I did. She had it coming…"

"Damn it, Jamie, do as I say."

"No way. She started it…oh, Christ. Fine, I'll do it." Jamie ended the call.

There really was not much of a plan for what lay ahead; everything depended on if Missy could get out of the city and to the bunker; they had lots of artillery stashed there. A rocket launcher would take care of the check stop. So, Heath had cut Missy loose and was hoping for the best, but he did not feel lucky. He felt ill-prepared. Heath covered the semiautomatic in the passenger seat with his coat. He would kill every cop here if he had to; he was not afraid to die for Elle.

He could see easily enough through the side windows of the Jeep; Jamie was facing her, and they seemed to be talking.

Heath punched the gas pedal of the sports car, revving the engine's rpms up. He let the clutch up slowly and inched closer to them, pulling ahead when space opened up between the Jeep and the car in front. Jamie kept getting closer to the check stop, and it was making Heath uneasy, because things were about to go boom.

He could not see any of the police cruisers anymore; a jacked-up Bronco had squeezed in front of him and obstructed everything in his path. The Bronco inched forward, and Heath let the distance between them expand. If anything was going to happen, the time was now. The Bronco was obliterated in a second, the explosion lifted the front end of Heath's car off the ground, and flames licked at the windshield, desperate for more. But they were on the outer edge of the explosion, and it was no more than a gentle nudge.

After a few minutes, Heath punched the gas pedal and sped into the fire and smoke. Most everything had been destroyed by the missile from the rocket launcher, and what was not was shoved aside by the front end of the sports car. He headed past Missy, lifting a hand in praise; she had done well. It would take the cops hours to regroup, and by then, they would be long gone. The Jeep Jamie was driving would stop for the rocket launcher. And Missy's darkened helmet and leather ensemble would never let Elle or anyone identify what she really looked like.

***

The wind blew in Elle's face; that is what finally woke her up. She tried to rise into a sitting position; the feeling that something bad had happened was almost certain. The quick movement brought a wave of dizziness. She leaned forward, putting her head between her knees. There was no nausea, just a groggy dizziness, the signs of being heavily drugged. After a count of ten, some of it passed; she lifted her head up to see where she was. She was in a car with tinted windows, probably the black car that had been following them. The sheet was still wrapped tightly around her waist and chest, and the seat was leaning as far back as it could go. The car was parked outside a gas station in the middle of nowhere. The seat on the driver's side was empty. The passenger door was ajar; she stepped out of the car into the bright sunshine. It took a while for her eyes to adjust to the sunlight after being in the dark car. But there was nothing to see, desert and a few cactuses, a broken-down gas station. Two dark figures were walking along the road; they were too far away to make out, too far to determine which way they were even going.

She remembered the pinch in her arm; she looked down to where the needle had gone in. But besides the slight soreness in her arm and a dull ache in the middle of her back, almost as if she had lifted something that was too heavy, she felt ok otherwise. She slid her fingers up her back, frightened by what she might find. This was getting creepier by the second. She could feel what felt like stitches halfway up her back along her spine. Elle glanced back at the figures, they were closer now, and they were walking toward the black car. One figure was easy to make out, it was Jamie, but the other figure was a dark smudge that, even as they got closer, she still could not make them out. The dark smudge came closer and closer, and it still looked the same. It was as if it were only a shadow and not the person that made it. Her eyes were wide, unblinking, even with the breeze blowing little bits of sand in them. What the hell was wrong with her eyesight; she did not think she was seeing things, because she could see everything else as it was, just not this other person. They had done something to her while she had been out cold; it was the only answer. It was as if she were wearing glasses and they had a smudge on them, a smudge she could not wipe away. Wherever she looked, the smudge would block out whoever this person was.

Jamie stopped to rest against the side of the car, squinting into the sunlight. The dark shape came to her side of the car, standing against the hood. And then it spoke, spoke clearly and not at all distorted. His voice did not sound at all familiar. At least she did not think it did.

"Don't worry; it's ok if you can't see me," he reassured her.

"What the hell did you give me?"

"A few sedatives just to make you sleep, to help you relax."

"I can't see you. Something's wrong with me."

"You're not supposed to. You can see Jamie; that's enough for now."

"Stop doing this. I want a goddamn answer for once."

"Boy, you were right; she does talk a lot," the shadow stated.

That first half of the statement was directed at Jamie, the second part at her. "Don't have a goddamn panic attack, sweetheart. You will see me, when it's safe for you to see me and not before."

"I told you it's better when all she does is sleep." Jamie said.

The dark shape walked around to the driver's side. He pushed the seat ahead, took out a blue-and-red backpack, and threw it at her. Elle caught it. She could see the backpack, but the rest of him was dark with no discernable features. He moved around the car back toward her side. She could hear him, sense him, but she just couldn't see him.

"Here, go change in the gas station." His voice softened because of her obvious confusion and fear.

He held a backpack out to her, but she did not move to take it from him. She did not want it, did not want to have to touch him. "Can everyone else see you?"

The shadow sighed. "Yeah, they can."

"So why not me?" Elle demanded. She was overwhelmed with these panicky feelings racing around inside of her.

"Because you're too dangerous right now."

"Why am I-I-I-I dangerous?" She could not believe she had actually stammered.

"Look, we're in a bit of a hurry, but if you want to stay dressed in a sheet for the rest of this trip, then hey, that's just fine with me. Although it might be just a matter of time before Jamie gets curious and wants to find out what is under that sheet. I ain't going to be riding with you to stop him, so I suggest you go change; we have a long ride ahead of us."

"I'm not going anywhere with you until you explain what you did to me and what you want with me."

"Fuck, stay in the goddamn bedsheet for all I care."

The shadow sounded like a him, although she did not know what the alien race sounded like. He moved an arm toward her, or it sure looked like an arm, as far as blurry arms go. He put his hand on her shoulder to try to push her back into the car. She resisted and shoved the car door at him. The door made a solid *whack* when it hit him; the shape stumbled back a few feet.

"Really? Is that the way you want to play it."

The figure bent down and seemed to be rubbing where his knees were. She moved away from the door, putting some distance between her and the shadow. Jamie was still leaning on the driver's side, not paying either the shadow or her any attention.

"I'm not a very patient guy; get in the car."

"No, you're not my boss."

"It's quite simple: we can do this the easy way or the hard way. I'll give you another sedative, and you can sleep the rest of the way. But it's your choice; however, I would assume you're hungry; you haven't eaten in, well, I'd say, over twenty-four hours at least. But hey, nothing I can do about it if you want to be like this."

Elle lost her temper. "Fuck you, and fuck your little sedatives."

"Jamie, we got a real live wire on our hands."

The shadow clapped his hands. Jamie didn't look up; he stayed looking away into the distance, maybe happy not to be traveling, maybe unhappy not to be. She turned away from them, her mind made up, kicked the sheet away from her feet, and headed up the road. When she was twenty feet away, the rocks digging dangerously deep into the bandages on her feet, she looked back at the shadow; he had seemed to shrink in height and grow in width with her eyes off him. Maybe he was in a crouching position. Then he was moving; she started to run, hiking up the sheet like the ladies did in the old days when they had long skirts. She did not get very far when he caught her; he knocked into her like tackle football; she went down on the gravel road, sheet and all, him on top. The dirt and rocks cut into her elbows and knees; blood soaked easily through the sheet. She struggled to get out from underneath him.

"Get off!" Elle screamed angrily at the shadow.

"Jamie, get another sedative."

Elle could not see Jamie from where she was lying, but she knew he was listening. "Do not do it, Jamie; don't do it. You're your own man; don't listen to him. This is kidnapping; you could go to jail for it."

"What kind of crap are you talking about, sweetie; he'll go anyway, not for kidnapping though, but for murder. Jamie, get me another sedative."

Jamie looked slightly annoyed; maybe he did not like the shadow's comments. "Get them yourself."

"Listen, you little pecker head, you better do what I say or else."

"Shove them up your fucking ass, boss."

"Yeah, fuck you too." Elle spat, spraying him. She was almost sure he felt the spray; she could imagine the disgusted look he had on his face; he didn't seem very patient or understanding. She could feel his weight shift, as if he were turning to look back at Jamie, as if to see if he was going to get the drugs or not.

"Going to have to wash your mouth out with soap after Jamie gets those sedatives," the shadow barked at her.

Her eyes narrowed at him. "You get anywhere near my mouth, and I'll bite your dirty fingers off."

"Jamie, Jamie, what the fuck you think you're doing?" the shadow hollered. "Get the fucking sedatives."

"I'm not a part of this, man. You told me to get Elle. I did that."

"Goddamn, you little pecker head, well at least throw them to me."

"Don't do it, Jamie!" Elle screamed.

"Shut up," the shadow snapped.

Something hit the dirt near her head. She looked to the right. There was vial of a clear liquid and a syringe in a ziplock bag that landed close by. The bottle was just far enough away that he would have to let go of one of her hands in order to reach the ziplock bag. She waited until he leaned in the direction of the sedatives before she threw her fist, hoping to hit him in the throat or some tender area. She hit his throat and he fell forward, off balance and choking.

He put a hand on the ground, leaning forward into her. Then he sat back, pushing her fist back to the ground with his right hand again. "Jamie, get the zip ties; maybe that will help her learn some manners."

Jamie appeared over top of the shadow's back suddenly, a compliant little servant. "Here." He held out the zip ties to the shadow. The shadow grabbed the zip tie and cinched Elle's hands together.

Elle could still punch him in the stomach, but it made it much harder. The shadow took the ziplock and syringe out of Jamie's hand; he filled the syringe with a clear liquid. Elle watched as if hypnotized, desperately pleading for someone to come to her rescue.

As if the gods had heard Elle' prayers, they answered her with a rumbling not far away, the sound of an engine gearing down to pull into the gas station.

"Help!" Elle screamed. She could not see anyone, but she screamed anyway. She scratched for traction, trying to escape from underneath the shadow, but he outweighed her easily.

A truck door closed, followed by footsteps crunching on the gravel as someone approached.

"There a problem here?" the trucker asked.

The shadow let go of her and got to his feet. "No, just so long as you get yourself out of here. Take my advice that this ain't somewhere you want to be, friend."

The trucker was a burly guy, the whole deal, with a beer gut overlapping the waistband of his sweatpants. The trucker started rolling up his sleeves with big, thick, meaty arms. He was at least two of what the shadow was or appeared to be.

"I don't think so. You and your friend like terrorizing young ladies wrapped in bedsheets? Don't think I can just walk away from that."

"Ok," the shadow answered, closing the distance between the trucker and himself. Elle gathered up the sheet before getting to her feet. She shoved past the shadow, intending to take a ride with the trucker. The wind whispered softly, and Elle turned slowly, realizing that the shadow wasn't just going to let her go. She looked back as he reached behind him for something. It was more than enough of a gun to put this trucker in a grave; it must have been tucked in the shadow's pants. Time slowed down, the shadow lifted his arm, and the gun in his hand Elle could see clearly. The only thing that was not slow motion was the bullet. The air whistled for a second before the splat. The bullet struck the trucker in the chest and whistled out his back. He fell backward into the dirt, all in the blink of an eye. The shadow's eyes were on her; she didn't need to see his face to know where he was looking. He killed so easily.

He came toward her, the gun loosely held in his hand, barrel pointed to the ground. He grabbed hold a of her arm. "Don't aggravate me. I have no problems doing what needs to be done."

She assessed the gun in his hand and then him. He hid from her, not because she had killed—he could kill and was more lethal than she ever would be. He hid because he was afraid, and that only made it that much easier for her to hate him. He grabbed her arm, trying to drag her back to the car. She ripped her arm out of his grasp, almost tripping on the bedsheet in her progress, but this time he let her go. Maybe this was his way of giving her one more chance.

He offered the backpack to her. "I had to do what I had to; maybe one day you will understand. Now hurry up."

She accepted it.

He reached into the car and pulled out a knife to cut her hands free of the zip tie.

There was a red mark on her wrists where the zip tie had been. The hand that held her, it was a real hand, real bones, tendons, and muscles. It was a real hand with calluses and skin. It was a real human touch, but there was no emotion in it—it was dead. And that made it easier, much.

She gave him a direct look—"Go to hell"—before stumbling in the direction of the gas station bathroom.

"Already been there," the shadow yelled to her back.

She headed into the gas station to change. It was an old Texaco station; long ago it had served families heading north and the regulars heading south. Somewhere along the way, it had gone out of business. At one point it had an ice machine and a small counter that dished up ice cream cones for sixty cents. The only thing left other than the building was the abandoned gas pumps out front. In the back was the bathroom; cigarette butts littered the doorway like a plague.

The old Texaco bathroom door squeaked open on rusty hinges. The air inside was stale and moldy.

The bathroom was nothing more than a closest with a toilet. Elle laid the bag along the sink; it had to hold either Jamie's or the shadow's clothes. But they were neither. They were her clothes—her favorite jeans. There was her T-shirt and electric blue sports bra, her underwear, and everything she would need. At the bottom of the pile were two pictures. One was of a man. He looked so young and hopeful. The second was a picture of the man and Elle when she was just a child. Elle guessed that she was no more than two or three.

She tried the tap; long ago the water had been turned off. The blood had completely soaked through what was left of the gauze on her feet. Elle was numb to the pain though. There was a shard of a mirror left still intact above the sink; even in the poor lighting, she could see the dark smudges under her eyes. The last few days had taken a toll on her.

"Hurry up." The shadow was banging on the bathroom door.

Slowly she removed the bandages and tore a few strips off the bedsheet and wrapped her feet with them. She wiped the blood off her knees and picked out a few pieces of gravel. Elle got dressed slowly. Hesitating, she got a glimpse of her back in the mirror, she was sure she had felt the stitches, why had she been cut open and stitched back up? What was the shadow hiding?

When Elle came out of the bathroom, the shadow was waiting to escort her back to the black car. Jamie was crouched down behind the car changing the license plates.

The shadow stopped to talk softly to Jamie; Elle walked over and looked at the trucker. He had been turned over, and on a strange impulse, she lifted the guy's shirt up to check the guy's spine, her father's words a jumbled mess of uncertainty in her mind. Along the dead trucker's spine were three black triangles; nobody needed to point out this interesting coincidence, to question why she was doing what she was. But at the same time, she realized that everything that she thought she knew was no longer; she was looking at the world a lot differently. Her father's words had sent a chill through her; she thought of what the triangles meant along the guy's spine; it was a brand, a way of keeping track of humans like they were animals.

She looked up, sure that someone was watching her reaction; she met the shadow head on. The gooseflesh popped out on her skin even though the sun was hot. A piece of hair blew in her eye; there was a very thin outline along the lock of hair; in that outline, she could see jean along the lock of hair; it was his leg. She looked a little higher up; there was an outline of skin along the hair. He was there. She just could not see him. For whatever reason, he was blocked from her eyes, and it was simply a glitch that had allowed her to see just a little fraction of him. Her legs straightened, raising Elle to her full height. The sand swirled around, almost whipping the shadow out of sight; she looked down at the body one last time, noticing something crawling under the flesh of the corpse. Elle jerked impulsively back, putting distance between the corpse and herself.

"Jamie, get the solution," the shadow called. "This guy is bugged."

Jamie popped the trunk to the car and threw a bleach container to the shadow. He poured it on the corpse, the corpse started to sizzle and smoke, and the flesh started to squirm.

Elle stared wild-eyed at it, she wanted to ask, but the thought died where it began.

When nothing else moved, Jamie nodded to the car, the shadow went behind the gas station, and she heard the engine of a bike rev. He whipped around and pulled up beside them. Elle looked once at the shadow before climbing into the black car. Jamie put the plastic jug back in the car, and they hit the road. The Harley passed them within minutes, but they never lost sight of it. Jamie had the look of someone who understood, because he knew what she was going through; she had entered a new reality—and she had become the hunted.

She had to ease into it slowly to try to draw out answers; she took out the picture from the knapsack and held it up for Jamie. "Is this my father?"

Jamie studied the photo briefly. "Boy, they did erase your memories, didn't they."

It was not a question; it was statement.

"Yeah, I think that's him."

"Where is my protector?" Elle questioned.

Jamie laughed, slapping at his leg. "Don't know if I would call him that; he's more of a pain in ass in my opinion."

Chapter 10

The hours passed before they met up with the shadow again. And it was about then that Elle realized she was starving, like the shadow had said she would be. The sun started to set; her stomach tightened from a mixture of anxiety and hunger. She had not been out at night for years, well, unless you counted when she blacked out. In a few minutes the sun would set.

The rock station had turned to static and had been shut off hours ago. She looked over at Jamie, he had taken off his sunglasses, and she could see the whites of his eyes. They were not as bloodshot as they had been in the hospital. He wiped at them, trying to keep them open. A few beads of sweat stood out on his face and dripped down his face and neck.

"Do you want me to drive for a while?"

A furrow dipped between his brows. "No."

"Why did the shadow say I was dangerous? I know you don't like all these questions. But, put yourself in my place for a few minutes. I supposedly killed my psychiatrist and another doctor, and I'm on a highway heading into no man's land. I'm freaked out over the last few day's events; all I would like are some questions answered. Is that too much to ask?"

Jamie looked at Elle briefly before returning to the stretch of highway in front of him.

"Ok."

"Why am I dangerous?"

"Because you might tell them."

"Tell who and tell them what?"

"Where you are, where we are."

"Do you mean the cops?"

Jamie eyed her with horror. The fear was easy to pick up on. He was not afraid of the cops; he was afraid of her. "Are you afraid of me because you think I killed those doctors?"

Jamie just looked ahead, refusing to answer.

"I wouldn't hurt you."

"Not intentionally you wouldn't; it's what's inside of you that we're afraid of."

Jamie's answer made Elle shiver. "Where are we going?"

"Don't know, just following."

A wall had come down; Elle had a feeling that Jamie had told her more than he had intended. They passed a sign on the side of the road. She looked at it to see where it said they were headed. But when the black sports car's headlights lit the sign up, it remained dark. The sign remained a dark, blotted-out shadow on a white post, dark like the shadow remained to her. She could not even read the road signs. "You cover your tracks really well, don't you?" she said more to herself than Jamie.

Jamie did not look at her. The glow of the bike was up ahead of them. It was leading them into the night.

The chills crept up and down her arms like spiders. Elle's belly growled from the tension and hunger. She could not even remember the last time she had eaten.

She looked ahead; the bike's brake lights flashed on, pulling off onto the side of the road. Jamie pulled the car off the road to the rest stop area behind the bike.

The dark shape put down the kickstand for his bike; he took off the helmet, hanging it from the handlebars. He took a few steps toward the car. Jamie got out and walked to the shadow. The keys were still dangling in the ignition of the car; all she had to do was scoot across the gearshift and into the driver's seat. Elle would have an expensive set of wheels. But how far would she get before they caught her? What if that letter really was from her father and everything he said about the protector was true? What if what he said about the aliens finding another means to extract the information was also true? Would they eventually just find that it was easier to dissect her and be done with the whole situation?

The darkness crept out of that part of her mind where it resided; when it did, she had no control. Unknowingly, her body was moving, crawling across the gearshift into the driver's seat. The keys were still in the ignition, her hand turned the key, and her foot pushed down on the gas pedal.

She was completely lost in her own mind, and the darkness evaporated to the sound of gunshots. Elle found herself in the driver's seat, clutching the steering wheel tightly as the rear tire exploded and sent the car skidding; tires caught on the pavement and spun the car around in a three sixty before she skidded off the road into a cactus patch. A dirt bank brought the car to a grinding halt, and Elle struck her head on the steering wheel. Blood poured down her forehead and across her cheek. She put her hand up to stop it. She heard the bike stop not far away. Then someone crashed through the cactus patch and ripped the door open. The overhead light came on, but it did nothing to illuminate the shadowy figure.

"Did you hurt your head?"

"I don't think it's too serious," Elle answered.

"Let's hope not. Hopefully it didn't damage your mind."

Jamie crashed through the cactuses and looked down at her. His anger was illuminated by the dim bulb. "I told you she was a lost cause."

"Fuck, Jamie, what kind of a dumb shit are you for leaving the keys in the ignition? If we lose the plans, I will crack your head open with my bare hands. Go get the emergency kit. Jesus."

Elle tried to step out of the car, but the shadow pushed her back down, bobbing in front of her face. The lights from the car shone into the night, forming an unwanted SOS.

By now the blood was flowing out from underneath her hand and running into her eyes. She could not see the shadow, but she did not need to to know he was pissed off.

Jamie handed the bag of supplies to the shadow. The shadow reached out and clasped the bag. It was mostly a shopping bag filled with antiseptic, needles and thread, bandages, freezing drugs, and some clean rags to soak up blood. He deposited the supplies in her lap and put a rag to her forehead; she dropped her hands to her sides. A headache was creeping up; it felt like one hell of a whopper.

"Elle, are you ok?"

"I don't know. I don't feel good," Elle answered.

"Sit up straight, and let's get a look at that cut." The shadow wiped the blood away. "It's not as bad as all the blood suggests. But you're going to need some stitches to close it up. Head wounds usually bleed bad."

The shadow's hand went into the bag and grabbed the needle and thread and some of the freezing drugs. Then he filled a syringe with the pale-amber liquid that would freeze the skin.

From the second the shadow had showed up in her life, she sensed this anger, a constant. It was a kind of hostility that was usually directed at her, for what she did not know, but now he seemed almost relaxed, except for the occasional swear under his breath, but even those swears were not for her but rather Jamie. It was a nice change of pace.

She would be lying if she said he did not scare her; she could not even see him. For all she knew, maybe he was one of them. But for someone so angry, he had skilled hands; they worked the needle smoothly in and out of her skin, closing the cut with only the car's interior light to guide him. When he was done, he examined it before putting the emergency kit back in the trunk. The shadow came back and held out a sandwich to her, almost apologetically. "It's all I got. I didn't want to stop anywhere too public, draw unwanted attention to us."

"It's ok." She took the sandwich; it was cool.

"It's safe. I'm sorry about Jamie; the guy ain't too bright sometimes."

"Fuck you, boss." Jamie stood ten feet away with his back to them.

"You're him, aren't you?" Elle inquired; she wanted to know so desperately.

"Him who?" the shadow asked.

"The guy my father talked about."

"I never met your father; I'm just doing what I've been told to do."

"Well, who told you to come for me?"

"He did."

"He who?" Elle questioned.

The shadow flashed a light in her eyes, then he asked her to follow his finger with her eyes. She followed his finger left, then right, up, and finally down. Seemingly pleased, he let out a sigh.

"If she died, we could've just cut the plans out," Jamie offered.

"You little maggot, how the hell do you think we're going to access the plans if she's dead?"

"We find a way."

"If she dies, we're all screwed. It's about time you start thinking about the course of your actions."

"She's a pain in the ass," Jamie answered.

"I don't care; start paying attention to what you're doing. Or I will end you."

The shadow hauled Elle over the gearshift and back into the passenger seat; she went willingly enough. He climbed into the driver's seat, and with Jamie's help, leaning and pushing on the hood, it only took a few minutes to get out of the sandbank and onto the road. The shadow and Jamie got to work on changing the flat.

The loud bang was caused from the tire exploding when the shadow had shot it. It was the noise of the gun that had brought Elle back from the blackout. Some of the nausea had subsided, but it was back with a vengeance. She was starting to feel sick to her stomach.

After the tire was replaced, they were almost ready to get going again.

Elle could feel her stomach convulsing. It churned dangerously; she retched, trying to vomit; however, she had nothing in her stomach and couldn't possibly expel anything. Elle gasped for air as the pain spread through her belly.

"What's wrong?" the shadow asked, looking in.

"I don't know; my stomach hurts. Oh fuck, it hurts." She tottered forward in her seat. "Owwww." She had broken out in a cold sweat.

The shadow forced Elle backward in the seat. He lifted her T-shirt out of her jeans to get a look.

"What?" She was afraid of the shadow's answer.

"Jamie, get the supplies; they put a jelly pack in her. Hurry."

"What? What's a jelly pack?" Elle questioned.

"It's a pack of poison that can be released into your system at any time they want."

"How did they put it in me?"

"I can only guess," the shadow answered.

Jamie was back with the supplies, and the shadow was moving about behind her. Her stomach wanted to tear itself apart.

"Do you feel like you're on fire?"

"Yes, and my stomach hurts. It hurts so bad." She was trying to curl into the fetal position and wishing that everything would just go away. When she opened her eyes to see what the shadow was doing, she opened them to thousands of eyes. They had surrounded her in the length of time it took to blink. There must have been at least fifty or sixty of them; some of them were tall, almost six feet. The tallest one reached out to her. Its skin was grayish blue, with a slight blackness. Its fingers were long, and there were only three of them per hand. She could see its veins running under its skin, but instead of blood, there was only murky black stuff. There was a network of spider web–thin veins that ran up their entire body. She looked from its outstretched hand toward its face. Their eyes looked through her and into her soul, and there was no end to their lifeless eyes, black holes that kept going on forever, with no irises or pupils. The only thing she saw in them was her reflection.

"We gotta remove the jelly pack, Elle. I'm going to have to cut you open."

No, you sick little bastards. The shadow was gone, and all she could see were the aliens. Then everything went dark. The aliens disappeared, and the highway was gone. She was in a blackness that was everywhere.

***

Back at the gas station, Heath could not help thinking that when she was staring at him, that it was not Elle looking back at him. That it was them. They had zeroed in on Heath. He had been about ready to try to shake off that scary feeling, tempted to suck in a deep breath; she would not be able to see it anyways. But she moved away to change into her clothes, and he felt relief. He was not afraid to fight, but he needed more time.

***

"Let go of me, you sick little bastards." Elle was screaming before she even opened her eyes. She opened them to the warm glare of the sun coming in through the side window; a warm breeze drifted in. The window was rolled all the way down, so she would not die of heat stroke, like a dog. She was surprised they did not leave her an ice cream bucket to lap water out of. The sun was shining, and she wondered if she had dreamt the aliens. They did not seem as real anymore. The pain was even gone; well, the bellyache was gone, but there was a sharp jab in her side. She pulled up her shirt to reveal an eight-inch gash that had been stitched up; it was not a hack job but smooth and evenly spaced stitches.

A cold sweat broke out on her skin when she tried to sit up; she panicked to see where she was. But the pain in her side brought her back down. She glimpsed the top of a building from her slightly higher perch, if only for a few seconds. It looked to be the top of café or something like that. She noticed the IV in her arm; the bag was hanging from the ceiling of the car.

92

The car door opened, and the shadow got in. He looked back at her. She did not know how she knew he was looking at her, considering he looked the same all around, but she knew he had turned his head to look at her. He had a coffee in one hand and a smoke in the other.

"Where did this gash come from?" She did not lift her shirt up because she knew he knew what she was talking about.

"We had to do an emergency operation on you last night."

"Who's we?"

"Jamie and I."

"Are you one of them? Is that why I can't see you?" Elle inquired. This was probably her greatest fear, that underneath that shadowy exterior was this grotesque mask, with a tarantula-type mouth and bug eyes.

The shadow ignored her question and sipped his cup of coffee, it smelled good, but she imagined it would be murder to her guts.

"So, you cut me open?"

"To remove the jelly pack."

"Jelly pack?"

"It was put into your stomach; they're lethal."

"I thought I was valuable?"

"You are; maybe they thought if they poisoned you, in your last moments, it would unlock the plans from inside your mind. They could download the blueprint, and you would just die." The reality of how close she had come to it all being over was scary.

"What do you look like?"

"Elle, this is not the right time or the right place."

"Cut the crap. Right before you cut me open last night, I saw them; there were at least forty of them or more. Did you see them?"

"No."

Jamie rode the bike, and the shadow drove the black car, with her riding in the back. The radio was playing.

They passed more buildings, but soon those disappeared, and mostly the only thing she saw was desert.

"Can we stop someplace so I can get something to eat? I'm hungry."

"I don't think eating right now would be very good for you, especially after your operation. You will get everything you need from the IV for now."

"You're an asshole," Elle stated.

The shadow chuckled softly. "I'm good with that."

"I want to make a call," Elle demanded.

"You are not allowed personal calls."

"You can't do this, hold me hostage."

"Actually, I can; you're too weak to go anywhere or pose much of a threat to me. So, until we get to where we're going, and remove the computer chip from your spine, you will do as I say."

"You think I have a chip in my spine?"

"I don't think. I know."

"How do you know?" Elle asked.

"Because your father told me."

"Grant?"

"You don't remember him, huh?"

"Have I ever really seen you?"

"A few times."

"When was this?"

"Years ago."

"You're fucking with me."

"Not yet I'm not."

"What?" Elle wasn't certain she had heard him right.

"Look, when we remove the chip, I will answer all your questions. But right now, I can't tell you anything more."

The shadow did not say anything else, and Elle didn't ask; she was desperate for everything she could find out, but it took to much energy. It was easier to sleep and close out everything.

***

The shadow did not stop the car unless it was for her to go bathroom or to get more gas. Unfortunately, the shadow came into the bathroom with her; she was too weak, and she suspected he had his head turned, but she was not entirely sure. She was too weak to care anymore; the life was being driven from her. No allowances were made to get her anything to eat. If she asked, they would not answer her. She relied on the IV in her arm to keep her alive.

94

She fell asleep, waking briefly during the stops at the various gas stations along the way. When she started to wake up, the shadow put some painkillers in her hand. She had avoided drugs as much as possible, only taking them if they were forced on her by a doctor. Her mom had always encouraged her to take what the doctors prescribed—the more drugs the merrier. That had never been Elle's motto, but now she downed them without hesitation. She went from one drug-induced sleep to the next; things happened and voices spoke; she heard fragments of conversations. And throughout it all, she felt the longing for it to end, here and now. But it did not; she kept going, kept moving, swaying and jostling over the bumps. Jamie and the shadow didn't need to tell her where they were going; she knew. They were headed straight for Roswell, New Mexico.

Chapter 11

Missy was waiting, just as she promised she would be. Heath said they would be in at 2:00 a.m.; it was fifteen past two now. What was keeping them? Had something happened? She should have traveled with them, then she would not be sitting here alone, worrying.

Missy already had on a white coat. Everything was sterilized and placed out on the tray. Years ago, she attended medical school, she was a quick study, and it had been a breeze for her. She was a natural, picking up so much just from her weekends spent with Heath. But no matter how hard Missy worked, she would never be as good as Heath. Heath had been programmed—he was more skilled than she was. She could do the procedure on Elle, if she had to. Heath would make her too nervous; if she screwed up, he would never forgive her. She was just there to assist him; this was his operation.

There was nothing parked in the driveway. She went and checked the back alley. Nothing there either. She checked herself in the mirror again. She should take the eyeliner and mascara off, but there was no point; no one would notice anyway.

A low rumble in the back brought her away from the mirror; she hesitated for a few minutes before she moved to the door that led into the attached garage. Missy left the door opened wide and walked out to the car. Heath got out and went around the side to get Elle. Missy went for her bag of clothes. The girl had not changed since the gas station days ago. She would probably be stinking from the long days of traveling. Heath had Elle in his arms; he carried her to the house, not even bothering to say hi to Missy. Elle was dead to the world again, which would make the second operation even easier. Heath had told her in minute detail, over the phone, how they had opened her up right on the highway to remove the jelly pack; that kind of operation Missy would have liked to have been present for. However, that had not been an option. She followed Heath inside. She hit the garage door button before she headed to the basement. Their time would be limited, depending on how discreet they all were.

"You need the light?"

Heath did not answer her. He was turning sideways to carry her down the steep basement steps. She flicked it on anyway. He looked grateful as one shaky foot found the next step in the dim glare. His whole body was shaking by the time he reached the bottom. Missy flicked the light off, putting the stairway back into darkness.

Heath laid Elle on the table. It shifted under the new weight added to it. Missy had put a white sheet on the Ping-Pong table earlier, the net was gone, and it seemed to suit the situation, as good as any medical table would have done.

"Thanks."

"You're welcome," Missy answered.

She knew he meant everything, the shuttered basement windows to keep out any unwanted visitors. She had been visiting this place for the last fourteen years, getting it ready for this specific day and time. The time limit had been vague as to when this day would arrive. The main thing was no big changes, so as not to attract any unwanted attention. Missy had visited sometimes, staying for a few months on end, pretending that this was little more than a summer cottage, a getaway, an escape from the everyday, rather than a surgical hideaway. Of course if you wanted an escape from the everyday, Roswell fit the description.

Missy could tell Heath was exhausted.

"We could wait until morning if you would prefer?" Missy offered.

"No." Heath headed to the bathroom. "They're already tracking us; we need to get it out now; besides, she'll need some time to heal before we're on the run again."

"Ok." Missy brought the tray close to the Ping-Pong table.

"Maybe you should get out of here after the operation," Heath offered, not looking at Missy.

"Where am I going to go?" Heath didn't hear the tremble in her voice, did he?

"I don't know, back to New York, someplace, any place; just start over. Home maybe?"

It had been a long time since Missy had been home, she would not consider it. "Heath, I have not been training to be a surgeon just to go back to New York. I promised that I would be here to help you do this. I'll be here, till the end." He said nothing; she could hear him washing his hands, his head bent over the sink, focusing on making sure to get every molecule of dirt out from underneath his fingernails, his neck exposed just above his collar and below his hair. "You don't really mean it, do you?" Missy questioned.

"What's that?" Heath asked.

"You know, about me leaving?"

There was no sound, just him fitting into his scrubs, then he would have to wash again.

"Heath?"

"I'm coming."

"You know, if you don't like my help, me hanging around…"

The only answer was the running water. A small trickle of sweat ran down her back, trailed her backbone, and soaked into the waistband of her jeans. He wasn't serious, was he?

"Why do you stay?" Heath demanded finally.

"I want to help," Missy said, a small smile on her lips. Did it sound like a likely possibility, a reasonable one? Would he believe it? He had to. He just had to. He was what she got out of bed for. It had never been about Elle, not once. Missy owed Heath for saving her life. They all did.

Heath had been the one who performed the first operation on Missy, to successfully remove the chip from her spine; to this day she was thankful. She did not hate Grant for testing on her, from picking her out of the hundreds of people in that shopping mall years ago; she and her mother had been looking for a miracle. At just the right moment, it happened. Missy had been selected specifically because she had the same chip in her spine as Elle did. Grant didn't think of it as a coincidence. How could he? He had taken it as stroke of good luck, an ace in the hole.

She could still see the look on Heath's face back then, reserved, hostile, and consumed.

Heath had removed the chip without a single glitch. That was the thing about this operation; if the chip sensed the removal, it would send out a strong electrical pulse and would fry the brain of the patient. That patient would be in a vegetative state for the rest of their life. Even with all Grant's knowledge, and he had vast knowledge, the whole US military's extensive files to be exact, that was something he could not reverse.

After Missy had recovered, she had promised Grant she would always be there to help Heath. He depended on her now more than ever.

For Heath to just set her free to live her own life was unthinkable. She would not hear of it.

Missy finished hooking Elle up to the IV, the IV would help keep Elle hydrated during the surgery, and they would give her a knockout drug in there as well. Closely examining where Heath had removed the jelly pack, she saw he had done an excellent job alongside a highway, but now there was always the fear of an infection. She rolled Elle over; the red mark lay along her spine and was the telltale sign that Heath had altered the chip, just a tweak to keep Elle from being able to see Heath. It was not 100 percent foolproof, but it was pretty reliable. And it was his best bet for now, to keep his identity hidden from the bad guys, if only for a little while longer, hopefully buying them a few more days.

Elle would be too young to remember when it had been implanted in her spine, possibly even before Grant had recruited Heath to be her protector.

Heath came out, looking more worried than he had in all the years she had known him. "Scalpel."

A goddamn nurse is what he was treating her like. He did not need her; he never had; he had only relied on her a handful of times when he was stretched thin.

She was the one who needed him, now more than ever. Missy had never wanted anyone as much as she wanted Heath. Saying goodbye would destroy her.

The blood shot up, soaking across Elle's back as the scalpel cut down into the tissue. Missy moved forward, cleaning it up, mopping the blood. Heath peeled back Elle's flesh after cutting through it.

Missy could see the chip carefully placed along the vertebrae; the chips were not just tracking devices; they had multiple uses, and only time would tell just what all the chip in Elle's spine was for.

The tattoos always bothered Missy; they were an outdated version of the chip. Three triangles tattooed along the spine were a reminder of what was out there. She tried to pretend that she did not have one. But almost everyone had one; they were being marked, for future purposes.

Elle, Heath, and just about everyone important had one. Of course, she had never actually seen Heath's. Somehow she doubted his was on his spine. She would like to know where his was.

"What's so funny?" Heath looked up in time to see a flicker of her facial muscles pulling upward in the corners.

"Nothing," she said, forcing her muscles back into a serious expression.

"Can you hand me those microscope glasses?"

She picked them off the tray, curtesy of Roswell General. She placed them on his nose. "Anything else, Doctor?"

He dug around in the vertebrae disc very gently until he located the alien fibers that were hooked up to the chip; he took a small set of tweezers and attached them to the chip. Pulling the chip outward, he used the scalpel to sever the threads of alien material. Each thread had to be cut separately, and it seemed to take a long time, one after another. With precision, he had to hold the chip perfectly steady, so as not to activate the exterminate sequence. When the last fiber was severed, Heath slowly removed it. He set it carefully in a metal bowl. There was a noise of friction and static electricity; the signal had gone off; it was now harmless without its host. However, they needed to be careful, a remote signal was still coming from it, and it could still be tracking them. Heath dosed the chip with an acid solution.

After Missy's operation years ago, Heath had waited to show her exactly what it looked like. Now as fascinating as basic science was, the technology was anything and everything far beyond what the human race could imagine. Missy had been lying on a hard table, much like Elle now, with a fiery pain burning its way up and down her spine. At the time, Missy cared not to look at the chip, but now Missy watched as if hypnotized by Elle's chip, watching as the acid melted the chip into nothing.

Heath sewed up the little vessels that were leaking blood; once that was done, he got to work sewing up the incision. Missy dabbed at the blood. Once Elle was closed up, Missy replaced the IV with a fresh one and gave her a strong dose of antibiotics.

"I'm going to go shower," Heath said, departing back up the steep flight of stairs. Missy could hear clothes dropping on the tiled floor just above her head. She did not care about finding that tattoo anymore; all she wanted was for him to understand. A moment later the noise of the shower could be heard.

Missy gave Elle a shot of morphine. Heath didn't tell her to, but she knew when he had given her the last one, and it should be wearing off by now.

Lying face down on a Ping-Pong table all night, even with morphine, would not be a pleasant sleep for anyone. But moving Elle right now was not an option.

The shower stopped; Missy headed for the stairs.

Heath was sitting on the couch with his wet head tilted back, his eyes closed, and only a white towel was wrapped around his waist.

"Heath?"

"Yeah?"

"I was wondering, why do you think Grant picked me?"

"Picked you?"

"You know…out of everybody else, to be the guinea pig years ago?"

"Oh, I don't know."

"Come on; there must have been a reason?" Missy asked, persisting.

"Not really, you had a chip implanted in your vertebrae like Elle; you were programmed to watch, record info. You were a guinea pig back then."

"You don't think there was anything behind it, fate, destiny maybe?"

He was looking at her with this placid look all over his face, but she knew how he could be, how quickly that serene demeanor could change, how he could misinterpret what she needed to tell him. And yet, sometimes he could be so dense.

"Never mind. I'm going out," Missy stated abruptly; she needed a drink.

"What, now? It's kind of late. About tomorrow, can you watch Elle?"

Missy did not answer; she picked up her coat and walked out the front door at 4:00 a.m., slamming it unreasonably hard. Things were not as easy anymore. There would be an uncomfortableness between them from now on, her doing nonetheless. Always her doing.

The cool morning air felt good in her lungs; the streets of Roswell were bare at this hour.

Missy's cell phone rang. Tyson Malone was on the other end of the phone.

"Missy, it's Tyson."

Missy sighed inwardly. "Hi. Tyson, what are you doing up at this ungodly hour?"

"Well, I swung by your apartment for a business meeting, but you aren't home."

Missy smiled devilishly to herself. Tyson Malone was the cop she had made good friends with to help her out now and then. That's where she had gotten the tear gas canister from, which Heath had set off in the psych ward where Elle was being held. He was young and a very appealing man, but she was only interested in what he could do for her. She did not feel dirty trading sex for information; she would do whatever it took to help Heath out. "Sorry, Tyson, but I flew the coop, had a job to do for my mom, and I am far from New York currently. But not too far away to discuss what business you had for me."

"You know about what you asked. I tracked the gun that Elleanor Mackowski used to kill those docs; she never bought it. A dude by the name of Chace Worthington, he bought the gun. Looks like our girl might have had an accomplice, but not much adds up right now. Both are missing."

"What about Elle's credit card? Did she use it during her hiatus?"

"Nope, wasn't used, but her prints are all over the crime scenes."

"Ok, can you keep me updated on this?"

"Sure thing, sweetie, but it'll cost ya."

"You know I always pay my debts, Ty."

Tyson laughed on the other end before he hung up on her. Tyson clearly believed her web of lies and was a very young cop; he probably felt like nothing could touch him and did not think anything of compromising an investigation. It worked out in her favor, but it made Elle look more dangerous all the time.

***

Heath kept up his watch until ten in the morning before he fell asleep. He had slipped back to when he was just a kid again—back to when it all started for him.

Grant Mackowski was in the prime of his life; he had been working on one of the top-secret projects, reverse engineering an extraterrestrial spacecraft. And it was that knowledge that helped him in treating Heath's highly unusual case of self-destruction.

"The jelly pack is like a two-chamber system: one chamber contains the fiery liquid; the other chamber contains a nitrous chemical; if released separately, they are only slightly harmful. But if they progress far enough to mix into the third chamber, they become deadly, they will completely shut down the human body as if in complete organ failure, and it is untraceable in a toxicology report."

"Once Elle's dead, they might be able to extract the plans before the neurons stop firing. But I think they will only do that as a last resort."

"How valuable are the plans?" Heath questioned.

"Protecting the plans is the most important aspect of your mission."

"So, I just sit and wait?"

"Not exactly," Grant answered. "Over time, having that much info in the central core of Elle's brain could start to break her down mentally. Weaken her grasp on reality."

"How long do we have?"

"Years maybe, there is no set time; it just depends on how strong her mind is."

"Why not just destroy the plans?"

"It's her salvation and yours too. This planet will be destroyed one day; we may need to find somewhere else to live. Those plans are your salvation."

It would have been easy to let the chambers mix and just end it all; he would not have to worry about keeping her alive. But Grant had rigged him up with survival mechanisms, and quitting was not in Heath's programming.

***

It was quite dark in the room, except for some light coming from a small adjacent basement window, what little that wasn't boarded up. The outline of a dartboard slipped into her line of view. There were three darts in it, and every one had hit dead center. She was lying on her stomach, on what appeared to be a Ping-Pong table. Elle looked to the far corner; yep, it was.

103

There was a couch with some paddles and a net stuffed in the corner. She tried to roll onto her back, but a sharp pain reached up through her back, paralyzing her on the table. Elle turned her head to the right, looking for another light source. A dim glow came from a night-light on a little table; it was in the shape of a unicorn jumping over the clouds with two bears riding it. How had this gotten here, and why did she remember it? A tear slid down her cheek, dissolving into the thin sheet covering the Ping-Pong table.

"Are you ok?"

Elle jerked her head away from the night-light to the stairs leading down into the room she was in. A woman had entered the basement; she had long, curly hair; it did not look naturally curly, more like she had done it with curlers or a curling iron. The woman leaned forward, examining Elle.

"I'm Missy," she explained; she had a nice bedside manner. "Don't worry; the pain will go away. Heath did an excellent job; the paralysis in your legs will disappear in the next twenty-four hours. There are no better surgeons out there. Heath is the best. Not even I compare to him."

"Who?"

Missy smiled at her. "You will meet him shortly. He'll be down in a few minutes."

"Can I lie on my back?"

"I wouldn't advise it—at least, not just yet."

Missy moved out of Elle's line of vision. Elle tried moving her head to follow her, but gave up after her stiff neck refused. Missy came back anyway.

"Here, take one of these; it will take away some of the pain."

Elle took the gel capsule; she shoved the pill to the back of her throat, accepting the straw that Missy held out to her. She swallowed the pill, lifting her head off the table a few inches. Down it went.

"Good." Missy seemed satisfied.

"How's she feeling?" It was the shadow's voice. Elle would know it anywhere after the time she had spent with him.

Missy turned to the voice. "She seems to be ok. She moved her toes briefly, no spinal damage."

The voice moved around her to stand looking into Elle's eyes. She stared at him. He sounded like the shadow, but he was no longer a shadow.

Heath was about six foot and had an athletic build, he had a cigarette dangling from the corner of his mouth, and his hair was somewhat long.

Elle was taken aback. "You're the shadow?"

"Yep."

"Why couldn't I see you before?"

"We'll talk about that later." He bent down to pick something up off the floor. His hair fell forward across his forehead; through his hair, Elle could see a faint line, not like a cowlick or a part in his hair, but more like a very old scar. His hair hid it nicely.

Slowly and meticulously, they moved Elle to the couch. The pills Missy had given her were strong; she was drifting half in and half out of consciousness. It was a relaxing feeling, without worry; she did not have to think or make sense of anything. Her eyelids closed softly. When she opened them again, staring at the opposite wall, there were eyes on it, big and black and staring out of gray faces, but one set stood apart from the others—one set was different; they were not black; they were dark chestnut in a black face, dark and calculating, predatory.

Elle squeezed her eyes shut; when she reopened her eyes, the faces were gone. But the fear did not pass, even after the effects of the drugs had worn off, and she could think clearly.

Chapter 12

Heath let himself drift back to simpler times, to the time when he lived on the street with his mother, Nadine. He was never told not to talk to strangers; perhaps if he had, the meeting with the Dark Man never would have happened. Or maybe that was just wishful thinking on his part. And without that chance encounter, life could've been a lot different.

After the Dark Man's touch, Heath disappeared and was replaced by this entity, and the following events ensued. Heath knew of the pain, but he had no way to fight it; he had become a weapon to be used against mankind. Blood was on Heath's hands, literally; blood dripped down his face and into his eyes. Two dead homeless people lay on the ground before him, and the third he had just stabbed. He was standing in a dreary warehouse. The skylight was too dirty to let much light sift through. Heath looked up, staring through a mask of blood and pain, he had a curved knife in one hand, and he felt crazy, not even conscious of who he really was anymore. He was moving forward simply by the pain driving him.

Someone walked out of the shadows and into the dim lighting.

"My name is Grant."

Grant was tall, at least six feet. He seemed like a giant compared to Heath; Heath was only three feet tall and was abnormally short for his age. Grant had not shaved, and he had a dark five o'clock shadow. Heath kept his eyes on Grant as he walked toward Heath. Heath felt pressure squeeze his heart, and he lashed out with the blade. Grant kept getting closer. He did not seem fazed by the knife Heath held. The pressure in Heath's heart and brain intensified, making Heath swipe out with his knife in defense, as if to try to ward off the pain. Before the knife could slash into Grant, the blade stopped instantly. Heath pulled back with his hand, but the knife was stuck. He reached his other hand out to try to pull the knife back to himself. But there was nothing he could do to make the knife move; it was stuck in the air as if it had stabbed into something invisible. Heath looked up into Grant's face in wonder. How was Grant stopping him? "How?" Heath finally questioned.

Grant looked down to where his hand was tucked inside his coat pocket and pulled out a chunk of metal.

Heath would do whatever it took to stop the pressure in his head; he would destroy Grant. Heath's head whipped around in the direction of the police sirens. Heath was panting; desperation was making him sweat uncontrollably. The cops would come, and they would know what he had done. Heath wanted to run, but he could not move. Grant spoke. "No."

Heath did not move; he was stuck. His eyes darted right and left, he did not like to be controlled, and yet he could not do anything about it.

"Do you want out of this? Or are you happy with the future that is laid out before you?" Grant's voice was gruff, laced with hatred. "You want to stop the pressure around your heart, in your head, and in your body. Come with me. But if you would rather wait and see what happens when the cops get here, then be my guest. They will not go easy on you just because you're still a minor. This is murder, no matter how you look at it."

The pressure squeezed down on Heath from within; it seemed to be coming from every angle of his body. All his organs pushed tightly up against each other. He fell into a tight ball on the ground, just wanting the pressure to stop. He opened his mouth in a scream. "Yeeeeeeeessssssss." It took everything in Heath's body to answer Grant.

Grant bent down over him, his face a wash of darkness. His hands felt along Heath's head to just in front of his ears. He reached into a pocket of his long coat and came out with a syringe; Grant flicked the plastic cap off with his thumb from the needle tip and stabbed it into Heath's head. The sharp jab of the syringe was a mere mosquito bite compared with the pressure and the pain in Heath's body.

Everything stopped, as if time had ceased to exist; the pressure was gone; Heath felt free, free like he had not been in weeks. He stood up, and together Grant and Heath walked out of the warehouse to a waiting car. It was that simple. Heath only had to make a choice, and once he did, he was free. Or so he thought.

Days passed, days when Heath was awake, days when he slept in a drug-induced coma. Sometimes Heath was conscious of the skin grafts to cover up the metal-plated alloy; they were essential to piece Heath's head back together. A big portion of Heath's skull had been damaged. When the plate was in and the skin grafts were finished, he felt like he was looking at Frankenstein in the mirror; the stich marks were a mess. They crisscrossed across his forehead and skull. But as time passed, Heath looked more and more human again. And then one day, it was as if a switch had been flipped; Heath felt more awake than he had in months. And yet there had to be a reason why Grant had saved him; nothing was free. But then it did not matter what Grant expected in return; anything was better than dealing with the pain and the pressure from the infection.

Heath got up and padded to the fridge. His blue jeans hung loosely around his narrow hips. He had lost a lot of weight; he was skin and bones now.

The fridge door opened, sending light into the room. It was fresh and bright, and Heath imagined that it was what really kept the fruit and meat from spoiling. That kind of light, if even for a few seconds, could ward off so much. When he was infected, he had longed for light; he felt like that might have kept him from deteriorating.

Heath chose an orange finally and closed the door reluctantly. He sat down on the couch and started to suck on the juice through the peel; it was so good he almost cried out in pleasure.

Voices from above spilled into the basement before the door at the top of the stairs opened and closed. Grant came down and sat in the armchair across from Heath.

"Am I going to jail?" Heath asked.

"No."

"What's going to happen to me?"

"You'll work for me now."

"For how long?"

"Until the people you killed can be forgotten."

"And how long will that be?" Heath asked.

"Not for a very long time," Grant said. "What the Dark Man did to you had damaging effects, irreversible. Your brain reacted to the infection as it spread, and your body was in survival mode. You would've been dead in a matter of hours if I hadn't found you. However, the part of your brain that was infected was so severely damaged that we had to alter it. It is impossible for them to get a hold of you ever again."

"Rendering me immune?"

"In a manner of speaking, yes."

"What's the downside?"

"Not sure there is an any downside to losing compassion. You are more valuable to me the way you are now—you won't let human emotions get in the way of your better judgment. That is priceless."

"When do I meet your daughter?"

"You don't; you don't meet her until it's absolutely necessary. When they come for her and she will accept reality without questions. You both will then need to work together, not before."

"Why not before?"

"Because they will kill you; it is safer for you if they don't know what you look like. Trust no one."

Heath looked a little uncertainly at Grant; if the last couple months had taught him anything, it was that the extraterrestrials had otherworldly powers. And that wasn't something that he wanted to mess with now. Immune or not.

"After I've finished training you, no one can know about you, especially Elle."

"How would they know about me if I met her?"

"She has a chip in her spine; everything she sees they see. They did it to watch over me, but it doesn't matter; they will never know what I know, so long as I keep the plans hidden."

"Where are the plans hidden?"

"Right now, they're locked in my subconscious. But soon I will implant them in Elle. I will wait as long as I can, until it is absolutely vital; however, when I do install them in her brain, she won't know about them, and she will have to figure out how to access them by herself."

"So, you're telling me that they would know about me if she knew about me?"

"Yeah."

Heath leaned back. "Why don't you take the chip out of her then?"

"It's safer for her if I leave the chip in her. If they knew I knew that it was there, they would start getting suspicious. But when you have to be right there with her, to protect her because they are coming for her, then you will have to take it out of her. If you aren't close to your facilities to perform the operation, you can tweak the chip, alter it, and it will buy you some time. It will black out your appearance."

"What good am I going to be to protect her? Right now I'm too young."

"Youth has its advantages. I want you to be young enough to do all the things that I would never be able to do. After all, I won't be around forever; they wouldn't think I would jeopardize my baby's safety and mental health by implanting the plans in her brain. I believe they don't know I have solved the solution to their magnetic-propulsion system."

"So why do I need to train now if they might not come for her for twenty years?"

"Because I don't know when they will come for certain, and you will need to be ready. After all, it's an assumption that they won't do anything, because even if they knew she had the plans in her, her mental stability would be too fragile to extract the plans from her. If they try to get the plans out of her when she is this young, they could destroy them in the process. My belief is they will bide their time, but only until they think they can get the plans without the risk of destroying them."

"It doesn't seem like you care about your daughter. What good are the plans going to be if she's dead?"

"That's where you're wrong; it might come down to those plans saving you both one day. My baby will be ok; she was always gifted that way; she has a lot of space up there." Grant tapped his head. "She's probably got enough space for two average people's memories. There won't be much of a risk, as long as I wait until it's absolutely necessary, when her mental development can't be questioned. But even if I did implant them now, it wouldn't be safe to remove them for at least ten years; it takes time for the mind to heal."

"How are you going to extract them from your head?"

"Very carefully."

Heath eased back on the couch; he stared at the TV. "If they're smart, why don't they just design their own plans and forget about you, her, all of us?"

"When I say they're smart, I mean they are an advanced race with special abilities; however, they aren't mechanically inclined. Another race of aliens built and designed their spacecraft; this race that is here is more like geologists; they fly around studying plant life, then crash and need a mechanic to fix their ship. I was their mechanic; they needed me to rebuild certain components of their ship. But when I reverse engineered their spacecraft, I came across data that suggested that our planet would be destroyed in our near future. Now, whether they know how to time travel, I can't say. But what I can say is their spacecraft is our best means for survival, if Earth is destroyed one day. We may need to leave."

Heath said nothing.

"To train you properly, we will need to begin immediately; tomorrow you will perform an operation on a boy about your age. I want you to successfully remove the chip from his spine."

"I'm not a surgeon. I'm a kid."

"Not anymore you're not; you will be everything that she will need you to be. You will be a blood donor, a hit man, a technician, a surgeon, and the most important job description of all, her protector. You will follow her throughout every aspect of her life at a safe distance. Now get some sleep; your training begins tomorrow."

Heath did not think he could sleep; he felt empty inside and afraid that he would not be able to do all the things needed of him. He was nothing special, and he never would be.

Chapter 13

Heath's Training

Grant appeared at the house; he had a big duffel bag slung over one shoulder; the weight caused him to limp. Heath followed him into the basement. Grant set the bag on the Ping-Pong table; inside was a little boy that appeared to be sleeping.

Heath stood next to Grant; he took out a handful of pictures from an envelope in a side compartment of the bag and handed them to Heath. Heath took them and examined the first picture. It was of a little girl with long brown hair in braids and bright-blue eyes. She was smiling; she had a big gap in her teeth where her baby teeth had been.

"That's my daughter, Elleanor," Grant said.

Heath knew why Grant had shown him a picture of her. Heath lit a cigarette before he took the next picture and studied it closely. She was familiar. She lived six blocks away from this house. He had seen her playing in her backyard when he walked to the store for cigarettes, something he was allowed to do now that he looked human again. Heath offered the picture back, but Grant held up a hand, refusing. Heath stuck the picture in his back pocket.

"You better hurry up and smoke that cigarette; we have an operation to do."

Grant rolled the boy over onto his stomach. Heath crushed his cigarette into the ash tray and came over to stand next to Grant. He exhaled deeply before he looked up at Grant. Heath studied the scalpel in Grant's outstretched hand and wondered what could be gained by this and how many of these kids Grant would bring him. Heath didn't feel steady, inside he was trying to escape, but his body wouldn't cooperate.

"I can take away your freedom," Grant spoke, almost accusingly. "Don't make me do that."

Heath extended his hand to accept the scalpel. His hand shook as it closed around the cool steel. He could not believe what Grant expected of him; he was not a surgeon—he was a boy.

Grant lifted the motionless boy's shirt over his shoulders. Heath moved closer; along the boy's spine were three black triangles. They were burned into the skin, almost like a brand. Heath looked at Grant in apprehension.

"It's ok; the boy won't know anything about this. Time is wasting."

"Maybe you could do the first one, so I can watch how it's supposed to be done, and I will do the next one." Heath hoped there would not be a next one.

"Ok," Grant answered.

Heath felt his heart slow down to a regular rhythm. He felt himself still inside. Grant lowered the scalpel in his hand to just above the three triangles on the boy's back. He pushed the scalpel deep into the boy's flesh. Blood squirted out of the boy's back and slid across until it dripped over his side and onto the table. Heath watched the scalpel go in deeper; Grant started cutting the flesh so it could be peeled back. Wedged into the vertebrae was a metallic chip about the size of Heath's thumbnail. This boy was used as a spy, without him even knowing it.

Grant pulled out the chip ever so slightly and severed the fibers holding it in place; he pitched it into the metal bucket; there was a crackling in the bucket and then silence. "You have to be smooth, so the electromagnet pulse doesn't go off and fry the patient." Grant started to sew the boy back up. It seemed like a simple-enough operation, if you could get through all the blood and cutting into flesh. But that was something that Heath was not sure he would be able to do. He felt his insides flip-flopping.

Grant called upstairs; a man came down; his hair was already almost all white. "This is Pete."

Pete nodded at Heath, collected the boy, and took the kid out of the room. Heath studied the pool of blood that had leaked onto the floor and then took out a cigarette. He lit a match, but his fingers were shaking so badly he could not seem to light the cigarette. Grant held the match steady so Heath could light his cigarette.

"I don't see what the big deal is. It's not like you haven't killed before. Like you have not been covered in someone else's blood. Avoiding this is not going to make it go away."

"It was different then; I wasn't aware of what I was doing; there was this force within me; all I could feel was the pain and the wanting to escape everything," Heath answered.

"But you're free of the pain and the infection. That must be worth something to you!" Grant stated. "The smoking could become a problem; try to cut back, if not quit cold turkey."

"Right now, I need it."

"But later it could be a handicap, jittery when you've got a job to do, and all you can think about is your next smoke. You may not be human, but an addiction is an addiction. It's simple; you won't be able to control it. You can't be selfish when it concerns her; every aspect of your life will revolve around Elle."

"The chip in the boy was along his spine; is that where the chip is located in your daughter?"

"Yes, the chip is lodged in her intervertebral disc, and it will take a steady hand to remove it but only when the time is right."

Heath nodded; everything that he would have to do would be ten times more difficult than in practice. And that is what it all boiled down to; it felt inhumane to dissociate himself from the kids Grant brought in here. However, there would be mistakes, and if he let it, it would destroy him. But it was human to fail, and he was not human anymore.

"You won't need to attend school in the fall; you will be here instead. I will teach you everything you need to know to keep her alive. You are going to have to grow up a lot sooner than most kids, learn to kill men, women, or children if they pose a risk to Elle's life. You're going to need to do everything from medical procedures to being able to build a bomb, wire a house with explosives, if need be, and repair machines. Become a skilled fighter; you need to put on weight and keep yourself healthy while watching her day and night. You name it; you're going to need to know how to do it."

"Isn't it going to be pretty hard to watch her twenty-four hours, and possibly up to twenty years, and remain unnoticed?"

"I did not pick you because I thought it would be easy. I picked you because most people in your position would have gone crazy from the pain you endured. You can do this and anything that comes your way."

"Is she going to be able to help?"

"My daughter will not be an invalid in this; she will know a lot of survival skills; you just worry about training yourself."

Pete returned, carrying another body over his shoulder. This was a little girl, two or three years younger than Heath. She was small and fine boned and practically blue. Heath wasn't even sure she was alive.

Pete set her down on the Ping-Pong table and left. Heath gazed down at her closed eyes. He saw her chest rise and fall, she was alive, but she was so blue it was frightening. He looked at Grant.

"Her chip is in her intervertebral disc; you will remove it." Grant rolled her over onto her stomach and lifted her T-Shirt over her shoulder blades. Heath saw the same three triangles burned in the flesh along her spine.

Pete returned and set down a clean tray of operating tools on the table before heading back up the stairs.

Heath stepped up to the side of the table. He reached out and picked up the scalpel. It felt like a chunk of ice in his hand. He lifted it above her body and placed the edge against her skin, right above the triangles. Heath pressed the scalpel deep down. Blood oozed up, spreading across the little girl's back, drowning the scalpel and the incision he had just made. Heath jerked back, his heart was hammering in his chest, and he felt like the room was spinning—he could not do this. Heath threw the scalpel away. It bounced harmlessly across the basement floor, spinning in a dizzying blood circle.

The stairs shrieked under Heath's weight as he pounded up them and out the door. The hot air dried the cold sweat from his forehead in one gust. He ran down back alleys and across driveways, making a zigzag pattern, trying to lose Grant. Heath ran until he found a high wooden fence to crouch behind. He stayed there, finding solace in the cool shade. A girl's voice drifted through the humid midafternoon heat. Heath looked through the boarded fence at the girl. It was Grant's daughter; his subconscious had betrayed him, leading him back to the life he was trying to escape. He sat there, watching the little girl play with her chalk, until the last rays of daylight had disappeared. Grant beckoned to his daughter to come inside for supper. But Grant was not looking at his daughter; he was looking to the spot where Heath was crouched on the other side of the fence. Heath turned, bolting; he ran all the way to the park, not even bothering to look when he crossed the street to the park entrance. Lights from a car blinded Heath momentarily when he landed in its path.

Tires squealed. "Hey, Moochie, that's the little fuck that slashed your tires a couple months ago."

Heath stared into the light, knowing someone had recognized him. "Hey, Bobby, I think you're right."

The car swung in Heath's direction, barely missing him as he cleared the gates of the park entrance. He raced through the sandy area toward the river. The river had been nicknamed the Burrow. You could hide practically anything there of reasonable size and not have to worry about anyone finding it ever again. The riverbank flooded yearly, washing old trees up, sucking away sand, creating dens, holes, trenches, and hideaways. The younger kids played hide-and-seek there during the summer months. Some of the kids were never found again; they went into the burrow and did not come out. It attracted the bigger kids as well. They had parties late at night on the sandbars. If he could get to the Burrow, he might stand a chance against the carload of guys.

Lights darted back and forth as he ran, some from the streets beyond, some from the car that busted through the chain-link gates and was bearing down on him. Halfway across the big, open stretch of park, Heath was out of breath already; the bank of the Burrow was a half-mile off at least. He turned to look behind him; the car darted across the sandy area overturning a swing set; they were trying to run him down.

"Run, little rabbit, run," one of the guys hollered at Heath from the open window of the car. "If you don't make it to the Burrow, you're dead."

Heath looked back; his body was soaked with sweat; he wished he would have stayed and done the operation. He did not want trouble. A loud bang erupted through the night; it was the sound of a tire blowing. "Fuck, another tire," one of the guys from inside the car yelled. The kids abandoned the car and proceeded on foot. Heath knew, if they caught him, he would die!

Heath could feel his heart hammering in his chest; when he felt like he was done, he found a burst of renewed energy, adrenaline he had not tapped into yet. The outline of the trees had completely vanished, a little voice whispered in his head, but it was too late—the young guy was already colliding with Heath. The flashlight flew out of someone's hand, highlighting the distance to the Burrow. The Burrow was barely forty feet away. That was the last thing Heath saw before his head hit something hard and the weight from the kid's dog piled on top of him. These guys probably were not more than 16 or 17, maybe 140 to Heath's 80 pounds. But to him, they were seven-foot-tall, beefy football players with hundreds of pounds, all dropping on top of him.

"Little rabbit, you didn't make it," one guy called out innocently.

A flashlight shone into Heath's eyes, practically blinding him. One guy pulled Heath to his feet and held him so he could not get away. There were five young guys circling him; a thicker guy came face-to-face with Heath. His face was round, and even in the poor lighting, Heath could tell he was drunk. Probably Moochie.

"So, you're the little puss jewel that slashed my tires, huh?"

"I don't remember," Heath said, wheezing, finally feeling like his lungs had started to inflate again.

"You slashed my tires, and you don't remember? What, weren't my tires good enough to remember? They weren't good enough, is that it?"

He shouted at Heath, accusing, as if Heath had slept with the guy's sister and had not bothered to remember her name. Moochie sounded like he wanted Heath to remember the exact time it had happened and the brand and year of the tire that he had slashed. Heath was drawing a complete blank; perhaps it happened when he was self-destructing, driven by the pressure and the pain. Moochie pulled Heath forward until they were so close they were almost touching foreheads. The other guys each grabbed an arm, spreading Heath out. Moochie took his first shot, punching Heath right in the stomach. Heath choked, gasping for air. The two guys held him firmly, letting Moochie punch him again and again. Finally, they released Heath's arms; he dropped to the ground. But it did not end there. They all moved in closer to him, and then they started kicking him in the body; his body jolted like electricity was coursing through it. He twitched from each boot that struck him. Each boot was pushed by hate, hate so powerful that it felt like it would kick his guts right out the other side of his body. The only thing that kept Heath's guts from coming out was the guy's boots kicking from the opposite side.

The beating stopped eventually; the pain distorted what was right and what was wrong. All Heath knew was that he was going to have to fight for survival.

"All right, little rabbit, this is your last chance to fess up for what you did."

That was so sweet; here Moochie was giving him the chance to make things right. But Heath did not need to make things right. Grant was somewhere nearby, and he had spoken so only Heath could hear. "*Verwandeln*." It was German for Heath to transform. Heath was not aware of the changes in him until the program was activated. A German command operated the program.

A cold feeling spread through his body in one sweep; he could hear the crickets from miles and miles away. He was getting to his feet, and the older kids allowed him to do this.

He became immediately conscious of a small knife in his jeans pocket; he reached in and pulled it out. The lock clicked, setting the blade into place. Nobody from the group of boys heard the clicking sound of Heath's pocketknife; their pants of exhaustion had drowned out the sound. They seemed more confused about how he could still be alive after the beating he had taken.

"You're going to die now, little rabbit."

Moochie reached for Heath, completely unaware of the small blade in Heath's hand. Heath's hand shot out, gripping the guy's arm to steady himself. With his other hand, he drove the knife into Moochie's stomach, to the hilt.

"You know…I think…I did…slash…your tires." Heath panted in Moochie's face.

Grant had promised that he would train Heath, but the part Grant left out was where Heath was lethal when pushed over the edge. Grant had altered one of the computer chips that he had removed from another kid and had put it in Heath's spine, sometime after Grant had rescued Heath. There was something in the computer chip, a bit of technology that amped up Heath's ability to fight, and no one could control Heath's rage. It turned and twisted him into a machine.

Heath ripped out the knife and dove at another guy; the knife gouged the guy deep in the throat. A spurt of blood sloshed out of his mouth with the fierceness of the jab. The guy's eyes remained shocked and open as they stared into Heath's.

The other three guys were backing up slowly, seemingly afraid to take their eyes off Heath.

Heath felt no remorse, not one shred, as he moved from guy to guy.

The rest of the group watched uncertainly as their leader remained frozen, holding his stomach. The other boy was dead. Heath lunged forward, striking Moochie in the chest again; he pulled it out in a sucking gurgle of air and blood. Everyone seemed to watch as if hypnotized.

Two of the guys finally turned to flee; before they could take more than two steps, they grabbed for their throats—a knife was lodged in each of their necks. They died on their feet. The third stood still; he did not even scream when Grant started slashing him apart.

A few minutes passed before Grant acknowledged Heath.

"Running away isn't a part of the job description, Heath."

Grant reached down for the body of the second boy that Heath had stabbed; he grasped him under the armpits, pulling him toward the Burrow. Heath reached down, grabbing an arm of a body, and pulled on the dead boy. He moved it ten feet before Grant was back; he grabbed the body out of Heath's grasp and took it. He went back and forth for the third and fourth while Heath rested on the ground, holding his stomach in his hands.

Cop sirens wailed in the distance. Heath stood up just as Grant stepped alongside him.

"It's a good bet someone will see you, if you head out of the park. We'll go into the Burrow and split up. You head upriver; I'll head down. If you have to kill someone, do it; everyone's the enemy; the line between good and evil doesn't exist anymore! There is no right or wrong; it's survival of the fittest from now on. When you lose them, circle around and come back to Pete's. I'll take a look at you and see how much damage those boys did."

Heath cringed while he moved through the trees to the edge of the Burrow; his body hurt. But he would not give in to the pain. The ground fell out from underneath Heath's feet; he dropped at least ten feet. There were easier spots into the Burrow than this path, but he did not have the time or energy to find them. He pitched forward into the sand, tears stinging his eyes from the jolt of the fall. He ground his teeth together to keep from screaming out; he did not lift his face out of the sand until he was sure he could keep from making a sound. He looked up to the sky; a few flashlights skimmed the bank of the Burrow; the cops were coming. He stood up, clutching at his side and moving slowly down the bank, looking for a place to hide. The loose sand slid easily along the bank in steep places. Heath ran blindly, slipping in the sand and over the driftwood. He fell just shy of the water's edge. Slipping silently into the water, he trudged upriver.

Heath's clothing became waterlogged; he ditched his shirt to lighten his load. The bank disappeared; the river must have turned or widened. He moved toward where he thought it might be, and he tripped on his heavy jeans just as the ground disappeared from under his feet. He'd never had swimming lessons. Panic replaced direction; he was just trying to keep his head above water now. But a mouthful of water was what he got instead. "*Schwimmen.*" Heath recognized the word, it was German for swim, and he could feel his limbs stretch out in front of him with newfound knowledge; he rose and swam with strength. He covered the distance quickly, the deep part of the river fell behind him, and the sand returned underfoot. He crawled forward on hands and knees, reaching out in front of him. Grant had saved him even from a distance; if Grant gave a command in German and Heath could hear it, and usually he could because his hearing had been altered in ways that elevated Heath far above the average human, Heath's body responded to the program.

Heath was far away from the cops and the sounds of the dogs, far away in what felt like another world. Heath crawled into a cave in the bank of the Burrow. The sound of the water lapping against the bank softened as the water quieted. Heath pressed his back into the farthest wall of the cave, making the sand sift down from above. Someone bent down to the entrance of the cave, looking in. Heath could see the whites of their eyes; their hand reached into the Burrow for him. Heath jerked…

***

"Stop," Heath mumbled in his sleep.

Elle was not going to stop—she pulled the gun from the waistband of Heath's pants. He reached for it with dull fingers, trying to shake off the shackles of sleep. But Elle was wide awake, and she had the advantage. She stood back pointing the gun at him, almost banging into the corner of the Ping-Pong table. She was a rather sorry sight, bent forward like a hunchback, pointing the gun at him. Elle did not know how to use the gun, was the safety still on? Heath leaned his head back, and he could not keep himself from laughing a little while she ran her hands up and down the guns casing, trying desperately to figure out how it worked.

The gun felt alien in her hands, she did not know what to do with the fucking thing, assuming the safety was on, and she did not know how to get it off. Once she had wobbled her way over to the couch and gotten it from him, she had almost fallen on her butt when his eyes suddenly snapped open; her face was practically in his; she had to bite her tongue to keep from yelping. Fuck, the pain in her back was so bad that she almost passed out just from that. Now he was laughing at her. "Shut your face. Mmm." She leaned forward, swallowing the warm bile that filled her mouth. She had to fight to swallow it back down. "Now listen to me, you son of a bitch. I want some answers, or I'm putting a bullet between your eyes. I'll be out of here before your little friend even knows you're staining the carpet."

"That's cute, my little friend."

"Call her whatever you like."

"What do you want to know?" Heath asked, leaning back comfortably on the couch.

"I know you're the enemy."

"You don't know fuck all." Heath dove at her; his fingers were inches away when the trigger was pulled back. Nothing happened, just an empty *clack*. He piled into her. The gun flew out of her hands, skipping across the cement. He retrieved it and pointed it at her. "I never load the first chamber! See this? This is the safety; know the difference—on and this is off." He shoved the thing closer, clicking the switch back and forth. "You understand?"

"Fuck you," she said through a mask of pain and anger.

That made him angry; he grabbed her by the neck of her T-Shirt and hauled her toward the bathroom. Once in the doorway, she tried jerking away from him, but he would not resist and pushed her toward the porcelain sink.

His breath was warm in her ear when he finally stopped shoving; the mirror reflected what he was doing, reaching behind himself for something. She tried bolting, despite the pain lacing its way up her back; he grabbed her around the neck, jolting her to a stop. She could not win, not now—especially with the red-hot fire racing up and down her spine.

He held up another mirror, nothing fancy; she could see the back of Heath and some of her back now.

"Now I want you to look."

He eased away from her, grabbing her T-shirt and ripping it upward in one smooth tear, exposing her back.

"Stop it." Elle threw fists and elbows at him. He jerked her body around, pulling the shirt off her shoulders so she could see her spine in the mirror above the sink.

"Stop acting like a fucking baby, and just look. You need to know the truth."

She stopped fighting him to look at what he was talking about. Her back was red in some places where he had pushed and jabbed her and especially red where the stitches crisscrossed where she had been opened up. But she saw what he was talking about. There were three black triangles along her spine, in a circle actually; they looked just like the triangles she had seen on other people, the trucker that stopped to help her. They were black, black like they had been branded into her skin, definitely not the work of a drunken escape gone wrong. There was nothing fun about these tattoos. She stared as if hypnotized; the startling realization of the truth was finally sinking in. Who was really the enemy?

"Do you see?" his voice was quieter, questioning.

"I see perfectly."

She looked back at him in the mirror; he nodded. There was a few T-shirts on the edge of the tub; she reached down for one, pulling it over the torn one she had on.

She could not escape from reality; she now saw what he wanted her to see; she knew what he wanted her to know. He relaxed, moving back to sit on the edge of the tub. Seemingly relieved, he took out a cigarette, crammed it between his lips, and dug in his pockets for a lighter. His attention was drawn away from her.

From all the excitement, Elle could feel the darkness creeping closer; she stepped back, connecting with the tile, then her head snapped backward, connecting with the wall. The jolt jarred her spine all the way to the back of her teeth. Her body slid down the wall; the room was replaced by a field; the darkness had settled down over the meadow. Little kids were running; they were everywhere, out catching fireflies in jars. And there were a lot of fireflies too, sparks of light bobbing and swaying through the tall, dry grass. Elle whirled this way and that, looking for the bathroom, for Heath. But it was all gone. It had been replaced.

An outstretched jar was thrust in her face, her hands reached out for it instinctively, but before her fingers encircled the jar, the little boy let it go, and the jar fell from his outstretched hand. The jar exploded into fragments when it struck the hard ground; the fireflies flew free. Her eyes followed them upward into the night sky. A dark figure rushed out at her; perhaps that was why the little boy had dropped the jar—he had seen it coming.

"You see them too?" she tried to ask the little boy. But it was too late; the night jostled until it came to a standstill; there were no more fireflies, no warm, muggy night, just the cold tile floor beneath her. Heath was staring intently at Elle.

"Sorry, Elle, they put them there after they abducted you." He caught her hands in his; he was referring to the tattoos.

Elle shook her head in disbelief.

"You think I'm lying? I thought you wanted to know everything."

"Everything but your lies—don't you think that if these tattoos had been there for at least twenty years or so, I would've seen them before?"

"Like you could see me? You don't seem to get it; they can control what you see or what you don't. That chip I removed from your spine can do more than you will ever know. It's like a command tower right inside you. Without it, they're not listening to you; they're not monitoring where you are or who you're with."

Everything she had been led to believe from nine years old had been a lie, one that her mother did her best to perpetuate; the little voice inside Elle's head kept saying that she cannot live in denial anymore, that they were out there somewhere, that they wanted her for what she possessed. The letter from her father was lost, but that did not matter! Heath was here and now, and he was more trustworthy than her own mother had been, than any doctor could ever be.

"You want to know why you're here, why they took you, and where your dad is—well I got most of the answers. All you got to do is ask and I will answer; there is no one inside you listening and watching me, tracking you. From here on in, it's up to us to keep you alive."

Heath turned away to head out of the bathroom.

"Wait, I want to know."

The cigarette between his fingers had been forgotten. He sat back down on the bathtub. "What do you want to know?"

"Everything."

"Ok." Heath shook the ash off his cigarette into the tub. "It was only when the blueprints to the extraterrestrial spacecraft were completed that Grant discovered how valuable they were, and he knew the aliens would come for them one day.

"They had been implanting computer chips in people for years, it was a form of control, and I was implanted a few years before I got infected. The placement of the chip in most of the test subjects is located along the intervertebral disc in the spine. It's where the Dark Man has the most control. The chip is small, maybe a quarter of an inch by a quarter of an inch. The chip records what you see once it's activated; you could be told what to do, as if you were a robot, and not even be aware of it. It did not take Grant long to realize what we were carrying.

"My mother was a drug addict; I was born on the streets. When I was only eight, the Dark Man approached me behind a fast-food joint. I did not have enough sense to be afraid. After the Dark Man touched me, he transferred a parasite into me; it caused an infection that spread rapidly throughout my body. The infection the Dark Man had given to me had its own purpose, to spread to others. But the infection mutated before I could spread anything, and it became a burden that only I could bear. The Dark Man realized that I had failed as a kind of doomsday device, a way to pressure mankind. I was self-destructing at an alarming rate. Right here." Heath pointed to a spot on his forehead and circled outward with his finger, indicating a much larger area than just his index finger could point to. "I bashed my head against the wall to try and get rid of the pain, the voices. I chipped away a large portion of my skull; it was your father who found me. I had killed two homeless people and had stabbed a third. I could not stop what was inside me. Grant offered me a way out. He implanted an extraordinary metal alloy into my skull to hold it together. The metal alloy definitely was not on our periodic table. The alloy absorbed the infection.

"Grant told me about them and why they were here. He told me about how Vincent Striker and Grant were assigned to the 'Project.' The Project was conceived by Willard Delaney and was deep inside the government. The Project's main objective was to get the crashed alien spacecraft up and running.

"Willard was not your average government employee; he had more clearance than the American President. Willard answered to no one; he ran the Project out of Area 51 in Nevada with one means, to get results no matter what.

"And for a while, Grant and Vincent were making headway, reverse engineering the alien spacecraft. But that soon came to an end when Grant realized who they were really working for. Everything the Project was supposed to stand for did not. Willard drew a line in the sand, to get the spacecraft up and running or lose your life. And for a while, Grant followed the rules out of fear, but fear can only be used as a means of control for so long. Grant knew the only way out with his life intact was to become deathly ill; if they thought he was dying, they might release him from the Project.

"Grant took sick during a brief hiatus; the compound became contaminated with a nuclear material that got expelled from the fuselage of the UFO. Willard discharged Grant, always feeling that Vincent was the true genius and would figure out the specifics that could get the spacecraft fully operational.

"After Grant got discharged, he focused on treating me, and my recovery was next to miraculous. Grant had been experimenting with the computer chips he had removed from kids and adults, and he was able to reprogram the chip. The metal alloy from the plate in my head connected with the chip, and I became a supercomputer of sorts, without human breakdown.

"The collapse came when you were nine years old. Grant feared for his safety; he injected the spacecraft's blueprints into your brain's interior core. One night, he disappeared, and I never saw him again. Speculation circulated for a while about what happened to him; some believe he had some kind of mental breakdown and ran off into the night, just as crazy as his father was. But I knew. I knew Grant very well, and I know he did not go crazy. A year after your father's disappearance, your mother picked you up and moved to New York. She pretended like Grant never existed. I think she was more afraid of the truth than anything. I did like I always do, and I followed you."

"Why did they come here in 1947?"

"Elle, they have been here a lot longer than forty-seven. When the forty-seven incident happened, it flooded the newspapers; the head of the military at the time turned it into a fucking joke, coming up with that weather-balloon story. As for 1947, that was their first attempt at going home. The original crash took place in 1906, we were undeveloped, and the Model T car was a few years off. When they crashed here, they were left with no way off. Our technology wasn't advanced enough to get them home. They watched us grow and develop, then they started to infiltrate the human race. The Dark Man can move among us, and you don't even notice that he's not normal until he touches you. Our minds are so easy to manipulate; subconsciously our minds can't handle the concept of an extraterrestrial life form—it's frightening. You were controlled, but now you are awake; you have a mind, and you can use it."

Elle spoke up, breaking into Heath's explanation, "After you showed me the triangles, I saw this field, a meadow, and I think it was a memory from when I was a child. I was chasing fireflies, and one of the aliens came out of the darkness for me. Another little boy in the field saw it too."

"Kids have an advantage; their minds are open; they look at the world and everything holds so much wonder; they're different than an adult. Adults are not open."

"So now what? We sit and wait?" Elle asked.

"Not exactly. We sit, and you heal, and we try and figure a way to get the plans out of you. If we can successfully do that, we got something to bargain with and possibly a way to beat the Dark Man."

"How do we get them out?"

"Sorry, but Grant never went into specifics—although, I'm not sure he ever intended to tell me that part. I kind of always figured that this might be something you might need to figure out on your own."

"Why bring me to Roswell? Aren't you just asking for trouble?"

"Roswell's special; their spaceship landed here before; all around Roswell is a hotspot; they can't track anyone when they're within a ninety-mile radius of the crash site, especially now that the chip has been removed and deactivated. It has bought us some time."

"Can you stop the Dark Man from taking me?" Elle inquired.

Heath's smoke had turned to ash long ago when he started to answer Elle's questions; he lit another one. "The Dark Man can't take me over, that much I can promise you. As for stopping him, that's something even I can't answer. He's incredibly strong, and his powers seem to be growing. I don't know what all he is capable of!"

Elle wanted someone to blame for everything that had happened to her, for the blackouts, the panic attacks, and it would be ok, to be able to lay blame finally, after all these years. But in the end, she could not blame Heath for anything; he was no more responsible for her crazy than she was. They both had a responsibility to the human race, whether they wanted it or not.

"I have been watching and trying to protect you my whole life, and before you were in it, there really wasn't much to remember. You are what I live and breathe for."

Elle couldn't imagine how tough Heath's life must've been for him, to miss out on everything. And yet she knew exactly how he felt, because she had missed out too. She was anything but normal, and her mother had made sure she knew that.

"You were dealt a bad deck of cards, but so was I; at least you got the chance to have a childhood; whether you remember it or not, you had it. At fifteen, other guys were going out on dates; I was learning how to hack into computer mainframes, learning about drugs and their interactions, surgery and genetics, breaking and entering, killing so as not to leave a trace. Maybe you think you've had it rough, thinking you're crazy, but it is nearly impossible to watch you every second of your life. I got a small fraction of humanity within me, and I have failings."

"So, you haven't had time to do anything?" Elle asked.

"I watch you from dusk to dawn. Usually, you're safe during the day so that I can get some sleep, so I can go make a few dollars to live off of. But anything that didn't contribute to your safety was and always will be considered a waste of time."

Elle considered it. "So are you still, like, a virgin?"

"Fuck off."

The tone in his voice told her he was not a complete robot; he was male, after all, and still had an ego. "Are you?"

"Yeah, I'm a twenty-nine-year-old virgin. So, you're starting to look pretty good right about now." Heath laughed with a shrug of shoulders. "Having a girlfriend isn't in the program."

There was something that Elle still had to know. "When we were out in the desert, are you sure I didn't see anything out there when the jelly pack was causing so much pain?"

"More than likely they were hallucinations; some of the toxins could've leaked into your system when the jelly pack was mixing; they could've caused such things."

"So explain to me why they need us to design and fix their spacecraft if they're a superior race?"

"You know, they just can't seem to comprehend the mechanics of their ship; their ship was designed by another race—a race far superior, that understood the quantum mechanics of the fuselage. Once they crashed, they needed our advancement to repair their ship."

"So why didn't Grant just repair their ship and get them out of here, let us be free?"

"When Grant was working on the Project at Area 51, he came across info when he was tinkering with their computer system; it controlled their propulsion system for the whole spacecraft. The info implied that the future of Earth was doomed if the alien spacecraft became fully operational, and they were able to escape. So, the alien spacecraft was capable of time travel, and they looked into Earth's future, only to find it extremely bleak. I only know what Grant wanted me to know—our lives are dependent on what you got in your noggin."

"If we couldn't see them, then how come we can see the UFO crash in Roswell, New Mexico."

"They thought they were going home; they released us; they set our minds free thinking this was their chance out of here, that we wouldn't be needed anymore. But they were wrong. They didn't even make it out of the Earth's upper atmosphere."

Missy interrupted the conversation. "You better not get too comfortable, boss. Pete's here."

Elle looked over at Missy; she could feel a frightening chill creep up her spine. It couldn't possibility be the same guy who had hypnotized her. And yet she knew that it was!

Chapter 14

Pete stood just a couple feet away from Ping-Pong table; it seemed that he had been involved in things as far back as Heath could remember. And he seemed to be on their side, at least for now.

Pete told Elle to focus on a spot on the wall, Heath was standing by, and Missy was there too, sitting on the arm of a La-Z-Boy.

"I want you to count back from a hundred."

"Ninety-nine, ninety-eight, ninety-seven," Elle said.

***

"Elle, as things become clearer, I want you to remember that you're a bystander in what you see; it's not really happening to you. No one and nothing can touch you. But you are you, and you can remember everything. When I clap my hands, you will wake up. Are you clear on everything I have said?"

"Yes, doc."

Pete didn't like that. Elle had gone under easy enough, her head was lax on her neck, but he was worried who might come out to play. "Now where are you?"

"I'm in my room in my apartment."

"What are you doing?"

"I'm standing in the middle of my bedroom, and I'm staring at the walls."

"Why are you standing in the room staring at the walls?"

"Because I want to paint something on it."

"What do you want to paint?"

"Things."

"What kinds of things?"

"Scary things."

"Why?"

"To scare Elle."

Heath looked at Pete; Pete looked back. There was a mutual look that passed between them, one that said, What the fuck is she talking about? But Pete thought he knew.

"Does it scare you, you know, what you write and paint?"

"Yes, that's the fun part," Elle whispered.

"Why?"

"Because I like to scare her."

"Who are you?"

Elle's eyes snapped open, staring into Pete's; it was so instantaneous that he could not stop himself from jerking back. Elle's eyes were wide open, and as weird as it sounded, her eyes were no longer blue. They had become an eerie hazel, and they were drilling into Pete's eyes.

"Hah, you know who I am Pete."

She looked at Heath out of the corner of her eye, a sly little smile playing across her lips.

"Elle, are you out of the hypnosis?"

"Of course, silly."

Pete's heart picked up forty more beats a minute, making it hard to breath. But it was not Elle who looked out of Elle's face. It was something else, something that did not need to be brought back through the steps of hypnosis. Something that had its own feelings, its own agenda, and its own trapdoor to come and go as it pleased. But make no mistake: keep your fingers clear of that trapdoor, because when that door decided to close, it would sever your fingers off at the knuckles.

"Elle, I think we need to try a different approach."

"You know goddamn well I'm not Elle."

"Ok, let's try to relax."

"You scared? Isn't this what Grant wanted, Pete?"

But Elle's head turned in the direction of Heath, her eyes lingering on his face, studying it as if she had never seen him before.

"Is that him?"

A quizzical look was what she briefed Heath with. She was enjoying this. Pete clapped his hands before she could do anything more. And hopefully it would send her back to where she belonged.

The resounding noise echoed in his ears. Slowly her eyes closed; she sank back into the couch, looking serene once again.

"What the hell was that? I thought you said you could get in?" Heath demanded.

Pete sat back, slicking his white hair down with both hands. He looked at Heath. "I thought I could. I can. It's just going to take some work; her subconscious is a mess. I think Grant put in a little insurance, a kind of backup plan, if you will. This other persona comes out when I try to get inside, a stronger Elle-type personality that has no fear, that can deal with things she can't. Who the hell knows how many booby traps Grant implanted; if he set locks on her subconscious, we may need passwords to unlock it. And how much of her memories did Grant erase when he implanted the blueprint into her? We could stumble around in her mind for hours and not find anything of value. You need to be patient."

"Well, I'm sorry, but the way she was talking, it kind of…" Heath trailed off.

Pete didn't want him to finish either. A cold sweat coated his entire body; he had not been expecting that reaction from Elle. Hopefully he could get back in without running into this other Elle again, because honestly, she was damn creepy. At least her eyes were blue again. Or had he imagined the hazel? He was pretty sure her eye color had changed. Was that mind over matter? Who knew anymore.

***

"We're going to have to take a different approach," Pete stated. Elle sat in front of him in a La-Z-Boy. She looked like she was sleeping, but she was just under.

"Do what you have to," Heath offered. He had a cigarette in his mouth.

Pete gave a quick nod of his head and leaned forward, rubbing the palms of his hands down his legs; his shoulders were hunched and tense. "Elle, when I snap my fingers, you're going to come back to us. Ok?"

"Ok," she whispered

His fingers snapped with fresh life, not the dry old fingers of someone who has aged. Pete stood up and moved across the room; he took a candle off of a small, dusty shelf and put it down in front of her. Heath handed his lighter over, and Pete lit the candle.

"I want you to stare into the candle, Elle. The longer you look, the brighter the candle gets. I want your attention to go into the candle. You are now inside it. But it's not hot; you can't be burned there; nothing can happen; you're you and no one else. You can speak of your own free will, and you do remember everything from your childhood; the lost years are as clear as if everything is happening now. You can speak; please tell me what you see, where you are, when you are, and why you're where you are."

"I see the front door of my home. I'm eight and half years old. I'm waiting here because Daddy should be home soon, very soon. Any minute," Elle declared; her voice had taken on an almost childlike quality.

"Where does your daddy work?" Pete asked.

"At home sometimes. And sometimes down the street in another house. It's off limits to me though."

"Tell me everything, Elle; it's like it's all happening; talk freely."

"Ok, Pete."

***

Elle had drifted into a time she could not remember, and it was like she was looking through the eyes of her younger self.

"Honey, move away from the door; you'll be in the way," Margaret warned.

Elle's daddy struggled with the door for a few minutes, she knew who he was, and his name was Grant. But to her, he was always Daddy. He had a paper bag in his hands. Probably his medicine—Daddy was very sick, not the kind of sick where he ever gets better, not one with the sniffles, coughing, and a sore throat. No, the kind where he does not feel good, inside, in fact so terrible some days he did not want to get out of bed. Those days are becoming more frequent. In fact, if Elle looked at her father, he looked old, much older than what he really was.

"Grant, is that you? Where were you?" Margaret asked.

"Just out visiting with a few friends," Grant replied.

"You shouldn't go out when you look so rough; you don't want people to know."

"It doesn't matter anymore," Grant answered.

Margaret turned away and went back into the kitchen. "Elle, how much space do you got upstairs?"

"Lots, Mommy's been cleaning up the attic."

"That's not the kind of space I'm talking about; in fact, that's very far from what I mean."

"Oh, Daddy, what did you mean?"

Grant looked up, catching Margaret's eye from the kitchen. Elle looked too, but that was just Margaret's normal look, upset and about to yell.

"Grant, what are you talking about with Elle?"

"Nothing," Grant answered. "Remember, Elle, never tell your Mommy about our project; it's safer if she does not know. Once she finds out, she might not be able to keep it to herself. Let's go down to my office." Grant took Elle's hand, leading her into the basement.

"Grant, where are you going?"

"To take my medicine. Elle's going to count out the pills."

"All right," Margaret answered reluctantly.

Elle followed Grant down to his office in the basement. It was basically a desk piled with paper, paper that was not good for coloring. If she did, Grant would not be pleased with her.

Grant moved slowly, slowly like grandpas did.

"I can beat you down the stairs, Daddy."

"No, just walk; it's never a good idea to run down the stairs."

"You're just afraid of the bad people; you think they might be waiting down in the basement. So you want to take it slow so you don't run into them."

"What bad people?" Grant asked, his voice quivering slightly.

Elle shook her shoulders; they both knew who the bad people were. Daddy could pretend all he wanted.

"Elle, what bad people are you talking about? You've never seen any bad people down here, have you?"

"Maybe I have; maybe I haven't. Hard to say what's real and what's make-believe."

"Think hard."

"Probably make believe." Maybe make believe would put him at ease.

"You sure?" Grant asked again.

"Sure I'm sure." Elle smiled her most real smile.

"Of course, you can't see bad people anyway," Grant said more to himself than Elle.

Grant set the paper bag on the desk. It jostled the pile of papers sitting there. They were stacked haphazardly; one small tremor disrupted the entire pile; they gave up their stance and sifted to the floor, falling in layers.

"Why don't you lie down on the table."

Elle looked at the table set up in the center of the room; it was a fine wooden one. She climbed up on top with her legs stretched out in front of her. Grant was fixing something at the counter; when he turned, he had a needle in his hand. Elle cringed from the needle. She did not want a needle. But Grant seemed to think she should have one.

The first needle he placed in her arm; that one was warm and hurt. It made everything go dim. The second needle was behind her right ear, and that one really hurt. She could hear someone tapping on the door.

"Margaret, I'm busy."

Tap, tap, tap, tap.

Elle could feel Grant's hands along the sides of her face. She could hear him whispering, but she could not see him; her eyes would not open. And as the tapping continued, she felt herself drifting further away. And as she drifted away, she felt something enter her mind and shove her aside; she could not see what it was, a quick flash of an image. And as weird as it seemed, it looked kind of like a diagram or blueprint.

Tap, tap, tap, tap.

"Margaret, I told you I'm taking my pills; bugger off."

Elle could feel herself coming back; how long she had been drifting, sent to the far recesses of her mind, she really could not say. However, as she came back, she could hear Grant, but she was also aware of a throbbing headache; it felt like her head was about to explode.

Tap, tap, tap, tap.

Elle opened her eyes and looked up into Grant's frightened face.

"Fuck, what the hell has gotten into you?" Grant screamed at Margaret; he stomped away from the table. Grant looked tired and old and very angry, like he wanted to tear into Margaret. He unlocked the basement door and threw it open; Margaret stood there, her head hanging slightly.

She looked different, like she had taken some very strong drugs, the ones that could make you feel unlike yourself.

"What do you want?" Grant demanded of Margaret.

"Daddy, there's the bad people," Elle called out.

Out of nowhere, the bad people seemed to step from the shadows.

Grant turned right into them. The Dark Man stepped forward; he grabbed on to Grant's throat. The touch of the Dark Man brought Grant to his knees in seconds. You could not really see the others that well; they were black shadows that moved, rushing out. There was nowhere for Elle to run to. A loud crack echoed through the basement when Grant's head struck the concrete. He didn't get up. They walked like humans; she supposed that was where she had gotten the idea that they were bad people, but the last thing they were were human.

"Daddy, get up; they're coming."

Elle tried to move, but she could not; she was rooted to the floor as if frozen, a deer caught in headlights, about to be mowed over.

There was something in their hands, something sharp and pointy. They came closer.

The Dark Man threw out its hands, her feet lifted off the ground, and she was thrown against the wall. When she hit, her knees came smashing against her chest; the power was infinite. The hold on her released, and she dropped to the floor. The Dark Man separated from the group of aliens, falling upon her. It rolled her over. The sharp thing went into her back; it was hot, fiery hot. It scorched her, igniting her flesh underneath the skin. When the Dark Man finally pulled the thing out, she was shocked she hadn't blacked out from the pain. The sweat rolled over her body. Suddenly she was hot everywhere…

Elle snapped forward in her chair like she was on a roller coaster ride, and the end of the ride was a jarring halt. She was wheezing, gasping for air as if it had all been taken from her.

"Hahhh."

Taking big, jerking lungfuls, her body shuddered in waves as she broke free of the hypnosis. Elle tried standing up, but her legs would not respond; her brain was trying to send signals to her limbs, but there was a malfunction. Elle could still see the Dark Man's eyes, solid black in the pale face.

"Maybe that's enough for now," Heath said, speaking directly to Pete.

The room was starting to get hazy, like fog was rising from the floor, through the cracks from downstairs. It was getting thicker, she could still see everyone, but somehow there was this mist drifting around them. Her chest was hitching up and down as she was trying to separate the past from the present. Reality was rapidly disintegrating.

She stumbled up out of her chair, looking uncertainly around the room; her eyes skittered over every occupant in the room, hesitating over Heath and Pete. She knew they could not see this weird mist from the looks they had on their faces. There were no chemicals in her stomach; the last painkiller was at least a day ago. That alone should have convinced her that the mist was not real. But common sense did not exist.

Heath and Pete were slowly moving toward her, their hands out as if she were a wild animal that needed to be corralled. Shushing noises whispered around the room.

"Now, get back, all of you fuckers. Now!" Elle shouted.

"Back up, Pete." Heath shouted over his shoulder.

Pete backed up; Heath took one step back, just one; that gave her a better view as she tried to sort things out. The mist got thicker, billowing around like they were in a swamp rather than an old house.

The air was not easy to breathe; in fact, it was becoming a lot harder by the second; it was like trying to drag pea soup into your lungs. Her lungs were slowly becoming crushed; her chest labored in jerking rasps.

Out of the thick mist, the Dark Man came for her; he grabbed Elle by the throat, lifting her off the ground. Their eyes met; his empty black ones bore into her bright-blue ones. He spoke into her head, "You have something I want." His voice was rough; he did not have very strong vocal cords, as if he never had to use them.

A burst of air filled her lungs as she fought back against it. "You'll have to tear my brain apart to get it out." She spat at him.

"Don't think I won't," the Dark Man whispered to her, and then he vanished. She dropped to the ground and could breathe normally again.

Out of the fog, something flew toward her, knocking her off her feet, and pinned her to the ground.

"Get the needle," Heath shouted.

Heath straddled her with his legs.

A tear slid down her cheek. Was hell ever going to end? Pete fell out of the fog just as Heath had. He had a needle in his hand, and he had a doctor's smile on his lips. "This won't hurt; it will make you better." Elle did not even try fighting them; from their perspective, she looked completely whacky. And for now, their opinion was ok, but if for just one second, they could see what she had, they would think a lot differently. How had the Dark Man found her, was he there spiritually, or was this something else? Elle had a feeling there was no limit to the Dark Man's powers. Pete knelt beside Heath and injected the needle into Elle's neck.

Her vision of Heath and Pete started to blur, sleep took over, and she left that world for another.

Chapter 15

Heath raked his hands through his hair. But it was not enough; he needed something to ease his nerves, something to calm. He took out a whiskey bottle, cigarette still clenched between his lips. He poured it straight and downed it in one swallow.

"Where did she go just now?" Heath demanded.

"I think somehow the memories followed her back from then."

"Will this damage the blueprint?"

"Probably not any more than anything else has; this kind of trauma is not good for the body though. It can put a great strain on her mental stability and her heart. If she can't stay in this world and she keeps drifting back into those dreams, who's to say if she will ever come back to reality. One time she could become permanently lost."

Elle lay on the couch; the red mark that the needle had made was already fading. But the drug had done its job; it had sedated her.

***

Elle watched the shadows skitter across the wall. The sedative was wearing off, and she was almost back to normal.

"Why didn't you tell Heath about the Dark Man?" Missy questioned. Her hands were on her hips. She looked angry.

"What difference does it make?" Elle mumbled.

"You don't seem to get it; if the Dark Man's mind is linked to yours, he could be tracking your every move. Chipped or not. Heath is no match for the Dark Man, even though he's been modified. I want you to give up what you know to Pete or Heath, before it's too late. Before the Dark Man finds you. Finds Heath."

Elle did not say anything.

"You know, Elle, I might work for Heath, but I know a hell of a lot more than he does. I don't assume anything, and I don't trust you."

"I'll tell Heath, when I think he'll actually believe me. Not now."

"You want to know why you saw the Dark Man and no one else did? For the same reason you saw the blood crawl toward the door in your hospital room, as if it had a mind of its own."

"How do you know about that?"

"Because I know how their blood reacts when their host is terminated—they need to find another way. I saw you yesterday after you broke out of the hypnosis, you were scared, and only the Dark Man could truly induce that type of reaction; you were talking to someone as if it were really happening. It wasn't just a hallucination—it was more than that. The Dark Man has powers out of this world, and it's my belief he has a strong connection to you."

"Can he really track me without the chip?"

"I don't know. I guess if the connection is strong enough, he can."

Did Missy notice the chill that went through her?

Missy turned. Heath stood in the doorway, a cigarette hanging from the corner of his mouth. He was shuffling an old deck of cards. His eyes strayed to Elle; she knew how she must look, pallid and fearful. She could not help betraying herself; there was no such thing as a poker face in her bag of tricks.

"What?" Elle questioned.

He looked between them, not saying anything; he had not heard Missy and Elle's conversation.

"Elle has something to tell you," Missy offered.

"Is that so?" Heath asked, an eyebrow raised slightly.

Missy turned and left, leaving the truth up to Elle.

"What?" Heath demanded; he was impatient, probably wanting to know what had spooked Elle so badly. Would he understand, when few understood, and somehow Missy did, ironically enough?

"Let's go into the desert and blow off a little steam maybe," Heath suggested.

Elle found herself in the passenger seat of the black sports car, the dents had been fixed, and it had a flawless new paint job, one that would not raise a cop's suspicions if they got stopped. Heath punched the gas, and the car responded instantly. They burned through the small town, heading out into the desert.

"So how'd you fix the car?" Elle asked into the dead silence between them.

"I used to work in a body shop. Jamie helped me pop out some of the dents while you were sleeping. Then a new paint job."

They drove for maybe twenty minutes into the desert, far enough away that no sound could be heard. Heath jerked the wheel hard, and the car skidded on the pavement and caught, tearing off onto a dirt road. When the main highway was far in the distance, he tramped the brake, skidding to a stop, got out, and took the gun from the waist of his jeans. He got seven tin cans from the trunk and set them about on a rock, then he stood far enough back for target practice.

"You and I need to be able to trust each other." Heath offered the gun as he spoke this.

Elle accepted.

"You also need to be able to hit a target; one day it could save your life."

Elle removed the safety, which Heath had pointed out a couple of days ago. She fired the first time, missing the target completely.

Heath stepped in, helping her aim the gun; this time the can hopped right off of the rock as a bullet tore through it.

Elle smiled, a small sense of satisfaction replacing the disappointment.

"Do you want to talk about anything?" Heath questioned.

"Like what?" Elle asked.

"Do you remember anything more after Pete hypnotized you?"

"You sure you want to know, or maybe you just want to shoot me up with some more drugs?"

"I guess I deserved that." Heath took the gun back and fired, blowing four of the six cans off. "Look, you were spiraling out of control; you were close to having a heart attack, simply out of fear. Pete thought it was the best way to get you under control."

"I get that, but at the same time, I'm getting a little fucking sick of being the guinea pig. They're coming for me; know that. Yesterday, when I broke out of the hypnosis, I saw the Dark Man. I don't know whether it was a telepathic transmission or something else, but he spoke to me."

Heath listened to everything she was saying, seeming to take it for face value, not as just the crazy ramblings of a nut.

"What did he say?"

"The Dark Man says I have something he wants." She turned, taking back the gun and firing, knocking the last two cans.

***

Four Days Later

Heath came down the stairs; he was all business this morning, shaved and clean, except his hair was still quite long. He did not seem worried about the length of it. Heath went into the bathroom for a T-shirt.

Missy looked over at Elle. This was Missy's last few hours with Heath; he intended to leave; after today he would be on the road somewhere, somewhere Missy did not know and dared not follow. Those were Heath's orders—the asshole actually gave her an order last night. Fuck, where he got off was beyond her. He had his secrets, and she had her own. They would meet up someday soon, at some point, whether he wanted them to or not.

Missy adjusted her sweater, straightening it so it fell evenly over her shoulders. She knew Elle did not want to talk about the other night, about what the visions meant. Hell, that was ok—she would rather not know the messed-up shit that was rolling around in Elle's mind on a daily basis.

"So how long have you and Heath been working together?" Elle questioned.

Missy answered easily enough. "We've been together for quite a while."

"I'll bet." A smirk crossed Elle's face. She seemed to think that was a funny answer.

Heath only knew Elle from a distance, from his vantage point as the protector. That really did not tell them anything about Elle or if she could even be trusted. What you see and what you get are two very different things. "What's that supposed to mean?" Missy demanded; she felt suddenly defensive.

"Just, you seem like the kind of people that are friends for life. I guess."

"Uh-huh." Elle's answer was logical enough, but it screamed of so much more. Elle was lying.

141

Elle smiled slightly, but it was not a genuine smile, and her eyes were not involved; it was flat and lifeless.

"So, are you coming with me to pick up the bike?" Heath asked.

"Huh?" Missy almost hadn't even heard Heath—she was studying Elle. Elle looked normal, and most of the time she seemed ok. But there was that frightening side to her, that side where Elle was not herself and she seemed almost unpredictable. "What do you mean?" Missy asked, finally tearing her eyes off Elle's face to look at Heath.

"Jamie has been missing since we fixed the front end of the car. I want to go get my bike. I think I would rather use the Harley when we fall off the grid. I thought Elle could stay here with Pete, and Pete could attempt to get in there one last time before we leave."

"Where do you suppose Jamie got to?" Missy inquired.

"Who knows. I paid him the other day; he probably went somewhere to get high. We'll be back in about forty minutes; be ready to go by then Elle. Pete, see if you can find the plans. Maybe we'll get lucky."

Pete nodded his head. Missy did not like Heath's attitude. "Don't you think you should go look for Jamie?"

"Why?" Heath asked.

"He could be hurt?" Missy stated.

"He's not my responsibility anymore."

"Meaning what exactly?" Missy could not believe how Heath was acting, as if nobody meant anything to him anymore. They had all played their part, and she had always thought of them as a team—dysfunctional maybe, but a still a team. Now she felt like she was questioning everything and everyone.

Heath left the room, jangling the car keys in his hand.

Missy stumbled after Heath. "That if he's dead, there's nothing you want or care to do about it?" Missy screamed to his retreating back.

"Meaning"—Heath stuck his head back in the doorway and looked at her—"what's done, is done, and when did you start caring about him so much?"

"He's still human; of course, you wouldn't know anything about being one, because you aren't." Heath had already turned his back on Elle and Pete, but mostly Missy.

Heath hollered from the garage, "Be ready to go before I get back, Elle."

"Sure." Elle nodded her head, polite, probably due to Margaret.

Missy did not like Margaret or this whole situation; someone goes missing and Heath barely bats an eyelash. Elle goes missing, and they all spread out to look for her. As for Jamie and Missy, the answer was quite simple: they were expendable.

Missy looked at Elle once before following after Heath. Elle was standing with her back straight, saluting him. Missy could not help smiling, but no matter what happened, she would not allow her initial instincts to be ignored; her instincts screamed to be careful around Elle, and that was exactly what she intended to do.

Heath was waiting in the black sports car for Missy when she entered the garage. She got in the passenger side. She could tell he did not wish to pursue the issue of Jamie's disappearance, so she didn't bring it up again. Heath stayed within the speed limit, checked the review mirror, stopped at all the stop signs, and waited for pedestrians. Today they were just a couple of people taking a Sunday drive through town. When they got out of town, Heath put the pedal to the floor; the desert passed in golden blurs. They crept closer to the end of their journey. And the closer they got, the more nauseated Missy felt. Heath did nothing to ease her anxieties. When they got to the storage lockers well on the outskirts of the county, Heath undid the locker and rolled the metal door up into the roof. He walked over; his fingers fell on the bike with a casual caress. Soon Heath and Missy would go their separate ways.

Missy closed her eyes; maybe if she did not see any of this, her stomach would settle down, probably not though. She was having difficulty saying goodbye—but why? Heath obviously did not care about her and Jamie. So why did she care about Heath?

Missy hopped out of the car finally, following him; it was all she had ever done. She could not remember a time or a place when she wasn't taking an order to help prepare, nor could she imagine a life without him, not now, not ever. He looked at her finally, kind of questioning why she was coming. But when Heath was focused on something, not much else mattered. He swung a leg over the bike and cranked it over. On the third kick, the bike roared to life.

"Heath." She had to scream his name over the roar of the engine.

"What?" Heath asked as he fiddled with a wire underneath the handlebars. He kept twisting the throttle, revving the engine louder and louder. "Look, I'm not good at goodbyes," he shouted.

"That's not it," Missy stated, at least that was not all of what she wanted to talk to Heath about.

"Ok, well why don't you tell me what this is about?" He killed the bike's engine.

"Heath, I just wanted to talk to you about some things before we go our separate ways."

"What things?"

Heath was impatient, and it was making everything harder than it needed to be. Missy had to spit it out. "I want you to be careful from here on in; you're entering different territory."

"How you figure?"

"They're smart, aren't they?"

"Incredibly."

"Then why do you think that once the chip is removed, that's it?"

He was evaluating her. Maybe he was shocked that she had said this to him, said any of it.

"If they're so smart, they would've had a backup plan."

"Such as?" Heath questioned.

"I don't know, but I'm telling you that just because the chip is gone, it doesn't mean that they haven't done something else to Elle, to ensure the safety of those plans. *Do not trust her.*"

He put the kickstand down and got off the bike. Missy pushed the hair out of her eyes as the wind whipped sand about.

"*Don't trust her*, those are very familiar words."

"Are they? Well maybe you should listen to them. Look, all I'm trying to say is, just because the chip is gone, you still got to be careful. You trust her because she's Grant's daughter. But you don't know her."

"Awful strange to be hearing this warning from you of all people; you like to go out to all those parties, do a little drinking, and go home with guys you don't know. Just who have you been talking with?"

Missy could not believe how Heath was trying to turn this around on her. "I'm not doing this. I'm not standing here and being accused of betraying you. I have not done anything."

Missy turned to head back to the car. Heath grabbed her arm, pulling her back; he was incredibly close, almost too close. She could see the worry in his eyes. He licked at his bottom lip, analyzing her the way he had always done to an outsider—not to his most reliable ally. Somewhere in his body, a bone cracked; he was loosening his body up for a fight, and Missy knew how every sense of Heath's was on red alert. She had seen him prepare for a fight, with his enemies. His eyes narrowed down to fine points, drilling into her as if looking for the truth. She had never been as afraid of him as she was right now. Oh sure, there had always been that aspect to him: he was a trained killer; if he thought for just one second that someone was betraying him, they would be gone. His purpose was to protect one individual, and Missy was not lucky enough to be that person. Heath had lost it before; if he did again, she would be dead in a matter of seconds.

"Who have you been talking to?" Heath demanded again.

Missy made her lips one thin line. "No one."

Heath had a death grip on her arms, one hand clamped around each of her forearms. Breaking free was next to impossible.

"I can't take chances on you. You know that?" Heath whispered.

Fuck, what exactly did that mean? His hand moved up her one arm toward her neck. That was the exact second when Missy lost it. She drove her knee in between Heath's legs so quickly that she caught him off guard; he had made a decision, and she had made hers. She was not dying due to his suspicions. Her knee connected perfectly with the vulnerable area— even he had one of those. Her free arm drove itself into his stomach, then upward at his face, palm flat, smashing into the bridge of his nose; it knocked his head backward. Heath had trained Missy to fight; he needed a strong team, no dainty flowers. They had battled for hours. Heath just never knew when something would happen; survival was critical; it was ironic to be battling Heath of all people. But doubt had tainted his trust; now it would be a fight till death. It was either him or her now.

Heath fell backward, almost pulling her with him; her feet spun for traction in the loose sand. She turned and ran for the car. Escape was her only option. She did not like to fight dirty, but it was not a fair fight, and it was not one she could win. Heath had the advantage.

The sand sucked at her shoes. It made getting anywhere seem impossible. She did not look back. Heath would catch her in seconds.

She did not stop; she slammed right into the side of the car and grabbed the handle, jerking it open. She got in and closed it quickly. Heath hit the door just as she closed it. His hand went for the handle. She slammed down the lock. Heath's face defied his killer instinct; only one wrinkle creased his forehead. He was without any emotions; it was somewhat unlikely that she could reason with a machine. A program had already booted up, and compassion was not built into the program. He reached backward, making a fist. Missy knew what he was going to do even before he did it. She tried to start the car, but it was too late—the fist was already coming through the window. Glass exploded into the car, showering her. His arm came through the window, grabbing for her throat. She skittered across the gearshift into the passenger seat.

He abandoned her for a moment; he locked his fingers on the door and pulled it from its hinges. She could hear Heath right behind her, she was not fast enough, and she couldn't stop him. A command came to mind.

"Stop," Missy shouted, throwing up her hands as if this were a game of tag that she did not want to play anymore. No, she needed the German command. What was it? "*Stoppen*." Thankfully, Heath responded to the command; he stopped, his chest heaving, and hers matched his beat for beat. "I haven't betrayed you."

"Then why were you running?"

"Because you were going to kill me."

"No, I grabbed your arm; you ran. You're acting suspicious."

"You scared me, just like you are scaring me now. Are you going to kill me? I fucking helped you; I goddamn fought for your cause, for years."

Heath lowered his hands to his sides. The command seemed to have paused the program, at least momentarily. He took a step closer to her. She matched his step but in the opposite direction.

"Jamie fulfilled his obligations—you could easily have executed him while you were supposed to be sleeping. And how would I know—maybe that's why you really brought me out here?"

"Missy, you have a life I can't keep track of, and I'm supposed to trust you without question?"

"You don't know Elle."

"I don't know you either."

"You're not human; you're dead inside."

"We're all going to be dead pretty soon; there's not much I can do about that."

"So why not me too, why take a chance, right? I'm telling you the truth, Heath."

Heath walked toward her; she didn't move; she held her ground, resisting the urge to flee. Heath looked Missy in the eye, then he walked around her and got on the bike, flipped the kickstand up, and tore out of the storage locker. Missy moved on shaky legs over to the car; she dusted the glass off the seat before she sat down. She had been an inch away from death. That was a little too close for comfort.

Chapter 16

Pete leaned forward. He wiped his palms on the knees of his jeans; he was so nervous; Elle could be unpredictable under hypnosis. "Elle, you are you and only you. I know how this scares you. I want you to see everything in the third person; no one can harm you. You are invincible. Everything comes easily, and there is nothing you do not remember. When you wake up from this session, I do not want you to remember anything that you have said or that we have talked about. Now, let's go back to the night when you had the longest blackout. Elle, what do you see?"

"It's after two o'clock in the morning. It's nighttime, and I'm afraid of the dark. I'm going to get Daddy, and he can help me get a drink of water. There is a light on in their room; it is coming from under their door. They must be up late like me."

"How old are you?"

"I'm just about nine, and I'm scared to open their door."

"Why? Are you worried that your parents will be angry because you are up in the middle of the night?"

"No. I'm just scared of the bad people. The light is coming from under their bedroom door, and it's so bright that it feels like it's burning my bare feet. I'm knocking lightly on their door. The paint on the door is flaking off; this is the third time this month that they have painted it. I knock again because I'm worried about Daddy. But Mommy won't like me waking them up. I wait but nobody answers, so I turn the knob.

"'Ow, the doorknob is hot, so I jerk my hand back. That light is starting things on fire. Daddy, fire, Daddy. I know what to do in case you start on fire. You stop, drop, and roll. But Mommy and Daddy were not at school the day the fire chief came and talked to us. I pull my nightgown over my hand and turn the knob. The door swings open, and Daddy is standing in front of the bad people. The bad people smell funny, like sour milk. I almost expect to see flies swarming around them. There are six of them, mostly charcoal gray, except for one; he's almost completely black. I am so scared that I don't dare look away."

"What is your mother doing?" Pete questions.

"She's standing by the dresser; she sees me in the mirror, and she is angry." Elle seemed frozen, as if unsure of what to do next.

"Elle, you stopped; what do you see; what's happening?"

"She's angry. She's turning away from the mirror toward me. Now she's screaming."

"What's she screaming?"

"She's saying, 'Get out; get out. Just take him. I've had enough of this; just take him and get out.' "

"Elle. Elle. Elle?" Pete grasped Elle's hands. She did not seem to feel Pete, or at least she made no indication she could feel him.

"She let them take him; she let them take him," Elle said, sobbing.

"Margaret? Elle, I'm sure you're confused. Margaret probably couldn't move because they froze her."

"No, she let them take him."

Pete wrapped his arms around her. But it did not matter. The tears came out anyway, tears that had been trapped for years.

***

Elle knew she was hypnotized, that this was not really happening, and yet somehow, it was. It was like she was locked in the days of yesterday, and she knew it. She just knew it, but knowing did not stop it from feeling less real or being afraid. It was scary because it was slowly unraveling like a movie, and there was no stopping it.

"Elle, what's happening? What do you see?"

Elle could see them, the gray aliens were standing everywhere, they stepped aside, and the Dark Man emerged from the mass of beings. The hypnosis shattered wide open, exposing the core of everything—Elle knew something. Pete was working for the Dark Man; she knew it deep down inside.

"Elle?" Pete was calling her name.

Pete was trying to console Elle, but nothing could stop the wave of disgust for the betrayal.

"Are you out of the hypnosis?" Pete asked, sounding a little fearful.

"Yes."

"Do you remember everything from this session?"

"Yes."

"How is that possible?"

"Because you did not put stops, you didn't stop me from being who I am, they scare me, and you know they do, but you did nothing to stop them. You sold out Grant; you told them he had the plans; you told them about me."

Pete looked scared. "No, I tried for years to protect him, to stall them."

"Here you are, almost twenty years later, still trying to give them the one thing they want. What if I die or I lose what I have? They'll keep haunting you, demanding that you help them."

"If I can't give them what they want, they will kill you. Please, for your sake, please try and work with me," Pete pleaded.

"It's too late for that."

"Honestly, I never really believed that Grant would put the blueprint in your mind. It was so risky; I thought surely he wouldn't take that chance with his daughter's life. Even if he did, there was no way to safely remove the plans without killing you back then. I almost thought they'd given up, and then the Dark Man paid me a visit. But it wasn't until Vincent called me and told me about all your problems that I knew that you had the plans. If they're not removed, eventually it will destroy your mind. Elle, I am your only way out of this."

She looked to the staircase.

"What?" Pete asked, alarmed; he seemed worried that Heath was already back.

"Oh, don't you hear that? Someone's knocking on the door."

Pete turned to look up at the staircase, as if that would increase his hearing range. Elle wiped away the tears from her cheeks.

"Heath probably locked himself out," Elle said, turning to the stairs. "I'll go let him in."

***

Pete knew Elle's mind had been made up the second she thought she heard something. There was nothing wrong with his hearing, because there was nothing to hear—no one was at that door. Although if Heath was back, Pete would have a lot of explaining to do.

Pete bent over the Ping-Pong table, studying the black-and-white pictures Grant had taken of the craft. The pictures were of the damaged propulsion system.

He heard the door open and close and footsteps on the stairs. Pete looked up from the pictures and his heart sank. "How did you get in?"

"Back door, somebody left it open." There was a smirk on her face.

"Not that you needed it," Pete said with only a slight tremor in his voice. "Where's Elle?"

"I knocked her out upstairs, but we both know I could walk through walls if I needed to."

"And I bet you would."

"Enough, what do you know?"

Pete sighed. "I don't think I can get in there. Grant's got her locked up tighter than a safe."

"Sure, that's just like him." Jeanie moved away from the table, to the small bathroom, stopped, and looked back at him. "Expecting any company?"

"No."

***

Jeanie entered the bathroom; there was a small tray by the sink, a scalpel, and other surgical instruments. She looked at them and at the mirror, and something changed in her eyes, a kind of resolve. She grasped the scalpel in her hand and hid it behind her back when she came out of the bathroom.

Pete stood with the wall at his back. Maybe that was the smart thing to do, although if he ran, he might have had a chance. But where could he go that she would not follow?

"The Dark Man was patient." Jeanie smiled; her hand slashed out with the scalpel. Pete blocked the blow with his arm, a reflex. The scalpel slashed into his forearm, but it kept it from cutting his body. He used his fist and punched Jeanie in the temple. She shook her head and slashed out with the scalpel again, catching him in the shoulder. Her arm shot out, balancing her, just as her right foot left the ground, kicking high; it caught Pete in the right temple, unexpected to him but trained for her. Pete stumbled to the side—his bloody hand reached up to stop the flow just below his elbow. Jeanie slashed out with the scalpel again, catching the

151

arm he was using to block her; he fell back into the wall, almost losing his footing. She stabbed him in the chest; she caught him just above the heart and embedded the slim steel blade to the hilt.

Her face remained passive; there was a bit of blood on her shirt, a light, misty spray. In the course of a smile, she faltered; Jeanie looked up to the staircase, thinking she heard someone.

She had better finish up and get out of here. "Goodbye, Pete."

She ripped the blade free. A fine squirt jutted out through the small hole the scalpel had made. She leaned back, taking a second stab; this one hit dead center, piercing Pete's heart. His mouth opened; no sound came out, just a few bubbles of saliva, but nothing else. His eyes were open in a stunned look; one last breath rasped from his mouth, followed by blood.

A clock ticked loudly, something like one of those grandfather clocks. It startled her, chiming loudly, almost shaking her feet out from underneath her. She looked up.

Right now, she did not need Elle to know about her; what Jeanie was trying to do was zero in on the plans herself.

***

Something flew at Elle; she saw it just out of the corner of her eye, it struck her in the temple. She succumbed to the darkness.

When the darkness subsided, instead of a warm feeling covering her body, it felt cold, almost as if the blood had stopped circulating. She remembered why her head hurt, something had hit her when she went to open the front door. The house was eerily silent, she headed to the basement to check on Pete. He was staring at her in an unblinking, hypnotic state.

Elle reached out a hand tentatively to check Pete's pulse; he was growing cold. He had been dead only a few minutes and was covered in blood. The room swayed from side to side. Elle turned away from him, heading for the door. She could not get enough oxygen into her lungs, then she felt her body jolt; she lost control of the calm she was trying for; she was not crying anymore but screaming for her sanity.

She closed her eyes, trying to shut the image of Pete from her memory. Elle crouched into a protective ball.

When something warm touched her face, she sprung away, sure that Pete had come alive and was touching her. But Pete had not moved; it was a warm towel wiping away the blood on her face. Heath had come back. She wanted to reach out and hug him close, but what stopped her was fear. Would he understand how this had happened? Probably not. She didn't even know. Heath bent down, looking into her eyes.

"What happened?"

"I was talking to Pete, then I heard someone at the door, so I went and answered it, and someone struck me in the temple. Whoever knocked me out killed Pete; he was already dead when I woke up."

"What'd they look like?"

"I don't know; they were just a dark shadow."

"They've found us. It's not safe here anymore. We're leaving. Now."

"Heath, where's Missy?" Elle asked.

"She's gone."

***

Days Passed

Just after noon, they pulled up in front of Linus's Garage and Trade Ins. Elle wrinkled her nose at the sight of the place. Heath could tell from her scrunched nose that she wasn't impressed; he tucked the gun into his pants.

"Stay here. I'll only be a few minutes." Heath walked to the garage; he felt suddenly nervous—it was ridiculous—as he stood just inside the garage door, trying to relieve some of the tension. "Hey, Linus, Linus McCall? Anyone here?"

Perfect, they had driven four hours to get here, and the fucker had ditched them. Heath had even phoned ahead to make sure he was going to be open this morning. "Sure, sure, I'm open," he had told Heath. "I'll be here all day, always willing to help someone out."

Or fuck them over. Heath wouldn't have stopped if he hadn't needed to; the feeling that someone was closing in on them was increasing, probably whoever had killed Pete. What he really wanted to do was just put the pedal down and head north. The Dark Man didn't like the cold; neither did the rest of them. In fact, they hated it, so that's where they were headed. But he would have to switch things up; a bike was not much good in a cold climate.

"Hey, Linus, are you here?"

From where Heath stood, he could only see a shadowy garage. Maybe something had fallen and squished the bastard. He kind of hoped it had; he would just hot-wire a truck or something and then take off, leaving the maggots to feast on Linus.

Heath stepped farther into the gloom of the garage; his eyes took a second or two to focus. Old car and truck parts littered the walls and floor. An old scrap heap was in the center of the garage. It did not look like it had been touched in a while; a fine layer of rust and dust had settled on the hood; no one had even started sanding it down. The rust was up the side panels, practically to the windows. A hell of a lot of work was needed. The paint and primer had vanished long ago.

Hopefully Linus had something a little better in back. The whole fucking point of coming here was to switch from his bike to something that could handle the winter elements. Maybe something custom, with a big grill guard on the front, so he could push his way through check stops.

Linus's garage had been the only place still listed in the phone book of the pay phone. The others had been ripped out and discarded somewhere along the dotted line of the highway. And using his smart phone to google anything was out of the question; one ping on that dang thing, and it would let the extraterrestrials know exactly where he was. He had built a program from the ground up; when the app was opened, he could not be tracked. But even using the app was risky; he didn't trust anything anymore. Heath was relying on the old-fashioned way of locating a used car dealer, through a phone book; it hadn't been destiny that landed him on Linus's doorstep but rather bad luck.

The garage and lot were surrounded by a ten-foot-high fence with razor wire at the top. The gate was opened slightly toward the lot. A sign hung from the gate stating that trespassers would be shot if found on the premises. In this kind of place, you usually found chop shops, not whole running cars or trucks. To look around for something that was a little better, well, they did not have the time, and the last thing Heath wanted to do was attract attention to himself. Word traveled fast in these kinds of places. As it was, he already felt antsy to be on the move. Maybe he would just steal something.

Heath had almost expected to have his head blown off at any second when he had entered the garage. No dog and no owner, this was so weird. How could his instincts have been so wrong?

"Hey, Linus, you here?" His voice melded with the sounds of the garage; something was dripping loudly. Heath stepped into the gloom, looking this way and that.

"Yep, I'm here."

Heath turned around quickly to meet Linus head on; he did not like being taken by surprise. The bit of sun that filtered through the grimy windows was in Heath's eyes; he couldn't see who was standing just in front of his only exit. And it was not Linus; he just knew it was not.

The man who belonged to the voice moved in front of the sun so Heath could see. Fucking perfect. Heath almost couldn't believe his eyes.

"Well, where the fuck you been, Heath?"

"I've been around."

"I'll bet, lurking around Roswell?"

Drip, drip, drip. It was subtle, but it caught Heath's attention. It sounded like water dripping in a sink, slow motion, each drop taking an eternity to fall and land. Once it did, it sounded like the loudest echo, water dripping off stalactites and stalagmites in a cave. The echo circled through Heath's mind, reverberations that just kept on echoing. The noise was not coming from a bathroom tap; it came from the rusty, old car in the center of the garage.

Heath's hand closed around the door handle. "What's in here?" He jerked on the handle, pulling it upward, and it gave a groan, a resigning appeal. The car door opened; metal ground against metal. Flakes of rust swirled in the air. A rotten smell hit Heath's nostrils; it made his eyes water; it was pungent and overwhelming. It replaced the regular smells of a garage. He had to take a step back to clear his mind. He saw Linus clearly now, Linus, a forty-something mechanic. He lay on the back seat in worn coveralls with little else underneath; through one of the holes Heath could see ample flesh spilling out through the unzipped zipper. Linus's hair fell across his face in a wispy comb-over that was now in disarray, a very pathetic attempt at disguising his baldness. His face hung in saggy pockets of flesh; below him something dripped through a hole in the car's body, and it was not an oil leak but rather blood.

Chace stood there calmly, feet slightly apart, his hands in his front pants pockets. Linus had been dead awhile—his tongue was black, and his eyes were swollen in their sockets.

"You next?" Chace asked.

Heath's eyes rose to Chace. Chace was the last person he expected to run into again. Heath's gun was partly concealed in his pants. "You're one of them, aren't you?" Heath asked.

"One of who?" Chace asked.

"You know what the fuck I'm talking about."

"I'm here for Elle. And when I get her, we'll be leaving together."

"She won't be leaving with you."

"Oh, I think she will."

The door to the office opened and closed. Chace smiled.

Heath could see Elle's face; she had come in through a side door. She was looking at him. She did not see Chace. Chace saw Elle though.

Elle put her hand up to block the sunlight and try to get her eyes to adjust to the gloom of the garage. "God, what is that smell?"

"Come here," Heath said. His eyes never left Chace from the moment she entered the garage. Heath took out his gun; he had another gun in the back of his pants.

Elle flinched when she finally noticed Chace by the big garage door. She circled around the car to stand just behind Heath. She trusted him completely, and that was good. This was only a slight hitch in the plans. How Chace had found them did not quite make sense. But he soon would find out.

Chace made no attempt to produce a weapon of his own. He looked relaxed, more relaxed than Heath had ever remembered the bastard being. "You armed?" Heath demanded.

Chace pulled a gun from his pants and held it at his side.

Elle shuffled nervously behind Heath. He felt relieved just to have her there beside him, knowing she had his back.

"Get my other gun; you might need it," Heath said.

Elle reached for the second gun hidden under Heath's jacket in the waist of his jeans.

***

156

Jeanie's eyes snapped open. The darkness receded. The sun was in her eyes; she had to shield them with her hand before she knew where she was: Linus's Garage and Trade Ins—and she was standing directly behind Heath.

She almost could not believe that Chace had been right all this time. There was someone watching Elle. Heath did not know that she had been trying to figure out who he was and what he looked like all along. And he did not know that she would take any opportunity to wipe him out. He was a little bug, he would try to stop her from getting the plans, but all bugs died when they got squished, and he was no different. She hadn't worked this hard to be stopped by someone like him. She had Elle right where she wanted her, in a dark corner where she could not move.

Jeanie reached for the gun Heath was offering, but of course he thought he was offering it to Elle.

"The safety's off already, point at the target, and pull the trigger. It is not any different than when you shot those cans off the rocks. Chace is trash just the like those cans; he will fall that easily," Heath said to her over his shoulder.

Jeanie clasped the cold steel in her hand with relish. Heath did not even look at her when she took the gun; his eyes were focused on Chace. The gun was in her hand; she stepped forward, lifting the gun to point it at the back of Heath's head, a hard *clink* as the barrel smacked against his skull. She could tell that Heath's breath stopped, and his heart probably skipped a beat or two. His eyes were probably wide with confusion. "Thanks for the pep talk, boss, but I never had any trouble pulling the trigger. I enjoyed killing Davis and Striker." She stepped forward, bringing her body against his. One arm slid up his body to cup around his shoulder stopping at his neck. Her fingers curled there, like a claw getting ready to tear out his jugular. She perched her chin on his shoulder and peeked innocently over at Chace. Chace smiled back at her.

"How would you like to be killed, Heath?" Chace asked.

"Hmmm, nice and fast, or would you like it slow and painful? How not human are you? Enough so that if I shot off your willy, you wouldn't feel a thing?" Jeanie asked, eyebrows lifting in brown question marks. Her lips parted, and she laughed, throwing her head back and letting the gun lift in joyances. "How about it? Would you miss it?" She looked comically around his shoulder, Jeanie's eyes innocent, the whites taking up most of her eyes while the gun pointed down at his crotch.

Heath was stunned into silence, and it enraged her to not have him acknowledge her. Just standing there looking over his shoulder at her, looking at the gun in Chace's hand, Heath did not even give her the satisfaction of looking worried, especially when they meant business.

Her eyes looked at Chace; he shrugged his shoulders. The anger was rising within Jeanie; she felt like she was about to lose it.

"Come to think of it, this will be the first time I kill you; maybe we need a practice shot to see just how easy it can be, how easy it is." She took a step back; throwing herself away from Heath, she leveled the gun and fired. The bullet tore through the air; it ripped through Heath's shoulder, spinning him around.

He staggered back a step from the close range of the bullet, yet he remained on his feet. Her finger rested lightly on the trigger, ready to shoot again if he tried anything. He did not; he dabbed a finger at the bullet hole; Heath seemed stunned to pull his finger away dripping red. He seemed to be in disbelief at what was really happening.

"You have no idea how easy that was for me," Jeanie said.

"Elle, what're you doing?" Heath demanded.

"It speaks." Jeanie threw back her head, laughing hysterically, throwing out her arms, spinning around in a circle, so carefree and delighted. The twirling stopped abruptly; what he had just called her had finally sunk in. Her head leveled on her neck, and she met him eye to eye. The smile slipped away so effortlessly as the happy moment dissolved. "It's Jeanie, not Elle."

After a few minutes he finally seemed to realize the truth; his eyes fell to the floor. When he looked back up, there was nothing remotely human left in his eyes. She knew how he felt in that moment, when realization struck so hard, finally hitting home. The panic he must have felt was turning and twisting his guts like someone working a voodoo doll. She had known that feeling all too well over the years, usually when she thought she had pushed at Elle too hard, that surely someone would figure out the truth, that just looking at her, when it was anyone but Elle looking back, that they would just know, and the look she had thought she had seen on Heath's face earlier, that he must know about her, had vanished.

"Surprised? I guess you could say I am Elle's nasty little secret, her evil twin. We're all rolled into one, and I don't think I need to tell you which one I am, do I?"

"I think I know," Heath said quietly.

"Thought so, you didn't know about me…before, did you?"

"No," Heath answered. "So, Elle really didn't have anything to do with killing Vincent and Davis. I thought they were just trying to pin it on you."

"Yeah, sorry about that, but the Dark Man wanted to try and break Elle with those murders; he thought the reality of what she had done would start a mental breakdown, a crack, and he could extract the plans from her subconscious. However, I never trusted Vincent, and I wasn't going to stay in that mental institution."

"Maybe that's where you belong."

"But that's never where I'll be."

"What about Pete?"

"Now there, I did you a favor; he was working against you; he was working for the Dark Man to try to get the plans safely out of Elle. But he wasn't any help. Grant had implanted too many booby traps in Elle's mind, and Pete couldn't get into Elle's subconscious to access the blueprint."

"So, you killed Pete?"

"Yep, Pete was expendable. And so are you."

Heath did not speak, just shook his head, seemingly dumbfounded by the reality of the situation.

"Got any last words?" Jeanie questioned.

"This other side of Elle sucks."

Jeanie chuckled softly. "Heath, do you know what the best part of me is? No clue, I'll tell you: the best part of me is that I'm her, and she's me. Elle and I are a part-and-part deal: if you get one, you get the other. There is no single person, no perfect ideal; we are wound together so tightly that no matter what side you see, you still see some of that other side. Maybe Elle likes you, maybe she even trusts you, but she isn't as innocent as she seems. She is here, and I am here, because she allowed me to come in. I'd, um, let you talk to her, but she just doesn't remember. And for your information, Elle was the one that killed the doctors just as much as I was. She could have stopped me at any moment, but she didn't, because deep down, she's scared."

"Why are you doing this to her?" Heath asked.

"Because she didn't want to deal with reality, so now I'm getting things done. I'm not going to spend the rest of my life with her. Do you know what it's like to share a body, hmm? Of course you don't; you don't have any fucking idea! Otherwise you wouldn't have asked such a stupid question? You have control only half the time; you're up there sifting through years of crap. I hate her, and I just want her out of my head, out of my body, and the best way to do that is get rid of you."

"But this is her body, and you're the intruder."

"Maybe so, but isn't there a phrase that 'life isn't always fair'? Well here's one of those instances, maybe not exactly a textbook situation, but I think you get the gist." Her neck felt tight; she rolled her head around, trying to loosen up her muscles. "It's such a pity; you were so careful to make sure that we wouldn't know what you looked like, to keep yourself hidden from us. You didn't count on me like I didn't count on you. But you know you're not very bright, Heath; if it would have been the bad guys that had killed Pete, they wouldn't have stopped at just killing Pete; they would've taken Elle too."

Heath nodded his head slowly. The color had drained from his face. He was still human maybe, just a little bit.

Jeanie cocked her head to the side. "How should I kill him, Chace?"

"Bullet to the brain should be sufficient," Chace answered.

"How exactly do you think you're gonna get rid of Elle? You can't exactly cut Elle out because she's cramping your style. And what was all that talk about you and her being a part-and-part deal, or isn't this part of the deal? Does Elle know what you're planning?" Heath demanded.

"Well, you see, I did lie. Elle doesn't exactly know about me yet."

"Well, if she doesn't know about you, then that means you don't have access to each other's thoughts, so that would mean you can't access the plans without her. Because if the Dark Man could access the plans, he wouldn't need you, and I'm assuming that he's known where they were for some time. And without them, you have nothing to bargain with; the Dark Man's not going to give you the time of day."

"Shut the fuck up." Jeanie struck out with the gun, slamming Heath in the temple. Heath fell backward onto the cement floor. She kicked him; her leg went forward striking him in the gut again and again. Beads of sweat flew off her forehead. She kept kicking, kept the pain from stopping. The anger had taken hold of her, and she couldn't stop it.

"Stop it." Chace had his hands around her waist and was trying to pull her back.

Chace fell to the back of her mind. The heel of her shoe connected with the bullet hole, Heath groaned, and she knew she had hurt him with that one. Hesitation was for the weak; she threw her body at him again, her boot ready to punish his lower intestine. Steel toes would have done the damage; stupid Elle, she didn't like them. One kick could've almost finished the job. His hand clamped down on her ankle, and he hurled her feet out from underneath her. She fell on her ass, smacking her head on the cement. Heath's fingers tore through the denim of leg of her jeans; drops of blood pierced the skin as he tried to crush her ankle.

"Let go, you motherfucker," Jeanie screamed.

Chace stomped on Heath's hand and booted him in the head before Heath could do any real damage to Jeanie's ankle. The gun was still clenched firmly in her hand. She knew what to do. The energy that coursed through her was hot and angry. His eyes fluttered open, looking directly into hers, a little bit of blood trickled out of the corner of his mouth, and a discoloration started to seep into his temple. He smiled at her.

"You're a traitor, and you'll get your own," Heath said.

Jeanie screamed and centered her gun on Heath's head. The bullet drowned out any other sound. Heath didn't know anything; he didn't know how the Dark Man would get the plans. But Jeanie knew, and that was all that mattered.

Heath's head jerked backward as the gun bucked in Jeanie's hand; she was splattered with his blood; it felt good, like a fresh rain. She never missed.

"Should we dispose of the body?" Chace asked.

She jerked her head up. "Nah, throw him in there with the other guy. Nobody will be looking for him anyway."

"What about the girl he was working with?"

"Missy, she'll be taken care of soon enough."

Chapter 17

Missy had been drifting; she had gotten out of Roswell and was heading north when her phone rang.

"Missy, it's Tyson," the young cop said.

***

Jamie had been driving around for a while, the bike was almost out of gas, and still he wasn't out of the desert. Drugs didn't come cheap in Roswell, and he needed it bad; of course, it didn't come cheap anywhere. It had taken him long enough to find someone who could help him out. The coke was good stuff. Jamie was practically an expert on good coke. He'd been around it since he was no more than seven or eight. All that mattered now was getting high and getting as far from Heath as possible.

The wind blew sand into Jamie's eyes from the west; he wished he had taken the helmet with the sun visor. He had to turn his face to the east to avoid most of it. A glittery thing shone out in the desert, winked its eye, and went dim. Then there was another flash of light in the distance; the light wasn't from the thing itself but from the moonlight glinting off it. The clouds parted, and the moon lit up the object like a beacon. He sped off the road, almost wiping out in the process. His foot dug down into the sand to steady himself, but at that speed, it almost tore his foot from his ankle. Jamie twisted the bike's throttle; the rear wheel made him fishtail as the engine screamed.

Jamie squinted into the night to try to make out whatever had lit up. But the closer he got to it, the more it still remained a question. The object disappeared when he got no more than twenty feet away. The clouds had blocked out the moon shrouding it in darkness. He looked self-consciously behind him; his bike tipped dangerously to the left, throwing him off balance. He tried to put his foot down in order to catch himself. Something struck his ankle; it sent needle pricks all the way up his leg to his throat. It would've been ten times worse if he hadn't taken a small sample of the coke before leaving Roswell. The jolt on his leg put the bike in a wobble. Jamie ditched, cutting a gouge in the sand; when the bike jerked to a sudden stop, he was thrown forward. He moved slowly; pain traveled the length of his neck; the needles in his leg were now gone; he felt nothing. He shifted about until he was sitting in the sand on his butt. By this time tomorrow he would still be digging the sand out of his ass crack, probably with a toothbrush. Bright-white bones jutted out of his ankle, a telltale sign of his stupidity. Shit, he needed it bad; he could turn this pain into nothing more than a bad nightmare. Blood splattered the sand in thick bursts around the exposed bones. He had fucked up majorly, but somehow he didn't care. He reached in his pocket for the ziplock bag; he lifted some on a finger to his nose and inhaled deeply. Sparks erupted in front of his eyes. A dreamy look crossed his face; as quickly as it came, it vanished. Jamie squinted into the night, something had just moved, and it wasn't the coke that had made him see it. Something with big, glistening eyes was watching him. Jamie rolled onto his stomach and crawled across the sand to his bike. He left a trail of blood, but what happened when he ran out of coke? Simple, he died. He reached into the night and grasped the spokes of Heath's bike, pulling himself forward onto the heavy thing. Jamie looked back into the night to see if the thing was following him. The ground shifted in front of the bike. The wind picked up, swirling the sand in his face, making it impossible to see two feet in front of him. The ground shifted again, the back tire of the bike actually rose up in the air, and Jamie tried to reach for it, but it was quickly pulled out of his reach. The sand shifted underneath him; he could feel himself falling forward and down. And he couldn't stop himself. The dust storm covered up any tracks he might have left.

He tumbled and rolled down through sand and over a rock. When he landed, it wasn't soft; it knocked the air out of him. He landed on his back on a gravelly rock-dirt mixture. Down here, the wind wasn't as bad; hardly any of the sand moved down here. Here he could look up and see how far he had fallen. It was at least a fifteen- or twenty-foot descent. Some of it was gradual, but the last five feet was a straight drop.

He looked down the length of the gorge for his bike, but it wasn't anywhere. Maybe it had rolled farther because of its weight. He looked up to the sky again; the thing stood outlined along the edge of the night, tall, dark, and malicious. He didn't know how he knew when he couldn't make out any details of its face. An inner sense warned Jamie of his impending doom. He tried to get to his feet and run, the broken ankle useless and unable to assist him. He crawled five feet before it stomped him to the ground; its foot was planted on Jamie's back. He couldn't move. Jamie turned his head, trying to get a look into the thing's face. The thing screamed into the night—Jamie lost his sanity, screaming into the little pieces of sand that were fitted in between the rocks. The things claws tore Jamie to shreds.

***

It was watching the human, broken and frail, injured, letting its life force seep into the sand. It wouldn't be hard to kill. It wasn't even one of theirs; it wasn't chipped, controlled, or marked; it was there and vulnerable for the taking. Now the human was moving away; panic seemed to fill the weak being. They didn't see; they didn't want to accept what was right in front of their eyes. Why? Because they couldn't handle it—just the concept of another species was too much for mankind to grasp.

Raleigh looked at the human on the ground; it was crawling onto the bike. The ground gave way; the human and the bike disappeared into the gorge. The sand whirled around, erasing any trace of the human.

It descended easily down into the opening in the rock; its feet traveled well down the steep slope to the bottom. It stood above the human without him even knowing that it was there. The human looked up into its face, and there was no doubt in Raleigh's mind that this human was just a little more perceptive than the rest, or maybe the white stuff he had pushed up his nose gave him a more open mind. Either way, he had to go now; he knew too much; when one human knew something, they were just dying to tell another.

Raleigh planted one of its feet firmly on the human's back, pressing him into the terrain. It shrieked into the night, a deep guttural sound from its belly, enraged, and territorial. To a human it might sound like the devil was let loose on the world. Its scream signaled the impending kill. Raleigh was one of the regular ones; it didn't have powers that the Dark Man had. It didn't need powers to deal with this human. Its claws extended and were razor sharp; its teeth snapped as its jaws watered. Raleigh clawed the human's back, tearing out the vertebrae. Raleigh feasted on the human's flesh. Its eyes rose up to meet the night, and it roared once again to acknowledge its kill, its pleasure.

***

"What is it, Tyson?" Missy said, waiting for the answers he had for her.

"Well, we located a surveillance video, one that was separate from the mainframe. And it looks like Elle did kill Striker; it shows her entering the house in a well-lit attached garage. There is no doubt about it."

"So, she did kill them," Missy said, more to herself than Tyson.

"We might not get so lucky with finding that kind of footage at Davis's place, but this is more than enough to go on. It links her, and no jury will go against the district attorney once they play this video."

"Thanks, Tyson." Missy hung up. It was what she had assumed. But how to tell Heath? He was off the grid and had probably ditched his cell phone long ago.

***

Missy had gone back to the house; she trashed the entire place trying to find some clue as to where Heath would've taken Elle, throwing his and Grant's shit around. That was something that they had never talked about, just where he and Elle intended to go after he had removed the chip from her spine. There was nothing here and nothing that mattered. She booked a flight and hopped on the next one that was headed to New York; it was a last-ditch effort.

Elle's apartment was exactly like it had been a week and a half ago, it still had police tape up, and she imagined that they had combed every inch of it again and again. But the thing was, she didn't need to find Elle. Missy needed to find Heath, hopefully before it was too late.

"Why in the hell did she paint this shit? Where the hell are they?" Missy screamed to the empty apartment; she shouldn't have let Heath leave with Elle. Why did she? Oh, that's right, he wouldn't have listened to her anyway—no matter what she did, what she said. Heath had been trained years ago for these next days, for this point in time. Nothing and no one was going to get in his way. But Elle was the one person he couldn't protect, that didn't want his protection. What if somewhere along the way, all the information that Elle had in her head made her mind become warped, twisted. Was it really just a blueprint to an alien craft that crashed almost a century earlier, or was there something crawling around in Elle's

165

mind? Was Elle being controlled by them even after the chip had been removed from her spine? Was it possible that the Dark Man had buried a transmitter somewhere in her body that Heath didn't know about? And if so, could this transmitter change channels? Frequencies? Basically, was Elle one person until she received a command? Or was this all nothing more than Missy's own paranoia? No, it wasn't, there were things that they didn't know about Elle, and the possibility of losing everything they had worked so hard to achieve had become a reality.

It felt weird, standing inside Elle's apartment looking at the wall of eyes. How could Missy help Heath? She didn't know anything, Heath had kept so much hidden from Jamie and her, and Grant had some dark secrets.

"Heath, what the fuck do I do?"

The apartment didn't know anything, and if it did, it certainly wasn't about to tell her. Missy lifted the lid of the garbage can in the kitchen. She saw a clown night-light sitting in the bottom of the trash can; she felt suddenly self-conscious, but no one was there, so she picked it out. She held it close to her face, looking it straight in the eyes. It felt out of place in a grown woman's apartment, but then Elle was afraid of the dark. Missy screamed in frustration and threw the night-light at the wall, and it broke into three pieces, right between the eyes and the third was a smiling red mouth and chin.

Missy headed back to Elle's bedroom; the eyes seemed to follow wherever you were in the room. That's where she needed to be right now. She slid down the wall to the floor, the rug flattening underneath the seat of her jeans. Maybe if she just sat there for a few minutes, a direction would present itself to her. She wasn't religious, never had been, but she believed that things happened for a reason. So, something must happen to direct her to Heath, because she believed he needed protection more than Elle.

"Holly fuck," Missy said out loud. Here was the sign she had been waiting for, a case of Smirnoff was sitting just within arm's reach. She pulled the case out from under the bed, pulled a bottle free, twisted off the cap, and threw it at the eyes. "We won't be needing this." Hell, who could blame her for this? No one. Heath had his release, his cigarettes when things got too heavy. This had always been hers; a little liquor in the blood took off that edge so she could relax enough to think calmly.

The first few swallows were guilty, but after that, they went down guilt free, one right after the next. Free of worry, no pain, just a warm feeling that passed through her head and made her feel dreamy. She could feel her body relaxing, going limp; she went willingly to the dream world without worry.

The warmth dissolved for a few minutes. Missy opened her eyes, she was looking at the wall crookedly, but it was clear, clear as if it had turned to accommodate her. Missy's eyes blurred just a little with each blink, just enough to get her attention; she stopped and stared at the wall with her eyes out of focus. She was staring at it like a drunk, and it was starting to make her nauseous, really nauseous. If she didn't get a handle on her stomach soon, Elle's room was going to change and not for the better. Vomit rose in Missy's throat; the wall would even be textured after she was done with it. She grabbed the garbage can beside Elle's bed and puked into it. The aliens' faces were painted over top of each other; it was just a fucking mess in front of her. *Bam. Bam.* It was almost as if someone had slammed her in the head with a sledgehammer. The wall jumped into focus, but the faces were still far back and sort of blurry; there was a kind of picture protruding from the wall of faces, kind of like one of those magic-eye things.

The blur of alien faces made up one alien, from head to toe, not just a head among many. It was scary. Even scarier than the oversized green heads with black eyes, this extraterrestrial was really looking back at Missy. And below the alien were numbers and letters, the numbers ran horizontal, forming a line.

To really see this thing, you just had to make your eyes unfocused, look at it from a different angle, and—*bam*—there it was. Of course, add a couple bottles of Smirnoff, and it was even easier.

She picked a felt pen out of her bag and wrote the numbers and letters down on her arm: 33.5264N111.3899W. It had to be latitude and longitude coordinates. Missy pulled her sleeve down over them.

Energy slipping away, she could feel her body getting sleepy again; this time she tried to fight the sleepiness; she wondered what was at these coordinates. It couldn't possibly be Heath, and yet it was all she had to go on. The mess of faces had been on Elle's wall for years. Finally, the endless possibilities gave way, and she slept.

After a while, the dreariness started to dissipate, and a bitchy figure popped out.

"Who the fuck are you?"

The words echoed in Missy's head; she was confused and couldn't place the woman standing over her. When her windpipe closed off, it jerked her from the drunken state in an instant. The older woman was stepping on Missy's neck with one of her army boots. She looked like one angry bitch, someone you didn't want to annoy. Missy reached up, struggling to remove the boot from her neck.

"Who are you?" the woman demanded again.

Missy struggled to say, "Get…off." But it came out more as strangled gurgle. Missy recognized Margaret clearly, even with the lack of oxygen going to her brain.

"What?" Margaret asked.

Missy ran her hand up the lady's pant leg and clamped her fingernails on the back of her calf. She squeezed with every bit of strength she had left. Missy didn't usually have much in the way of nails, but they were in good shape, and she had let them grow a little longer than usual. Her nails sank into the flesh easily. The lady's calf blurred in front of her eyes before the foot jerked off of her neck.

"Ow…you…bitch." Missy gasped when she could breathe again.

The air was fresh and clean, her strength returned, and in one jerky motion, she was climbing to her feet as if someone had pulled on her marionette strings. In a way, someone had. This bitch meant business, and Missy was filled with a rush of adrenaline. Margaret was taller and heavier; those odds weren't in Missy's favor.

Missy lifted her arms, pushing back at Margaret.

"Who are you?" Margaret demanded.

Missy freed an arm and punched Margaret in the face. Margaret stumbled backward a couple steps. Missy rubbed at her neck while she reached behind her back to the waistband of her jeans—it was empty; her gun wasn't there. Shit, it must have fallen out or been taken, Missy looked to Margaret, and there were no clues there.

Margaret punched at Missy. Missy blocked the shot, bringing her arm up. Margaret slammed into Missy, knocking her back against the wall; there was nowhere to go.

"Looks like you ran out of room."

Missy glared at Margaret as she pinned her to the wall.

"Now, who are you?" Margaret demanded.

"I'm not your concern," Missy countered.

"You're in my daughter's apartment, and she is wanted for murder. Do you know where Elle is?"

"No, but consider yourself lucky; she's a fucking whacko anyway."

"Bitch," Margaret whispered.

"Right back at yah."

Margaret jerked out of Missy's grasp and grabbed a broom by the door; she held the broom horizontally and rushed at Missy. Missy braced her feet and held her arms out to catch the broom handle. For an old broad, Margaret was one nasty woman. Missy shoved back at the handle, ducked beneath it, and tripped Margaret. Margaret fell, and the end of the broomstick stuck into the wall.

Margaret ripped the broomstick free of the drywall and whipped it at Missy. She had to step back to avoid getting smacked. They locked eyes on each other, and Margaret pushed Missy backward, swinging the broom at her.

Missy dodged the broom and dove into Margaret; Margaret stumbled backward and smacked her head against the wall. Missy had never killed anyone in hand-to-hand combat. However, Margaret was a spy for the Dark Man, and letting her live wasn't an option.

Margaret ran at Missy, Missy tried to block her, and Margaret bodychecked her. The broom went skidding into the wall. Missy couldn't stop Margaret, but she could slow her down. Margaret was out the door, running for the coffee table. Missy was on her; she stuck the broomstick between Margaret's feet and tripped Margaret, sending her sprawling on the ground just shy of the coffee table.

"I guess I'll get a penalty for tripping." Missy planted a boot in the middle of Margaret's back, stomping her to the ground. She leaned forward, just able to grasp her gun from the edge of the coffee table. Margaret must have taken it from Missy when she had fallen asleep.

Margaret eyed Missy over her shoulder, what little Margaret could twist around to see. Margaret's eyes were huge, a snarl twisted her features, and she tried bucking Missy off. But Missy held Margaret down firmly.

"This is the end of the line."

Missy put the barrel against the back of Margret's skull and squeezed the trigger twice.

With that task done, Missy got up off Margaret's body and sat down against the wall, gun still in hand. Remembering the coordinates, Missy slid up her sleeve; they were directions to something. She googled them; it was a location somewhere outside of Phoenix, Arizona. She booked her flight to Phoenix.

When she looked back over at Margaret, Margaret's head was a mess. Missy undoubtably had blood all over her. She headed into the bathroom to get cleaned up. Missy knew what she had touched, and she knew how to handle these types of situations; Heath had left nothing to chance. After quickly cleaning up any trace of her fingerprints in the apartment, she moved on to Margaret. Grant had developed a solution that could erase foreign skin without destroying the body. The solution was undetectable, it evaporated into the air, so there was next to no evidence that could link Missy to the crime. The only thing that remained was Margaret's body, and no amount of hunting could bring back evidence that no longer existed.

The coordinates were a longshot at best, but she had a feeling this might lead her to Heath—or at the very least, the Dark Man.

Chapter 18

Jeanie dabbed a tissue at the corner of her eye; dark-red blood stained it. A smile pulled her cheeks upward. Heath bled, and that meant he could die just like other humans. With a soft sigh, she followed Chace out to his Bronco. She got in, closed the door, and leaned her head back.

Jeanie remembered the turn of events that had led up to today. There was a long list of them, but the very first and truly the clearest memory of something more came through the darkness. It settled before her like an oasis in a hot, dry desert. It was a sketch, and then it wasn't; it was as if it were a 3D model with lines, and parts fit together in just a certain way; the lines were black and sketched with a deft hand, one that must have been drawn quickly and with reason. She wasn't very mechanically inclined, and she didn't understand what the lines and pieces were for, at least not at first. She had only brief glimpses of it, maybe two altogether; each time she saw it, it was for maybe one or two seconds, before it was like a door was slammed shut in her face. She would be struggling through the darkness to the light, and there it would be, right in front of her, glowing like something made out of precious gold, even though the lines were harsh and black, smudged a little around the edges. It had this valuable feel that couldn't be ignored. It took years for her to realize what it was; she couldn't remember the exact intricacies of the pieces or parts and how they were put together, just that it struck her with a feeling of great importance. She remembered a few words scrawled at the bottom, *Not for alien eyes.*

Jeanie believed that she had been created when Grant had installed a kind of backup plan, a side effect when the blueprint was initially installed. The backup plan was a program designed to fight anyone who tried to extract the blueprint during hypnosis, which would be the most likely way to unlock the plans from the inner core of Elle's brain. But this program had created a major flaw in Elle's mind, and Jeanie had been created from that.

For years Jeanie was captive in Elle's body; sure, she had her moments of freedom, but they were brief and momentary. At one point, she was certain that she would never again see the light of day, at least until the Dark Man paid Elle a visit, and after that, Jeanie knew it was possible to get what she wanted. Elle couldn't deal with the reality of the Dark Man and the extraterrestrials; Elle's sanity started to break down. Jeanie used her foothold—when something was too much for Elle to deal with, Jeanie appeared. But even though Jeanie would appear from time to time, she wasn't the safety clause Grant had installed—no, that was something else, a personality so strong, stronger than Elle and Jeanie put together, almost untouchable.

As Elle became more and more fragile, Jeanie stepped into Elle's shoes more often. And it didn't take Jeanie long to realize she didn't want to be a bystander in her own life. She wanted to be the front-runner, and she didn't want to share their body anymore.

Elle couldn't remember the first nine years of her life, but Jeanie did. It was strange how each had gotten hold of certain memories and time frames; every day that Grant was there, Jeanie remembered. Elle could only get glimpses of the past under hypnosis, and even then it was a struggle, because the safety clause would block anyone from getting to the plans, from unlocking what needed to be kept hidden.

Most of the time, Jeanie didn't get to look out at all, unless of course she had complete control of the body. But sometimes, she could take over when Elle wasn't paying attention or was almost asleep. It was like she laid down her guard, and Jeanie jumped forward, taking over the reins.

Jeanie had no problem taking what she wanted, dealing with what Elle didn't want to remember, because bad things happened to good people, all the time. And soon, very soon, something bad would happen to Elle, because Jeanie was here, and she wasn't just going to go back into the dark. And if Elle had a problem with it, well, fuck her. Fuck everyone that got in her way. She looked over at Chace; he smiled at her; she smiled back. He would probably have to go too. They would all probably have to go, but that was ok.

She slipped into an unconscious darkness, but it wasn't an empty darkness; there were words there, fears and pain. And they couldn't hurt her.

"Now, sweetie, I have to go away for a little while," Grant said.

"Why, Daddy, why?" Elle asked.

"Because some bad people are going to come for me, and if I stay here…they'll get me."

"Maybe the bad people are already here." She was very perceptive, able to know when something was going to happen. Or when they were going to make a move, Elle could see them.

"Huh?"

"Maybe they're all around you. All around us."

"Elle, where are they?"

Elle stared up at the roof. "They're outside."

Grant was scared; Elle didn't feel anything; nothing was left inside her. Grant looked at the window and then to her; he moved back, heading for the door. The room filled with light; the curtains barely filtered the brilliance out; it was strong and hot. Jeanie felt like the light was going to burn out her retinas, but of course she wasn't really there; she was just experiencing one of Elle's memories, one that Elle didn't want to remember anymore.

Elle was very perceptive, sensitive, tuned in to what was going on around her. Or at least she used to be, until she had given up her memories; she had given up a lot more, certain instincts and strengths. Elle probably still had a feeling once in a while, but now it was a lot more subdued. Now Jeanie had the advantage over Elle, and it was a pretty big advantage.

The lights brightened until the bulbs exploded; the room fell into darkness. Elle stood there alone in the room. Grant was gone, like he had been beamed up. But Grant got a one-way ticket, and he wasn't coming back no matter what.

Elle laid down on the floor, curled into the fetal position; the TV clicked on. She laid there, staring at it all night; she had known they were coming, and yet she had done nothing to warn Grant.

***

Twenty past one o'clock in the morning, a Bronco pulled in front of a motel. Jeanie was still covered in Heath's blood; the night clerk eyed her nervously when she had first pushed the bills across the counter. He shook his head but quickly changed his tune when she followed up with a gun pointed at the plastic-shielded window. He jerked back a foot in surprise. She didn't care if he called the police, this place likely hustled drugs, and

173

she was the least of his concerns. In fact, it probably cost a bit to get the cops to give this place a wide berth, to ignore the drug trafficking going on.

Jeanie reached across the counter for the key card the night clerk held out to her. She knew she scared the shit out of this scrawny guy, and she really didn't care. She lifted her finger up to her lips and made a *shhh* sound. A smile cracked her lips into a malicious grin.

She unlocked the room; the fluorescence washed the room in a dull brilliance; not very many people stayed here. It was off the beaten path and far from the Holiday Inn, more like a urine-soaked crack hole with dirty sheets. But it wasn't the ambience she was after; she knew this place was a lot safer because of its location.

Chace was leaning against the Bronco, his hands stuck low in his pockets, Heath's gun tucked into the band of his jeans. It might not be a bad idea to confiscate Chace's gun before anything else happened. This little crusade that Chace was on was stupid; he believed that they were mankind's salvation. If he wanted to believe that kind of crap, well, fine. She went along with it in the beginning because he could be useful at times; he was an outsider when she was trapped inside Elle.

***

Elle's mind was weakened by the plans, creating an almost distorted reality; the panic attacks and the blackouts could consume her. Elle eventually entered into therapy to try to get a grasp on reality, but behind the scenes, Dr. Davis intended to institutionalize Elle when her sanity crumbled. However, Elle was stronger than they had initially assumed; she fought mentally for control, to keep the darkness within her at bay. Institutionalizing Elle seemed to be the only way to break her mind; shock treatment and a lot of other twisted techniques offered a plethora of options. But the idea of Dr. Davis and Striker playing mad doctor with Elle's mind frightened the Dark Man; he thought they would do more harm than good—and the plans would be lost forever. That wasn't something he wanted to take a chance on. Now or ever. Soon Elle would be the Dark Man's.

***

174

Dr. Davis and Vincent Striker had become expendable; Jeanie didn't want Elle's mind to be harmed—Elle's mind was Jeanie's mind. She wanted Elle gone, and she wanted it now.

Something trickled down Jeanie's upper lip; she reached her hand up, startled to realize there was blood dripping from her nose, fresh blood. Elle's mental stability was deteriorating, and if Jeanie wasn't careful, her body could be damaged; the brain was the powerhouse for the body, and without it, she had nothing.

Chace had been trying to keep an eye on Elle, to try to figure out if anyone was there to protect her. They all had their theories. However, he could never pinpoint just who it was. The fact that Chace's own employee was Elle's protector was just one of those weird coincidences.

Jeanie knew the Dark Man had absolutely no use for Chace, and she didn't care; Chace had served his purpose.

The walls in room G8 were painted teal, probably painted over thirty years ago with lead paint. Even as bad as the paint job was, Jeanie noticed that the paint wasn't flaking off the walls. That meant the Dark Man hadn't been here yet. Jeanie and Chace were early.

The TV didn't work, the toilet barely flushed, and there were water stains on the roof, or were they pee stains? Could somebody piss and defy the laws of gravity? Mold encased the windows in a rotting black mess. The smell was disgusting, old pot, urine, beer, and cigarettes. Jeanie pulled a chair into the center of the room, dusted off the bugs, sat down, and stared at the wall. They would be coming soon; it was almost dusk.

The clock ticked loudly—*tick, tick*—Jeanie's eyes felt weighted, and slowly they closed. How had that happened? She jerked awake; she had almost fallen asleep. Or is that what Elle wanted her to do? Was she trying to get a hold of her body again? Maybe she was; maybe she was trying to initiate a takeover. The sound of the clock was getting increasingly louder, but of course, eventually Jeanie had always faded into the background. Jeanie admittedly was the weaker of the two personalities at times; she had done only what she wanted to be forced into the darkness time and again. Well now she wasn't leaving, and if she had to fight to be here, she would.

The noise of the clock got even louder; the little hand seemed to be growing in size, filling her mind as it turned. The high-pitched *tick, tick,*

tick, tick seemed to scream that time was running out. Jeanie wasn't even conscious of the feel of the gun leaving her waistband; she didn't feel it center on the clock; all she really felt was the ticking inside her. The gun bucked in her hands; the plastic encasing the clock shattered. Chace jerked to his feet, alarmed. Jeanie glanced briefly at him, then turned back to the clock. She could hear Chace sit back down in the easy chair again. "Fuck, get a grip," he demanded.

The clock didn't stop; the arms still ticked; they still moved, pushed without electricity or batteries. They were pushed by another force altogether.

There was a soft thud, like someone passing out or drifting off to sleep and falling out of their chair.

Chace leaned back and closed his eyes; his breathing became steady and even. He had fallen asleep again. Jeanie moved across the room, she stood by the door, listening for a minute or two, the ticking pushed far back in her mind. It took a great amount of effort to drown the sound of the clock out. As the seconds passed, nothing seemed to move outside; Jeanie's fingers clasped the crappy chain and slid it back in a moment of defiance. She held the gun in the other hand as she slid back the dead bolt and stepped outside the motel. A glistening layer of sweat covered her from head to toe, the night was hot and muggy, and the flies swarmed around her, as if bewitched.

One long cement sidewalk encircled the motel; it was still hot from the day's warmth. The bottoms of her jeans brushed against her ankles as she walked across the cement in bare feet. After ten feet, she didn't feel the heat anymore. Just like the ticking, it had faded out, disappeared. What was important now was what she had heard.

She approached the vacancy sign that hung outside the office. Nothing seemed abnormal about it. She could hear the TV from inside the office; the dialogue was clear; the scrawny guy liked love stories; this was a B movie at best, probably hadn't even made it to theaters.

Jeanie could see through the window now, she could see the TV, but no one was sitting in front of it. A cool breeze blew her sweaty hair off her neck. Her head swiveled so she could see over her shoulder—nothing there.

"Hey, are you there?" Jeanie asked; her voice sounded raspy. Her throat was dry; her tongue came out, lolling at her lips. Speaking had been a mistake; she knew that now; the thing was not to alarm them; they acted quickly and without thinking at times.

A warm liquid was running down her nose and over her lip; Jeannie wiped it hastily away.

The sidewalk receded into gravel; the rocks bit into the tender heels of her feet. As she got closer to the desert, the ticking started up, louder, thundering in her head like a grandfather clock amplified. The thudding brought tears to her eyes.

Why was she here? Why was she doing this? The answer quite simply was to get control of her life once and for all, so she didn't have to watch from a far corner of Elle's mind. Was it risky putting all her faith in a race that was far from human? In a way it was, but she didn't have many options.

Jeanie returned to the front office when she saw nothing out in the desert. She decided to ask the night clerk if he had seen anything. She jerked her hand away from the doorknob; the knob of the door was extremely hot to the touch. The skin on her palm bubbled up in a third-degree burn. She bit down on her lip, shoving the pain aside; pain was for the weak. Ok, she thought, as she gathered her T-shirt into an oven mitt, not quite as insulated, but it will do. She turned the knob and threw the door inward, getting back in case fire should rush out at her. There was no smoke and no flames. Her oven mitt was replaced with the gun; she gripped the gun, completely numb to the pain.

Something trickled down Jeanie's upper lip again; she reached up and wiped away the blood; her nosebleeds were getting worse. Maybe it was the dry heat that had caused the nosebleed, but she knew the stresses of her split personality and the blueprint were actually damaging this body.

The office consisted of a small, cluttered desk and key card rack, but the hall that led away adjoined it to a small apartment with a bathroom, kitchenette, living room, and bedroom. Chip bags littered the floor. Crumbs crunched under the soles of her feet. A small pile of coke dusted the top of the coffee table among the beer bottles. Thick, dusty drapes enclosed the apartment from the outside world.

The place was a mess, not as if someone were looking for anything, but as if the guy were a fucking slob. Jeanie sighed, looking around for the night clerk. The small bathroom door stood slightly ajar; all you could see were bathroom tiles and a sink. She walked across the gritty rug and stopped in front of the door, leveling her gun. She kicked the door in; it hit and bounced shut. Her hand clasped the knob with the already-formulated oven mitt and pushed it slowly inward. It opened easily to a point, then seemed to stop, as if something were blocking the door. Jeanie didn't feel any heat from this door. She unleashed her hand from her T-shirt, using her left hand to push the door wider. One finger slipped delicately onto the trigger, her nerves tingling in anticipation, getting ready for what lay behind door number one. Nothing moved; she slid her foot across the linoleum and peeked around the door to the small sink and toilet. The edge of the sink had blood on it, and in the far corner was the night clerk. His back was against the wall, his knees drawn up to his chest for lack of room in the closest-sized bathroom. He looked to be asleep, but that wasn't the case; the veins of blood were spider-webbed and stood out as if a bad infection had spread through his body. She reached forward to touch him; his body fell apart into pieces—arms, legs, torso, and head. The maggots were in full swing, as if he had been dead a long time. Jeanie turned away in disgust, heading back to her room.

Chace still slept in his chair, undisturbed and unknowing of anything weird. She looked up at the far wall; something scratched against the far corner of the motel, like a mouse—or was it a rat in the wall? It started high up, almost to the roof, then it quieted down and became faint. Jeanie saw what had made the noise; something was protruding through the motel's wall. It looked kind of like a black claw, a sharp black claw that withdrew before her eyes. When it reentered, it slid down the wall, cutting through the wall as effortlessly as a knife through butter. It slid in one smooth motion all the way from roof to the floor; the claw twisted on its side, sharp and glistening as it changed to a horizontal cut. Jeanie knew what was on that other side of the wall, but it didn't stop her from being afraid.

She waited as the teal paint drifted around the room, floating lazily on the air current produced from the small fan. The wall shuddered as it was pulled outward like the flap of a tent, and that was when Jeanie made eye contact with it. *It* summed up this thing in just one word; it wasn't male or female—it was just it. Through all the memories that Jeanie had taken from Elle, this had never been one of them. Sure, there had been the memory of her lying on the table and getting the implant in her spine; she had seen something black shift past the table, drifting just out of reach. But it had been the Dark Man who had put the chip in Elle's spine; she had never seen this thing. Suddenly the pizza she had eaten earlier wanted nothing to do with being digested; it wanted to come back up.

The thing slid through the opening, graceful, unmindful of how terrible it looked. The clock had long been forgotten, but it started ticking again, and Jeanie almost let Elle take over. But if Jeanie did give in, Elle would surely fuck it up, and that was the last thing Jeanie wanted. There was that piece of Jeanie that was twisted and disturbed; she was obsessed with the extraterrestrials almost as much as Chace was, maybe more. Chace wanted to see them, to know that they were real, and in his own fucked-up mind, he believed that they were the answer to mankind's fate. It wasn't just her freedom that Jeanie wanted; she wanted power like the Dark Man—maybe that was what she wanted most of all, to be unstoppable, to be what no one else could be. And it was possible; she believed in that with every fiber of her being, that the Dark Man could make her so much more than she was.

Crouched not more than five feet away, it turned its focus on Chace. Its hands were curled slightly; it had a total of three fingers and what looked like a thumb, but longer and thinner, resembling a fourth finger more than anything. The fingers didn't have nails; it had animal-type claws. It stood taller, at least six feet, much taller than the aliens people had claimed to see. It reminded her of an inkblot come to life.

***

It could see her there, standing still, staring at it; it hunkered down; its eyes shifted over the room in an untrustworthy motion. Then it moved; it slashed the male human apart; he did nothing to stop it. Then it turned toward the woman; this was the one it had come for. It moved forward until it stood over her, a dark shadow that swallowed her up.

Chapter 19

Missy picked out her rental; she wanted one with navigation that could tell her exactly where to go. Linus's Garage and Trade Ins fit the coordinates. A fat, potbellied man handed over the keys to the rental car.

Instinct told Missy that this wasn't going to end well, even before she stepped into the garage. The smell of rot was so strong it made her take a step backward; the thought of the fresh air outside made going into the garage that much more difficult.

The coordinates from Elle's wall had been a one in a million shot, but she didn't have any other ideas. And that had been enough for Missy. It had been as good a choice as any to start with.

"Anybody here?" Missy called out to the empty garage. The garage was a fucking dump, not a successful business venture at all.

Slowly her vision became somewhat accustomed to the poor lighting; the windows were dirty and hadn't been washed in years. She could just make out the corners of what looked like a desk enclosed in glass partitions, probably the office.

There wasn't anything of value in the office, old work orders and a few Playboys. Missy found the main breaker, only to realize that the lights in the garage didn't work. It was one disappointment after another. However, in the top drawer there was a twenty-inch flashlight made of heavy steel. The weight of the flashlight was comforting; it was the kind you could thunk your ex-boyfriend with if he became a problem. The flashlight wavered back and forth across the garage; it settled finally on the old car sitting there. The old car had once been chrome and red paint; years ago it had been replaced by rust and tarnish.

Something was inside that car—she reached for her gun, shuffling the flashlight to her left. Her hands reached out in front of her.

Her eyes strained to see through the windows of the car; as she stepped up to it, the light from the flashlight couldn't penetrate the layer of dust covering the windows. Missy stuck the flashlight between her thighs; gun in hand, door handle in the other, she tore the door open. The stench of rot poured out of the car. She had to cover her mouth and nose with her shirt to keep from vomiting. And even the need to gag was almost uncontrollable.

Missy retrieved the flashlight and swung it into the car, blinding anything in the back seat. Her eyes soaked up the scene before her in seconds. But it took longer to register in her mind. She contemplated the oodles of maggots that were withering in a heap; they saturated the whole back seat and floor of the car. Missy desperately wanted to turn away, but something held her there, an instinct or feeling maybe; she was unable to turn away. They were snowy white and oozed over one another, so many, many not even touching what they were feasting on.

Missy got a glimpse of heavy material; someone was under the sea of maggots. She took a deep breath, reciting a prayer, as if that would help anything. "Oh no, Heath, Heath!" It couldn't be, but then…oh god, her mind was screaming.

A crowbar lay off to side of the garage; she picked it up and shoved it into the maggots, snagging a piece of material. The material pulled free and came out of the maggoty pile. It was blue coverall type material, not usually the type of clothing Heath wore. He was a jeans-and-T-shirt type of guy.

A cell phone dropped to her feet. She picked it up, mesmerized by it yet repulsed by the squishy, wormy goo covering it. Why was she here? That was one question Missy couldn't answer. What was the probability that Heath had been here? Not very likely. Missy had gotten this garage's address off a wall, a wall that had been painted years ago by a crazy person. It didn't mean anything. It couldn't. And yet…

She wiped the cell phone on a rag that had seen better days. Missy turned it on; the security code had been deactivated. The phone buzzed weakly; she clicked on the voice mail icon that was flashing. She listened to the options; after the message started to play, Missy's heart stopped. It was Missy's voice, she had called Heath from New York, and it had gone to voice mail—this was his phone. Was she too late and missed him or…

It was a last-ditch attempt, her calling him; Heath would've more than likely discarded his phone, and yet he hadn't.

What else was under that sea of maggots? Was Heath in there? He had been here, and more than likely, he still was. "Oh fuck." Missy wasn't even conscious of diving into the maggot pile; she shoved her hands into the disgusting, wriggling mass and pulled and dug.

Her previous meal tried to resurface, making her gag, her stomach rolling. She had to choke it back. "Oh god, oh god, oh god, oh god, oh god."

A body started to surface in the sea of maggots; the flashlight was held between Missy's legs as she dug into the mass. Out of the twisting maggots surfaced a decayed and swelled face. Oh god. Wanting desperately to turn away, Missy gagged and pulled on the body. "Christ, you're one ugly fucker." She wasn't about to let him plunge back into the sea of decay; she was just strong enough to pull him aside. Maggots and guts spilled out of the car onto the cement floor of the garage. She got a glimpse of material, of something beneath the dead body. The flashlight was dimming, what was left of the battery had cut the light to a dim glow, but it was enough to see the man lying in the back seat, at least from the neck down. Her eyes were brimming with tears as fear settled into the pit of her stomach. "Heath!" she screamed. She scraped at the mass of maggots still covering the body's face.

Missy had never expected to find Heath, let alone this way. She figured that if anyone could beat the aliens, it was him. He would disappear, just Elle and him somewhere up north, and Missy would go back and live out the rest of her life always wondering. But there had been a snag in that plan, an unwavering feeling of uncertainty surrounding Elle—a feeling Missy couldn't shake.

Luckily the maggots had been hard at work, otherwise Missy would never have been able to move whom she assumed was Linus off Heath. How Elle had the strength to dump Linus's body on top of Heath, she had no idea.

Missy climbed into the car, squashing maggots under her bootheels. Bending down over top of him, placing the flashlight on his chest, she saw his eyes were closed and dark. There was a definite bluish tinge to his skin, like he was frozen; the top of his head was caked with blood and matted hair. A few maggots wiggled around in the mess, but they had done a good job to keep the infection from setting in. Thank God for small wonders. Under normal conditions, one would assume that he was dead; however, he wasn't decaying. Missy gingerly reached out to touch the side of his face, almost hesitant to touch him; touching him would make this all too real. It was definitely Heath's blood. He had sustained a major head injury. Missy held her breath, hand lowering to find a pulse in his neck, if there was one…

***

"Elle?"

Jeanie could see it getting closer; she held her ground and let it reach out one of its claws to her.

Out of nowhere, the Dark Man appeared, looking expressionless, just like he always did.

***

Elle's heart was beating so fast, it felt like it was malfunctioning and ready to explode. Elle was desperate; she couldn't understand how she had gotten here. The blackout must've come, and it had been strong this time, taking over and throwing her into that black void with no way out, a prisoner in her own body. Elle had this strange feeling she'd done something, something really bad. But of course, it wasn't her; it was whatever took over when she was in the darkness. Where was Heath? Was he ok? And why did she feel like something bad had happened?

"Hey, over here."

Elle swung around, she couldn't see anyone, her vision was blurred, and it was out of focus. "Who's there?"

"Don't you know?" the voice questioned.

"No."

The voice laughed, cackling like a witch; it gave Elle the chills.

"Do you know where Heath is?" Elle asked the faceless voice. She was really worried about him. She was almost certain something bad had happened to him.

"Boy, you don't know much, do you? I'll give you a little hint; he's worm food right about now."

"Nooo!" Elle could feel the world swiped out from underneath her feet. The sobs wracked her body.

"Yep, do you know who killed him?" the voice questioned Elle.

Elle was crying uncontrollably. "Who?" Elle asked finally.

"You did it, Elle."

183

"No." Elle turned around, trying to find the person that was talking to her, but she couldn't get her eyes to focus; it was just a blurred, dark mess. "I would never do a thing like that."

"But you did."

Elle shook her head in denial.

"Yes, you did, but you don't have to remember that. You don't have to remember any of it."

"I would never hurt Heath."

"But you did, I guarantee it, it will all come back, and it's not something you want to remember. I can take it all away."

"How?"

"Just let me in, let me into that darkness with you. You let me in once, not that long ago. Don't shut me out; after all, you owe me."

"Who are you?"

More laughter, it was definitely a woman's voice. Out of the corner of her eye, she could almost make out someone, but they disappeared instantly.

"I'm you. I'm your other half."

"That's not possible."

"I think it is; in fact, I know it is. I'm here, and you're here, and I remember all that you don't want to remember. I gave you an option years ago; I gave you the chance to get rid of those memories, the memories you couldn't handle. However, I could give them back just as easily as I took them away. If you don't want that, all you've got to do is show me into that dark space you occupy."

Elle felt so much uncertainty, she wanted out of the darkness, but she also knew that she wasn't giving this woman what she wanted. If she did, bad things would happen. "No, I won't let you in."

"Ok. You're on your own from here on out."

Elle snapped her head around; her vision cleared in one quarter turn of her neck.

The voice quieted; that's when the flashes started blowing up in front of her eyes like fireworks. The flashes were pictures, things, happenings, people, and some that were not people. One after the other, some of them snapping so quickly, it was like watching flashes of your life blow up in front of your eyes. With each snap, she remembered the past, each memory she had forgotten. One after another, they picked up speed; they were coming so fast they were now a blur.

The images stopped finally, and the Dark Man was before her; she knew who it was without anyone needing to tell her. His hands were on her neck, and their eyes were locked. Elle wanted to turn away, but she was unable to move; she desperately wished for the darkness; anything was better than having this thing staring into her soul. Now its hands were moving down her neck, across her shoulders. It was a very unpleasant feeling, cold, extreme cold penetrating her body, almost like being touched by death. The cold circulated through her body in surges. She became aware of a digging sensation, digging through her subconscious, and it was almost worse than the cold.

Something pierced the skin on the back of her neck; it dug down deep, ripping through the flesh. "Aaaahhhh. Aaaahhhh. Aaaahhhh." It hurt so bad; it felt like her flesh was being torn from her bones. Thousands of thoughts were rushing through her mind, crowding in so quickly that it was hard to make them all out.

No one needed to assure her that everything was going to be all right, because it was very evident that it was far from ok. Something moved past her, something black, blacker than even the shadows could be. She wished she could block everything out; it just got worse and worse, magnified to an unbearable level. But she was wide awake. The pain moved down her back to just above the end of her rib cage. There the Dark Man's fingers stopped, and something pierced into her spine; it threw her arms and legs into convulsions; she wasn't sure how she could even stand. The Dark Man laid her on the bed in the crummy motel room; her back arched like a bucking bronc, as another surge of pain made her body contort.

"Oh, the pain must be hard to take. However, I can take it away; I can take it all away; all you gotta do is let us in," the Dark Man said throughout her mind.

There were flashes from the first nine years of her life, of her and Grant. The flashes stopped, she remembered everything, and she was deathly afraid of what came next. Her eyes looked clearly into the Dark Man's; the shadows surrounding her were moving, jiggling; they were moving toward her. The Dark Man's hands reached out and grabbed her just behind her ears. She could feel him tearing her apart; he was destroying her mind and shredding her memories one by one, looking for a way in. She couldn't keep him out for much longer.

Chapter 20

"Heath, you come back to me."

Heath drifted away from reality, as if he were a ship floating on the ocean and it was moving farther and farther from land.

Heath sat outside Pete's house on the grass; he had a cigarette in his hand. Even the cigarette couldn't stop the shaking. The little girl—he thought—she would be all right; the surgery hadn't gone well. Grant had to take over. Heath had become overwhelmed, the blood blurred to black, and he felt the pressure on his heart, on his brain. Or at least he thought he had felt the pressure; it was hard sometimes to separate memories from reality.

Heath couldn't take it anymore; he got up to leave but stopped when he heard Grant and Pete talking. "What if Heath can't perform the surgeries or any of the things I need him too? What if I don't have the time to train him?" Grant asked.

"Maybe we are overthinking this, some things he could be trained to do, but if we reprogrammed him, he would be unstoppable," Pete answered. "A new program would add insurance, if anything damages Heath beyond the point of no return. Heath becomes a lethal killing machine, to protect Elle and the plans."

"Guess it's kind of ironic, to reprogram the one that was intended to kill us all," Grant stated.

"You have the plans, and as soon as the Dark Man figures it out, you won't live long. I think reprogramming Heath is our only option. Humans make mistakes, but machines just follow the program."

***

"Heath? Heath, come back to me."

There was something else, someone's face staring expectantly at him in the dim gloom. It sounded like Elle, it almost looked like Elle, but it wasn't her. And if he had looked carefully at her in that instant when he had handed the gun over, he might have noticed the change. How she held herself, how she had looked at him should've been more than enough. He had gotten sloppy somewhere along the way; he had relied on a very human emotion—trust. Trust no one, that had always been Grant's motto, and Heath had ignored it. Heath had trusted Elle completely, assuming that, because she was Grant's flesh and blood, she could be trusted once the chip had been removed. How wrong he had been.

Elle was never commanding, and this other Elle was.

All those faces Elle had painted on her wall, he had always thought it was a cry for help. But in reality, it wasn't that at all. It was because someone else was doing it; another personality was calling the shots from time to time.

"Heath?" Someone was calling his name. He was clawing his way to the surface. "Heath?" He tried to grab the neck of the woman standing over him, but he felt as weak as a kitten. She disappeared, and he sank back into the darkness.

"Heath, come back to me."

Heath tried to speak, but he couldn't.

"Heath, listen to me; you've got to come back to me."

Heath fought out of the darkness; he grabbed the woman who was hovering over him by the neck. His mouth was dry; it felt like all his spit had been sucked out. And something else was missing, something important.

Her name was missing; everything came back, jarring him to the soles of his feet. Her name was Missy. "Elle tricked me," he said through clenched teeth.

Missy's eyes bulged from the hands encircling her throat, she grabbed at his fingers, and slowly he released her. She coughed and looked uncertainly at him.

When he made no more aggressive moves toward her, she reached out to pull him into a sitting position. "Sit up."

Heath did, and it felt like his head was about ready to explode. He started to lie back down.

"No, sit up; you've been down for quite a while." Missy disappeared and came back with a cold cloth to put on his forehead. It relieved some of the dizziness.

"Where are we?"

"Linus's garage, don't you remember coming here?"

"Jeanie was playing us from the beginning. Elle suspected someone was watching over her, but she had no idea who."

"Who the hell is Jeanie?" Missy questioned.

"Elle."

"Huh?"

"Jeanie's Elle. Elle's Jeanie. She's got one of those, what do you call it…split personalities. It's like Elle has an evil twin."

"Oh, this isn't good."

"No, it's not."

"Ok, then why did Elle/Jeanie wait so long before she made herself known? Why not kill us both?"

"They don't know I'm not dead, and as far as Jeanie knew, she thought maybe I knew how to get the plans safely out of Elle without damaging them. I think that was her problem all along. Maybe Elle really didn't kill Davis and Striker; maybe Jeanie killed them."

"So, Jeanie was trying to get the plans? What value would they have to her?"

"She wanted complete control over Elle, over their body. She didn't want to share it with Elle any longer. She figured maybe the Dark Man, being a higher intelligence, that he would be able to get Elle out of her head, and the plans were something to bargain with."

"What about the jelly pack? If that thing had mixed, Elle would've been brain dead, split personality or not."

"You got me, unless maybe Jeanie agreed to it without realizing the consequences or maybe she didn't know about it. They clearly didn't have access to each other's thoughts. Otherwise she wouldn't have shot me in the metal plate in my forehead, the one place where I couldn't be killed."

"Sounds like the Dark Man double-crosses whoever he wants," Missy offered.

"If they abducted Elle, like they had done many times before, Jeanie might not know about the jelly pack. Maybe Elle could block things from Jeanie, and Jeanie could block things from Elle; she must've been able to, because Jeanie couldn't access the part of Elle's brain that held the plans."

"Hmm, that makes sense."

"Sure, Jeanie waited to see if I could tell her anything, then when she realizes, *wham*, I know as little as she does, she decides she's had enough and she tries to kill me."

Missy let go of the cloth, now in Heath's own hands, and she moved away.

"You mind telling me what happened to you?" Heath asked Missy.

"Margaret happened to me."

"Elle's mommy?"

"Do you know any other Margarets?"

"Where did you run into her?"

"Elle's apartment."

"What were you doing there?"

"I couldn't find you; you were gone; I thought…it doesn't matter. If they're getting ready to tear Elle apart to get the plans out, then there isn't much time left."

"Yeah."

Something occurred to Heath. Missy said he had been down for quite a while. When the bullet struck the metal plate in his head, it must've caused a bleed in his brain, and it would take hours, possibly days, for his body to repair it. The program had a safety mechanism that could speed up the healing of cells, but the abilities were limited, and any extreme injury, Heath wouldn't be able to come back from it. "Just how long has it been since we split in the desert?"

"Five days I guess."

"That means they've had more than enough time to study her."

"Should we be worried?"

"I am."

"Grant was smart, wasn't he? Did he really know for sure that mankind would be exterminated if the Dark Man got a hold of the plans?"

"Come on, Missy; we're all grown-ups here. You think they flew eighty billion light years to crash land and then just go home as soon as their ship was repaired? They want to wipe us off the face of the Earth, but first they need their ship repaired. The ship they crashed here was built by a superior race; this race that is residing here is just simple geologists, no opposable thumbs, so they need us to do it for them."

"What do we do?"

"What else? I'm going to go after Elle."

"Will you listen to yourself? If she wants to be with them so badly, then let her. Grant would ensure a backup plan."

"Elle was the backup plan."

"No, Heath, let her go. Drop the training; just walk away now before it's too late."

Anger, dangerous anger was swirling around inside him. "I'm not leaving her to them. I'm going to do what I was trained to do. They have her now, but it's not the end."

"And if you're wrong? If they have what they want from Elle already, you could be walking into a bloodbath."

"Then it won't matter; we'll be dead in a matter of weeks, possibly a month, or however long it takes to repair their ship. The only problem is I don't know where to look for her. You got any ideas?"

"They've got to be out in the desert somewhere."

"That really doesn't narrow it down any."

"What about the Roswell crash site?" Missy suggested.

"Why would they still be there?"

"Not sure, but there is this electromagnetic charge out there; it's a weird anomaly; the surge is being picked up by a mapping app on my phone. It's just as good of a place to start as any other."

Heath nodded.

"Try to avoid coming face-to-face with the Dark Man, Heath. They're not all geologists; he's extraordinary; he's lethal. I think he's a hybrid of more than one alien species," Missy declared.

***

Less than ten minutes later, Missy was behind the wheel, and they were speeding toward Roswell, New Mexico, in her rental.

Heath's head was a mess; when the bullet struck the plate, it shattered and tore the skin up. He would need significant skin grafts to fix the mess, but there were bigger problems than blending into society. Things had changed—possibly forever.

As Missy drove, Heath worked on a project in his lap. With each twist of the screwdriver, each wire carefully put into place, he came closer to his destination.

"And what is that?" Missy inquired, absently glancing over after hours of driving.

"A bomb."

"A bomb. And what do you need a bomb for?" Missy asked anxiously.

"I don't know, blow up some outer space crap. This bomb has a ten seconds' allowance before it goes off."

"Why not put a detonator on it or a remote?"

"Nope, they might be able to tinker with it. I can't take the chance."

"Ten seconds isn't enough time to get you safely out of there, Heath."

Heath didn't comment. He didn't think he needed to. It was pretty obvious this was a one-way ticket.

"Why you?" Missy demanded.

"You know why. I got nothing to lose."

"Heath, listen, there's something we need to talk about. I think if you need to do this, there are some things we need to discuss first."

"I think the thing we need to do is alter me a little more, take away anything that's even remotely human." He hoped he could stop himself from doing anything he might regret, without a human side.

***

Tears welled in Missy's eyes—a kind of sad resolve replaced her need to tell him anything more. "Ok."

Just outside of Roswell, New Mexico, Missy cut the engine to the car. She got out a surgical scalpel, and while Heath leaned against the car, she made the adjustments he requested to the chip. Then with the skilled precision of a surgeon, she sewed him back up, it only took about twenty minutes or so, but it was more than enough to know she had changed him. When he looked at her, there was nothing even remotely human about him; he had an agenda and would do whatever it took to fulfill it—or die trying.

***

When the change happened, it was like being given a drug and not really knowing when it had started to take effect. This other sort of control snapped into focus, without him really becoming conscious of it. It was like someone else was in command, and you know they are, but you can't think around it; you can't quite stop yourself from becoming someone else. It was scary to not have any morals, and you don't know how to stop yourself from doing something you normally wouldn't do.

When he stopped the car just shy of the crash site, he reached behind the seat for the bottle. Missy got out, looking off into the distance, as if searching for a direction that they should head in. Missy didn't seem to see the rag he was twisting in his hands nor the liquid that he had poured on it. He turned to look at her; she was clearly distracted by the thought of him strapping that bomb to himself and detonating it. She was shaking her head no, maybe realizing how this was supposed to end. Her eyes slowly drifted down to the rag in his hands. Heath couldn't stop his arms from reaching out for her. His fingers were numb, and yet he could still feel her flesh under them. He couldn't stop himself; he spun her around, putting her back to his chest; one arm slid around her waist so she couldn't go anywhere; the other came around just over her right shoulder, the rag clutched in his hand. The smell was strong, overpowering, crippling, but not reaching his senses in the least. The rag covered her mouth and nose; she fought with her hands, flailing and clawing to breathe. Her fingers dug into his arms and hand, tearing and ripping at his flesh. The rag covered her breathing; he ground it into her mouth and over her nose, making it the only thing she knew.

Her body went slack in his arms, the fight leaving her almost like she was dead. The blood dripped off his arm where she had clawed him; a small tremor raced through her body, and he danced with her, a motion that set the stage.

"The more I think about it, the more I think you stayed not because I wanted you to but because you wanted to. I could snap your neck. I could make it so no one would find you, so no one would even blame me, but someday I might want to know why you stayed with me. So, I won't end your life," Heath stated.

The hold he had on her body released, and her body slumped to the ground, lax as rag doll.

He shook his head as if trying to clear it, but there was only his mission, now and forever.

He packed the shotgun, bomb, a long-bladed knife, binoculars, a radio, and a set of headphones. He set out on foot, headed in the only direction that he thought they might be, that rock formation in the West.

***

Raleigh stood in the dark, watching. He could feel the human, the human that wasn't human at all. They were usually so predictable. Raleigh knew Heath was coming for them, but once he stepped past the line, that invisible line that divided them from the land of make-believe into the real world, Raleigh would strike.

There it was, the human; even from the distance, Raleigh could smell it. The human had blood on him. The saliva in Raleigh's mouth thickened; it was hard to swallow.

The human couldn't see Raleigh; he was crouched behind a rock. The others would like to know that the human was coming. But this one human wasn't worth alarming the others. This one would only take seconds to deal with.

Or would it?

The human was talking to itself; Raleigh could hear it even from this distance, whispering, but the words weren't clear. They were jumbled up, barely above a soft whisper. Raleigh had learned the human language shortly after their ship crashed on Earth. It was a simple dialect. However, they couldn't speak it; they didn't have the vocal cords to pronounce the syllables that humans had. They didn't need to make the sounds; the high-pitched screaming was all they needed for communicating. Plus, when the Dark Man was around, they could all communicate telepathically.

The dry lightning had hit the spaceship, in one thunderous, electrical crack; the ship's computer grid had short-circuited. The crash had been almost instantaneous; the ship's crew members were knocked unconscious on impact; two died from their injuries. Over the course of the days that followed, they had to hide. Raleigh and the crew had entered uncharted territory, and they had no intel on humans. It took a few days to complete their analysis of mankind, and the analysis stated that humans were weak, mentally and emotionally. Only then did the Dark Man feed on the two dead crew members; the alien flesh amped up the Dark Man's magnetic telekinesis, the power to control thoughts, and communicate without speaking. It wasn't normal, they all knew that, to eat the others, but it was a way to control mankind. The downfall came when the Dark Man lusted for the flesh of his own kind. Raleigh sensed how much the Dark Man craved the alien meat. But the Dark Man resisted the urge; instead he had to satisfy his hunger with human flesh, a poor substitution. The aliens relied on human meat to survive.

Raleigh observed the human closely. Jeanie had told Raleigh everything that she knew about Heath. She was more than willing to sell out one of her own. As for Elle, the Dark Man was still having trouble breaking into her subconscious to extract the blueprint. However, it was only a matter of time; Elle's resistance was crumbling.

Human minds were a sea of ideas, thoughts, memories, and the forgotten. The forgotten was what Raleigh craved, what he needed. Almost every human had something that they were hiding, something so valuable that they would do almost anything to keep it secret. And that created problems—the aliens needed to unlock the whereabouts of the blueprint. They had been here way longer than intended, and they couldn't dig through everyone's subconscious—most human's mental stability couldn't handle the process. The digging. A plan started to arise from the ashes: if they infected a host with an extraterrestrial parasite, they could use the infection to manipulate mankind into giving up the blueprint. It was the key to unlocking everything. Or so they thought. They had never counted on Heath creating such a hostile environment for the parasite, the parasite infected Heath's brain, and he started to self-destruct. The Dark Man turned his back on Heath, certain that Heath's own injuries would kill him within a day. No doubt Grant had helped Heath but that made him even more frightening—this was one human they couldn't control.

The parasite was useless and the infection couldn't be passed on. Years later, with so many failed attempts to locate the blueprints, they turned finally to Grant's daughter; it was locked up tight in her subconscious; she had been the one all along.

***

A whistling sound pierced the silence, as if something were flying, slicing through the air. Heath was struck in the chest; he flew off of his feet and fell on his back. The oxygen was knocked from his lungs in an instant. The pain that rippled through his heart was fierce. Heath gasped to catch his breath. He opened his eyes slowly; they wouldn't focus at first. Raleigh was right in Heath's face, and yet he could barely make out the alien's features. Heath's chest cavity had been punctured; Raleigh was going to kill him, crush his heart in one of its long-hooked hands. The other hand held him down so he couldn't move. Heath hadn't seen it coming, but he could see Raleigh now. His vision was clearing. The pressure slowly increased around Heath's heart; he knew now what a heart attack must feel like—Raleigh was squeezing the life right out of him. Each body part ached for fresh blood, but the supply had been cut off.

Raleigh was a cold, lackluster army green; its big eyes drilled into Heath from its hairless body. Some eyewitness testimonies described the aliens as almost frail, but that couldn't be further from the truth—this alien was agile and quick, six feet tall.

A sex wasn't evident, and yet Heath knew that Raleigh was from their male species. There was nothing for genitals except a hole, a few shades lighter than everything else. That had to be where the fucker expelled its waste from. It had hips like people, but they were sharp and pointy, no fat anywhere, even where its rib cage started and stopped. The skin was pulled taut, outlining each rib. But there was a kind of mottled color to the skin, so slight that at times it looked almost one color, then another.

The pressure increased on his shoulder where the one hand was holding him down; its fingernails clenched even harder down on Heath's heart.

Heath's eyes finally lifted to its face. He should be afraid, but in Heath's current state, he feared nothing.

This motherfucker was just hideous, far worse than anything Heath had ever encountered before. For as long as he lived, this moment in time would be at the forefront of his memory. However, he probably wouldn't be alive that much longer. Slowly Raleigh drew back his thin lips, displaying a tarantula-like mouth.

The alien was talking in Heath's head; it snapped at Heath, coming just an inch from his face with its canine-like teeth. Heath's hands were up, keeping it off of him as best he could. But it was impossible to do much with his heart in Raleigh's claws.

Raleigh was talking in Heath's head; it was working deeper into his subconscious, looking for anything, info or details on Elle. But whatever Missy had done to him was enough; it kept his thoughts few and far between. There wasn't much for this creature to try to steal from Heath. But even one mental slip, and Raleigh would latch on tighter, sucking Heath's thoughts from him like a leech.

Heath was weakening; Raleigh got a mouth of flesh off of Heath's shoulder; the blood curdled instantly in the wound, soured from the poisonous venom that dripped from Raleigh's fangs. Heath reached down, pulled the long-bladed knife from the sheath, and drove it into Raleigh's midsection. Heath bucked Raleigh off of him, and he stumbled to his feet, putting some distance between them, but he knew Raleigh could close the space between them in seconds. Thankfully Heath's heart had remained in his chest. Raleigh had retracted his claws when Heath had stabbed him.

How many more awaited? Raleigh wasn't the only one, more were there, and he couldn't possibly fight them all. Cold resolve would be needed to tear them apart, one at a time.

Raleigh stepped back, and three more stepped forward and replaced him. The drool that ran down the alien's chin was slightly bubbly and frothed with Heath's blood.

Chapter 21

The metal plate in Heath's head was almost completely uncovered; it looked like his hairline had drastically receded into a steel dome. He probably looked more robotic than human, but his life no longer belonged to him, and he didn't much care what happened from here on in. A glitch in Heath's program, or maybe it was finally entering the here and now, whatever the reason, a smile spread across his face. Blood poured out of the hole Raleigh had made in Heath's chest, and his steel plate glinted in the lengthening shadows. Heath lunged forward, smashing his head into an alien as it rushed him. He crippled it; he unloaded the shotgun; one dropped. He pulled his knife out and sliced his way through the aliens. He turned to see Raleigh grab hold of him; they wrestled in each other's grasps. Heath could feel its nails digging into his biceps; Raleigh knocked the shotgun out of his hands and sent it flying. Blood and spit were running down Heath's chin.

***

Grant could see the edge of the valley; his friend was waiting out there somewhere for him. The valley always had a glow of its own under the moonlight. Not many people came out this way, but Grant knew where the valley was, had known his whole life. And as long as his dad didn't find out, everything would be ok.

Ever since Grant was a boy in the sixties, there was a deep, dark secret within his household. Delmar, his father, had laid down the law early on when Grant was no more than six: no going out at night. Delmar kept up a nightly vigilance, his gun at his side, watching the windows and sky. On this particular night, Delmar had fallen asleep early, and Grant had taken this opportunity and had crawled out his window. Perched on the edge of the roof, he had dropped twelve feet to the ground, just barely missing his mother's rosebushes. Grant slipped away into the darkness, fearful of his dad but mostly of what waited in the valley. Common sense said to stay home, but curiosity had infected him, and it was impossible to ignore.

The valley was where Delmar had been called to years earlier; Delmar had been a sergeant in the military. The story was that something had landed in the valley, and they were checking it out. Delmar didn't return home; a colonel eventually informed Jean that her husband was sick, and he had to spend some time in a hospital. It was a year before Delmar returned. When asked, he would not speak about what happened in the valley, nor about his stay at the army-base hospital. Delmar had been released with a dishonorable discharge, and it became something else they didn't talk about in their household.

Delmar had developed an undeniable fear of the dark; he insisted that everyone in their household be in the house before nightfall. The valley was a place of question, mystery, of wanting desperately to know, and it was more than an invitation—it had become Grant's obsession.

Grant's friend Toby was supposed to borrow his dad Carl's pickup. Carl was a heavy sleeper, at least since Toby's mom had died—whiskey likely had something to do with it. Grant had walked down the driveway, darting a few nervous glances over his shoulder at the darkened windows. Once out at the road, he waited for his friend. An hour passed before Toby drove up in the pickup, his feet barely able to reach the pedals. Grant piled in, and they drove the twenty-nine miles to the valley. When they pulled up, only a sliver of moon shone through the clouds, although they didn't need the moon because they both had flashlights. The sand overflowed the tops of their sneakers and sifted down into their socks and between their toes as they walked.

As they neared the edge of the valley, it glowed bright orange and metallic purple. Grant hesitated, assessing everything carefully. The moon blinked out as the clouds blocked it completely.

"Come on, scaredy cat," Toby called as he was rushing down the side of the valley and up the other side toward a rocky outcropping.

Grant moved to the edge and slid ten feet or so on his butt. The loose sand sucked him into the valley. He slid and crawled down slowly, hesitating to look around; once at the bottom, he moved up the other side toward the rocky outcropping, the sand shimmering at his

feet. Grant had heard stories of pirate's gold and ghosts, but the fear of where they were wasn't enough to deter the boys. If anything it only tightened its hold and drove them farther. They were doing what nobody else had dared to do.

The sand and rocks ended on a ledge hundreds of feet above the bottom. Toby scrambled up toward the ledge, leaving Grant far behind. Grant turned back, his head twisting over his shoulder to look up at the sky, but only a small sliver of the moon had returned. It worried him a little, not being able to see much of it. Something moved out there; Grant could see an outline against the sky; it was of something standing just above the edge of the valley.

"Toby, maybe we should head back," Grant called to his friend.

He could see Toby briefly hesitate, looking toward the top of the valley. Toby clearly couldn't see anything, as he plunged toward the lithe figure standing above him. It was watching both of the boys.

Grant screamed, trying to alarm Toby, and he turned, making a run for it. He was slipping in the sand and rocks, and the thing had already caught up to Grant and grabbed hold of his ankle. Grant's feet were whipped out from under him, and he was dragged back into the valley.

"Grant!" Toby screamed, but it did little to no good. The thing wasn't going to be scared off.

Grant ground his teeth together; the thought of getting eaten alive gave Grant the shivers. He briefly looked back over his shoulder at what was dragging him. The rocks and the sand scratched him up and were very rough on his exposed skin. But the worst was the claws that were clamped to his ankle. The brief glimpse of the creature was haunting at best; it was tall, towering easily over six feet; the creature's back was mottled in a camouflage of navy, green, and black.

Cloud cover blotted the valley out into complete darkness, Grant twisted around trying to grab on to something, a sharp old tree root scraped his palm, and Grant grabbed hold. The force of Grant holding on to the tree root momentarily jerked the creature to a halt; Grant was frozen in terror as he looked up into the creature's tarantula-like face. It screeched at him. Out of the darkness, Toby came with a fossilized tree trunk that he used to strike the creature. The creature turned on him. It grabbed Toby by the throat and threw him almost twenty feet, as effortlessly as if he were a toy. Toby didn't move.

Grant didn't need to be a grown-up to know that this wouldn't have a happy ending. Toby and Grant were going to die in the very valley that had haunted Delmar for so long.

The creature flipped Grant over, and something sharp pierced into his skin; it felt like Grant had been paralyzed. The valley temperature dropped drastically; Grant could see the puffs exiting his mouth into cold air as he lay there panting, fearful, and rigid.

The clouds drifted apart, making a pathway for the moon. The light filtered down into the valley, highlighting everything. Grant was conscious as he screamed for his mother, for someone to help.

"Aaaaahhhh!" Grant screamed into the night as something like a hot coal erupted under his skin. It felt like it was smoldering and burning there.

"Go fucking home."

Grant looked up just as the butt of his dad's shotgun swung through the air. The thing looked up as the stock of the butt struck it. The crack of the gun striking the creature resounded through the valley. The creature stumbled backward, shocked; Delmar had stunned the son of bitch. But Grant's father didn't stop there; he swung the gun into position, one hand falling onto the trigger, the other holding on to the stock. Both gun barrels blasted at the creature. The gunpowder stained the air with a sulfur smell. Delmar was quick to reload and pulled the trigger a second time, hitting the creature dead center in its chest. It flew backward fourteen feet, hitting the ground on its back, digging a trench as it skidded in the sand.

Delmar spared Grant only one glance before moving toward the creature. He moved like someone who had dealt with them more than once. He stopped by its head. It lay still, but he probably just knew this motherfucker wouldn't go that easily.

The creature's hand snapped upward, ripping into the thick, meaty flesh of Delmar's bicep. Delmar didn't seem to pay any attention. It was like he felt nothing.

"Dad!" Grant screamed.

The explosion of gunpowder lit up the smile on Delmar's face, and he unloaded another shotgun of lead into the creature. The creature cringed as the buckshot tore what was left of its chest to shreds. The hand loosened on Delmar's arm and fell away. Blood laced the two scratches made on Delmar's arm; he wrapped something tightly around the upper arm, a tourniquet to staunch the blood flow. It looked like his father's blood had gone bad after being exposed to the air. Delmar poured a strong acid all over the injury. The flesh twisted, and the infection was eaten from the wound.

"Is it dead?"

Grant could feel his feet slowly trying to work under him, but he wasn't sure he could stand. "Don't know. For all I know maybe the fucker can regenerate, put himself back together," Delmar offered.

"Can it?"

Delmar poured the acid on Grant's back. It stung bitterly.

Grant slowly got to his feet; the hot coal under his skin had been pushed to the back of his mind. At the forefront of his thoughts was getting the hell out of there.

Delmar finally answered, "I don't think so, but you want to stay and find out?"

Grant hobbled toward the opposite side of the valley. "What about Toby?"

"He's dead. His head struck a rock when he landed."

At the top of the valley, the old Dodge was parked maybe half a mile away. They were both dog-tired when they reached it. Delmar drove with the lights off on the ride back to the farmhouse. Neither spoke for the longest time.

When Delmar finally did, it was with resignation dripping from his voice as the truck sped down the road. "They've made their mark on you."

Grant looked over a little uncertainly at his father.

"Dad, I'm sorry. I didn't know what was out there."

Delmar said nothing more to Grant until they were back at the family farm. Delmar headed into the house and set the shotgun on the kitchen table.

Grant stood just inside the door; he was unsure of what to do, of what not to do. Tears stung Grant's eyes, he wanted to wish away this night, but he knew that wasn't possible.

He held his hands out to his father in attempted plea, trying to say he was sorry, knowing that there was nothing he could do. In the end, Delmar didn't give a shit. Delmar's exterior was impenetrable.

"I'm still me," Grant offered.

"You know the rules, no one allowed out after dark. You broke those rules, I saved you tonight, but it was for not; either you die now at my hands, quick and easy, or you die at theirs, slow and painful. Betraying your people will become your way soon enough. I can't stop what's been done to you. I could only slow down the infection. Be a man, and take death as a beginning, not an end. Face up to what you've done, what you're about to do."

The tears streamed down Grant's face; Delmar slid a bullet into the chamber and turned the gun on him.

"Couldn't you cut the mark off my skin, burn it out, and let me disappear into the night?" Grant pleaded.

"I can't do that; their ways are in your blood; it's only a matter of time before you turn against your own kind. I'll kill you now and save you from tomorrow. Less suffering for everyone if you die now at my hands."

There was nothing left to be said, Grant didn't turn away, and he didn't run. He stood there facing his father, remembering the first time Delmar had given Grant a sip of beer, of the hunting and fishing trips, of the good times they had together, of Christmases long past now. Delmar seemed to have no nostalgia as he stood staring down at Grant. Nothing mattered anymore, Grant had never understood, until now, how the dishonorable discharge had affected his father, how the fear of what was in the valley had become like a sickness in Delmar, and it couldn't be undone.

The gun bucked in Delmar's hands; Grant wasn't conscious of closing his eyes. It was instinctual, and when nothing hit him, he cracked an eye open. Jean, Grant's mother, had come out of the living room into the kitchen and had grabbed hold of the shotgun, sending the buckshot into the roof of their house.

"Get off me, woman!" Delmar shouted. But Jean didn't back down.

"Grant, ruuun!"

Grant didn't hesitate. Delmar threw Jean to the side and took another shot at Grant. But Grant was already out the door and had launched himself off the deck; he hit the ground running. Grant ducked into one of the outbuildings; once inside, he headed for the small hole in the back that he had used to sneak through. Once through, he headed for the juniper and sagebrush. The hills and valleys of the desert were his only refuge.

The sound of the shotgun blasting in the distance was enough of an incentive to never return; he would be killed on sight if he did. Grant fled into the night, not really conscious of heading in any one direction, so fearful of his dad for the first time in his life. He had known of fathers that beat their sons, that got drunk and slapped them around, but this was completely different.

After running for hours, Grant crouched behind a thicket, five miles from home. He had nowhere to really go. When the first rays of morning peeked through the sky, Grant could hear his mother calling out to him. And slowly Grant backtracked his trail. His mother was wrapped in a blanket and had some nasty bruises on her face—no doubt her punishment for disobeying Delmar.

Grant and his mother walked beside one another; the police cars were just leaving when they reached the yard. Delmar was in the cop's custody, viewed as a danger to his family. The sun was starting to climb high into the sky, and Grant's night of hell seemed to be behind him.

Jean and Grant stayed on the porch, huddled together under the blanket the cops had given her. It wasn't just the state of shock but the coolness of the desert—the day hadn't warmed up yet. Jean's face was swollen, and her lip was cut from trying to fight Delmar, but she didn't want to go to the hospital, hadn't wanted to be tormented by the curious looks from various strangers; she just wanted to stay there with Grant.

"He's just a crazy old man; he will never hurt us again. Remember him not how he is but how he used to be."

Later that day, a military vehicle pulled into the yard; Colonel Williams had gotten out and approached them. Grant had immediately gotten to his feet and saluted him.

"Ma'am." Colonel Williams tipped his hat at Jean.

"Hello, sir," Jean replied.

"May I talk with this young man?" Colonel Williams asked Jean.

"Absolutely," Jean said. She wasn't interested in denying the colonel's agenda, he had heard about Delmar's aggression toward his family, and it had prompted his visit.

Grant fell in pace with Colonel Williams; he had seen military personnel enough to know to respect them. Freedom was never something to take lightly.

"It's a terrible thing how the events of the valley years earlier changed Sergeant Delmar. I think, however, that his heart was in the right place. I questioned Delmar earlier at the cop shop where he was briefly held, and I understand that you were attacked by the creature out there. I think there could be a few complications if we don't handle this carefully."

Grant's pace stopped as the colonel's conversation faltered. Colonel Williams grabbed Grant by the neck, knocking him to his knees. He pulled something from his pocket that Grant could barely make out. There was sharp stab to Grant's neck; the pain brought tears to his eyes almost instantly. After a few seconds, the colonel pulled the needle out of Grant's neck. It was a big needle with a long tip that had gone deep into Grant's neck muscle.

Grant could see his mother running from where she had been waiting on the porch, but it was too late. Colonel Williams held up his hand, as if to say for Jean not to bother. Grant took a deep breath and tried to get to his feet; it took a great deal of effort to do so.

"What I gave you is just a little something to fight off whatever that creature might have infected you with. You will feel some pain throughout the day, but it is far less severe than the infection would've been. I wish you and your mother well. Good day."

Colonel Williams left after that; Grant had trouble walking back to the porch; he felt like his senses were on fire and his ability to walk was being hindered. The feeling was frightening, and it was just one more sense of reality that he had to deal with on top of everything else. Jean had to help Grant to the porch; it was evident that his temperature was rising as the syringe's contents worked its way through his body.

After two days of pain and the sweats, Grant's temperature returned to normal, and he went back to school; he would never forget what was done to him and what he might have become.

***

In an instant, Grant's life dissolved before Heath's eyes. When Heath had connected with Raleigh, he had reverted to a time he had no previous knowledge of. And it was like Heath was looking out through Grant's eyes, as if Heath were actually experiencing Grant's childhood and the night that led up to Grant's father almost killing him. It was strange how the creature was so powerful and how strong the connection was between them.

Heath glared into Raleigh's eyes; he drove him backward into the rock wall. He slashed at Raleigh, then turned and sliced at another alien or two. There were so many; the cave was filled with them.

"Where's Elle?" Heath demanded.

Even though they couldn't speak, Heath knew they understood him. He ran forward, stabbing, and stumbled over his shotgun where it had fallen when Raleigh knocked it out of his hands. Heath picked it up and unloaded the barrel into two aliens. The shotgun worked well, the buckshot spraying out and catching more than one of them at a time. The bullets cut them up pretty good; their skin wasn't quite as tough as Raleigh's; he was definitely the alpha of the group. But even Raleigh was nothing compared to the Dark Man.

"Having fun yet?" Jeanie said as she walked into the cave; she ducked her head at the low opening of the doorway. The other aliens seemed to sense her importance and backed off.

Heath was running out of time, he was soaked with blood and sweat, and he could feel something wet running down his pants. His body was letting go, giving up, giving in to them even though he wasn't human.

"You don't look so good," Jeanie quipped.

Heath shook his head. Was he actually seeing this? Or had Raleigh connected with him again, and this was only a vision? Jeanie was standing just a little to the left of Raleigh, staring at Heath. If this was a hallucination, it was damn real. She looked like she had when she had shot him in the head—confident, evil, and very dangerous.

"Are you really here?" Heath said through clenched teeth. The program was glitching, every now and then there was a surge, and everything went dark, like turning a TV off. It was momentary, and then power was instantly restored.

"Of course I am, Heath. I am as real as you are," Jeanie said.

It came out of the darkness, hunkered down and slightly pigeon-toed, in a blur, one minute standing twenty feet away and the next before Jeanie. It lashed out, grabbing her head in its claws. It knocked Jeanie to the ground, crushing her body underneath it.

As if summoned by a far-superior being, the creature stopped; the Dark Man seemed to almost materialize out of thin air. He knelt down over Jeanie and helped himself to her memories.

Chapter 22

Jeanie was no longer on the ground, but Elle was, and Jeanie looked on as if she were uncertain what to do. It was her body, and she wanted it to be only hers.

The Dark Man seemed not to notice, not to care, as Elle moaned softly, blood trickling out of her ears. Huge ruptures had started to spread through her brain. Jeanie was at the Dark Man's side, trying to make him stop, but its hand plunged into Elle's chest.

"Nooooo!" Jeanie shrieked.

"Uhhhhhhh." Elle's last breath caught in her throat. Her chest rose and fell and then stopped. Jeanie saw it stop, and that was it…

Jeanie turned, looking at Heath; he was frozen in place.

"You're not really here, are you?" Heath said, shaking his head as he looked at Jeanie staring down at the body she used to share with Elle.

"No, and soon you won't be either," Jeanie answered sadly.

"How is that possible?" Heath demanded.

"Raleigh, he connected with you; the second he touched you, you were in his head; he's taken all your thoughts, feelings, memories—he's like a vampire; he sucks you dry. That's why I'm here, Elle, Grant—hell, even Jamie is here. You don't have to be afraid; these are just the things he wanted me to tell you, what he is really telling you.

"Why did he kill you? You had the plans?" Heath questioned.

"Had." Jeanie laughed, almost comically. "Grant didn't trust his own fucking daughter enough to install the whole blueprint; he only put half in Elle's brain."

Fuck. Heath could feel more pee leaking down his legs. His body was malfunctioning.

"Heath, are you paying attention?"

He looked up at Jeanie, but Jeanie wasn't there anymore. Elle had replaced her; she was looking at him with concern.

"Do you know you're lying there, listening to people who aren't really there? And if you don't do something, you'll die inside Raleigh's head, and you'll never get out; your memories will be the Dark Man's forever. You'll never live again."

Elle had only half of the blueprint; what Grant had done with the other half, Heath had no idea. But the possibilities were endless. Grant could've installed the plans in someone else; he could've downloaded them onto a remote server. He could've locked them up in a safety deposit box in a bank or buried them in a hole in some deserted lot. Wherever they ended up, it was up to the Dark Man to find it so the blueprint could be whole again.

The Dark Man had successfully extracted half of the blueprint from Elle's brain without damaging it, but he still needed the other half to repair their ship. This couldn't be the end of Heath. Who would protect the other half?

Everyone was there, Grant, Elle, Jeanie, and even Jamie; they were all trapped in the Dark Man's mind, held hostage in his subconscious. Memories that had once been important to each individual now belonged to the Dark Man for him to twist and manipulate.

Heath turned from the people that stood before him and flexed his arm, making it move; he reached up, grabbing hold of Raleigh's arm. Heath was not even sure how he knew Raleigh had his fingers embedded in his flesh. He pulled it free, turning its claws on itself. Every ounce of strength went into turning its claws against Raleigh, driving them into the creature's heart. The claws, sharp and deadly, cut through its black, leathery flesh like a knife.

The last thing that Heath got from Raleigh was an image of a cord being severed, as if harming Raleigh had freed Heath. Everyone else in the cave vanished. Heath was free from this brain-sucking leech.

Raleigh recoiled from Heath and Heath as much from him. There was only one voice in Heath's head, and it was his own. Raleigh circled around him like a boxer, his knees slightly bent, hunched forward eagerly, eyes assessing Heath very carefully, seemingly trying to calculate Heath's next move. Black blood dripped out of Raleigh's chest where its claws had been embedded.

"I can see you now, motherfucker. No more hiding."

Heath picked up the gun that had been knocked out of his hand. He pointed it at Raleigh, just like Delmar had pointed his gun at one of the other aliens forty years earlier. The pain for Raleigh would be the same.

The noise exploded in the cave, echoing off of every corner. Heath was able to fire at least six shots before he was out of bullets. However, Raleigh wasn't dead yet—he kept coming.

Raleigh's arm came up, smashing Heath with a powerful backhand. It almost ripped Heath's head right off his body; Raleigh's strength was mind numbing, especially after the bullets had torn up his chest, yet he didn't seem to be slowing down any. Heath smiled back at Raleigh, displaying big gaps where his teeth used to be. His body was almost done; the light behind his eyes flickered again, dimming for at least thirty seconds.

Thump, thump…thump filled his ears; there was an irregular beat to his heart; it wasn't in good shape; he had lost a lot of blood. There was no way he was going to make it out of there alive; he had suspected as much earlier. The bomb had had its purpose in the beginning and would in the end. Whatever safety measures Grant had put in place to protect the other half of the blueprint would have to be enough.

He thrust his arm upward, fingers clawing and digging, clinging to Raleigh like he was Heath's lifeline. The other hand explored the cave for the canvas bag, and it was there, just within reach.

"Zerstore sie."

Missy spoke as if she were right beside Heath, but of course she wasn't—she was nowhere near him. Her command was in German and spoken from a great distance—it meant destroy him.

The bag tore away effortlessly; he found the switch, previously set for ten seconds, and armed it. He chanced a look up into Raleigh's face. Raleigh started flailing, trying to get free of Heath. But Heath's fingers were locked in a death grip; they couldn't be undone. Raleigh dove his hand into Heath's chest to try to break himself free. Warm blood was spraying everywhere; an important blood vessel had been severed.

Raleigh couldn't get free of Heath; he was latched on as tightly as a bronc rider; Heath had sent one last vital command to his arms, to not let go no matter what. The bomb quickly counted down; Raleigh was franticly screeching, trying to shred Heath to pieces. But Heath's arms had become steel vices, and Raleigh couldn't free itself from Heath. Heath's mind was so damaged that the program was barely idling; there was nothing left to work with, to try to manipulate.

"You fuckers flew a long fucking way to get here, but I bet you're not fucking fireproof," Heath said. His voice had taken on a robotic tone.

The 1 on the clock blinked, Heath didn't see the other aliens when the bomb blew, but he saw Raleigh, and just knowing that it killed him was satisfaction enough.

***

The explosion blew up Heath and Raleigh in a simultaneous blast of power. The cave blew outward, falling in on itself. The others had fled down another tunnel hollowed into the solid rock. They were ok, but Raleigh was dead.

The Dark Man slipped away into the night; this was not his battle. His battle would come later, against another species that was searching the galaxy for the Dark Man and his tribe of aliens. The alien race that was hunting for the Dark Man and his race were far superior in almost every way imaginable. To be captured by that alien race would mean being tortured for centuries. If by some miracle they could get their ship repaired, they could erase any trace of their existence on Earth. But with the essential part of the blueprint still missing, that was impossible. What Grant could've done with it was anybody's guess. The Dark Man had scoured Grant's mind years ago; everything had been erased from Grant's memory very carefully. However, someone somewhere had to have the other half of the blueprint; it was only a matter of finding that special someone and soon, hopefully very soon, so they could get off of this stagnant rock.

Any humans who still bore the mark were a window of information. The Dark Man reached out with his mind, connecting to every controlled soul. The Dark Man whispered in his mind, *"Go, and bring the other half of the plans."*

In the end, Grant's past had caught up with him, and the Dark Man had torn out his heart. Grant had been smart to hide the plans; putting them in Elle was pure genius. He must have done something equally intelligent with the other half of the blueprint.

Anyone not baring the mark would die soon enough; closing day was nearing. How soon? Possibly ten days or ten months.

***

The cobwebs were still clearing from Missy's head as she lifted her face out of the sand; she knew she had spoken the words: "*Vernichte ihn.*" She hoped that Heath had gotten clear of the explosion.

Epilogue

The dust settled over the valley; something that was unexpected had silenced everything. The explosion could be heard all the way to Roswell. Missy was sitting in the sand, trying to break free of the fog in her mind; she finally got her legs to cooperate. The effects of the chloroform were finally receding. She headed in the direction that the explosion had been for no reason other than closure. She was still wobbly, but with each step, she was more herself and less disoriented. Tears streamed down her cheeks, clearing tracks in the dust covering her face.

How many aliens had Heath killed? It would be hard to tell; there would be nothing left of their corpses—of Heath's body if he was caught in the blast.

A figure came into Missy's line of sight. Missy stumbled, falling to her knees in the sand. She was almost certain that she wasn't seeing the figure. Strands of black hair flipped about in the wind, smooth as black ribbons. The figure turned to face Missy. She was dressed entirely in black.

"Have they all fallen?"

"I don't think so," Missy responded.

"The Dark Man?"

"I'm not sure."

"Heath?"

"I think he's dead."

"You sure?"

Missy looked up through the tears.

The figure showed no emotion; they nodded their head in understanding. "Bill is coming out to help you collect Heath's body."

"He's dead," Missy answered; that much she was certain of. Deep inside there was a strong feeling in the pit of her stomach.

"I want physical evidence."

Missy shook her head.

"I want physical evidence. Bring what's left of him to me, even if he's dead."

"You blame me, don't you, for him dying?"

"You shouldn't have let it happen; you shouldn't have let him out of your sight."

"He changed; he didn't care what I said anymore; he would've killed me too."

"Dig him up. I want that body."

Missy shook her head sadly, knowing that there was nothing she could've done to prevent Heath's death. The alien race had already fled from the cave; they would want distance between themselves and this place. Within the hour, an excavator showed up on a low boy with all the needed attachments to dig through solid rock. Bill got out; Missy had known Bill for years; he was an old family friend of her mother's. The dark figure turned and left, black ribbons floating on the dry air.

Missy stood watching as the backhoe started tearing into the rock.

Heath could still be alive, a small voice whispered up from the dark recesses of Missy's mind. But she knew Heath was dead; she didn't need to see his body to know this. After Jeanie had shot Heath, he had changed; his mission had been forever altered.

One Week Later

Missy stood looking down at Heath's body, or what was left of it. He was easy to identify with the metal plate that had held his skull together. That couldn't be destroyed no matter what.

At least a few aliens had been caught in the blast; their corpses had become a fine white ash. The dark figure would finally be satisfied now that Bill and Missy had found Heath's remains. That left Missy free to go home. She had been in New York way too long, following Heath, following after Elle.

Soon it would all end, and that was all that mattered now.

They would be hunted, but Missy was not running anymore. She'd had enough of that.

Bill loaded up the excavator and headed out of the desert; his job was done. He left Missy alone with Heath's body. It had been a long week searching for Heath.

Missy knelt, hovering over Heath's charred remains, tears cascading down her cheeks.

She didn't hear the sound of the footsteps in the sand. The stranger stopped, standing over Missy, placing her hand on Missy's shoulder. Startled, Missy looked up uncertainly into the face of the stranger.

"What are you doing here?" Missy asked.

"It's time to come home."

"It's over," Missy stated.

The stranger's long dark hair blew softly into her face. It was glossy, like silk ribbons. "No, the revolution has just begun."

Together they wrapped Heath's remains in a garbage bag and put the hot, dry air of Roswell behind them. Even if you're not with me, I'm with you.

To be continued…

www.ingramcontent.com/pod-product-compliance
Lightning Source LLC
Chambersburg PA
CBHW060316310726
48976CB00007B/2343